Praise for L.E. Smith's Writing

"It was Stanley Elkin who taught us that 'the great gift of fiction…is that it gives language the opportunity to happen.' L.E. Smith, in *Views Cost Extra*, has taken that opportunity and given us a remarkable collection of short stories, fiction that exploits the miracle that is the English language. He torques it, turns it upside down and inside out, maims it into brilliant particulars that ask us to downshift and pay fresh attention. Smith knows his world, its physical make-up—'Peel an apple skin with a knife, go all around in one unbroken ribbon, it's like that—driving roads that hug the mountains of New Hampshire.' And he understands the human heart in its mythical quest for 'the quick of significance.' Often hilarious, always original, these are astonishing stories that reshape the known world."
—Darrell Spencer, author of *Bring Your Legs with You* and *One Mile Past Dangerous Curve*, Professor in Creative Writing at Ohio University

❧ ❧ ❧

"A new breed of story-teller is loose in the land: heedless and headstrong, enraged by the fey and the unambitious, dismissive of the wan and merely well-mannered. L. E. Smith is a member of that good and necessary tribe. His are the stories that result when the imagination is blasted from the ancient ice of convention and effete tradition. *Views Cost Extra* is made of rubble and shards and splinters and infernal dreams and splintered hopes--all of it less typed than shouted on to the page."
—Lee K. Abbott , author of *All Things, All at Once*, Professor of English, Ohio State University

❧ ❧ ❧

"L.E. Smith takes the Novel of Ideas in his two hands and then, in masterly fashion, proceeds to rip its guts out -- replacing those guts just as deftly with all the mystery and sex and incomprehensible violence that powers the best thrillers. The result is something like a dialogue between Nietzsche and Plato and James Joyce, a dialogue conducted in a dark room about to be consumed by fire, and slowly filling with smoke. Smith gets Burlington right, Vermont right, Boston right, and his characters always feel painfully human for all their philosophical confusion and existential peril. Best of all, as the mystery unfolds Travers Jones finally does manage to transform into the warrior philosopher that all thinking readers have, at one time or another, struggled themselves to become."
—Philip Baruth, author of *The X-President* and *The Brothers Boswell*

☙ ☙ ☙

"I can think of no other novel so dense with image, concept, and language; every sentence is rich and toothsome. While in arc it's a mystery yarn, *Travers' Inferno* is much more: it's scholarly, sexy, philosophical, crazy, and full of troubling and amusing characters. The telling reminds me of Frank McCourt (*Angela's Ashes*) because its humor strikes first while irony and pathos slip in unobserved. But L.E. Smith must also have genes in common with the brilliant Flann O'Brien (*At Swim Two Birds*) and with Gully Jimson, the hero of Joyce Cary's *The Horse's Mouth* -- similar absurdity, language play, and mad, wise rant.

Throughout runs the terrible, powerful image of the mysterious burning churches, echoed in Travers' epileptic seizures. The churches, the relentless moral predation of evil Uncle Gerrit, and the implacable menace of the murderous brothers Quebecois, are reminiscent of Howard Frank Mosher's best tales of Vermont's Northeast Kingdom. Take time reading *Travers' Inferno;* chew on the language and savor every bite."
—Daniel Hecht, author of *Skull Session, The Babel Effect,* and the Cree Black series

The Consequence of Gesture

A Novel

L.E. Smith

Fomite
Burlington, VT

This is a work of fiction. Names, characters, places and incidents are either the product of the author's imagination or are used fictitiously. Any resemblance to actual persons, living or dead, events or locales is entirely coincidental.

ISBN-13: 978-1-937677-49-7
Library of Congress Control Number: 2013941206

Fomite
58 Peru Street
Burlington, VT 05401
www.fomitepress.com

Cover Art - Nathania Rubin
Front cover - The Dakota Building, NYC
Back cover - Heads of Mark David Chapman and John Lennon
www.nathaniarubin.com

Acknowledgements

Many thanks to the Byrdcliffe Arts Colony of Woodstock, NY, for their residency accommodation during which much of this book took shape. And thanks again to Nathania Rubin, a talented artist whose work has graced the front, and back, covers of all my books to date. Finally, to the unique personality and warm heart of my wife, Andrea Donahue-Smith, and to my son, Calvin D. Smith, for his continued support and inspirational love of the world at large.

About the Author

L.E. Smith lives in Vermont, writes books and teaches English, has tried to make it as a tennis pro and as a recording artist for Columbia Records, has trained guard dogs, worked as a security guard for the Metropolitan Museum of Art in New York City, delivered mail on the back roads of Vermont, worked as head chef in a restaurant, and for one day sold Fuller Brushes door-to-door in Los Angeles.

The Consequence
of Gesture

Chapter One:
Mason Fisher in Bogota

Bogota, Colombia, December 2000
(twenty years after the murder of John Lennon)

What happens when you destroy the thing you most love? I can tell you. It's the worms of conscience eating your guts. It's walking two paces behind a round, assertive tummy that most skinny, nervous types accept as evidence of your prosperity. What I carry in front of me accommodates a host of memories gnawing with tiny, hungry mouths. Because I have violated Andy Warhol's *Four Marilyns*, a painting I once loved beyond reason. And I have assisted in the murder of John Lennon. Terrible things. From these offenses come riches, notoriety and exile in Colombia. Because I am very "wanted" in America. Take note, Raul, Mason Fisher is *wanted*. What hurts most is that I'm not wanted by my lover Raul Vega, whom I followed to Bogota to this tangle of whispering back streets where even the shadows bask in green.

This beautiful, sensual, pulsing Colombia, where songbirds fill the courtyard of my love nest in the terraced gardens of Bogota. They perch in cashew trees beneath which I sit. They preen and sing and feed on the sugary cashew apples, on the red juicy marañóns, and they shake to the ground, all around me, the drupe that embraces the seed, the seed shaped like a tiny penis encased in a poisonous shell. These tiny seeds that fall around me chasten me. I sit here beneath cashew trees naked and swollen, pendulous of limb, sweating in the humidity, and I wonder – who would have thought to burn away the toxins to eat the delicate nut within?

Mostly I wonder, who would have thought Raul Vega would still service the cock of Mason Fisher? I would have, yes even now, despite having become an old man with eczema and swollen joints. Because of my disease, because of my advancing age, because of the infectious properties of the rain forest and the gesture that sent me into exile, but mostly because of Raul's dalliances, I have become a whiny malcontent. I would like most to complain to Raul of his lack of attention. But I fear losing him. Complaint has become my song. It is Raul Vega's love for me that used to move me to song. I am an old queen settled into Raul's abuse like the vintage taxi he drives. I have lived in Bogota with this man since the spring of 1981. Raul is seven years younger, a boy of nineteen when we first met. Raul Vega is achingly handsome, his teeth strong and white, his face damply dark and smooth, his voice a rapture of trilled r's and at one time the softest vowels of feminine gender when applied to me. I still love Raul. But I must qualify his part in this relationship as opportunistic. I fell in love with a cock sucker who has become a blood sucker.

I have become an artist of international renown. I have become very rich. I have long felt a stranger in Bogota despite my notoriety as an artist and as an outlaw, maybe on account. I am sought and feted by the elite of academics and journalists and by the wives of wealthy industrialists. I go off reluctantly in silk threads to elaborate dinners to sell my paintings. I am not accepted, not really trusted and included. This despite having taken a lover native to Colombia. I spend many hours in this courtyard pondering my separateness, the songbirds flitting overhead, the cashews dropping around my pudgy and flatulent self seated at a trestle table of antique wormwood. I embrace this table as if it were here to save my life. Maybe it is.

There are deep scratches like furrows in this table from the nails of some 18th century buccaneer relative of Raul's. Raul tells me of this man, of whom he is so proud, this man who had clung to this table in the frothy surf of Santa Marta after scuttling his own boat to collect the bounty on his drowning freebooter brethren. He was a pirate who became rich and legitimate through betraying intimacy. Raul seems to have inherited his relative's penchant for cashing in on a brother. There is a painting of this pirate become politician hanging somewhere in the offices of government in downtown Bogota. Raul brought me to see this man once. He sits in a chair of carved curlycue that dwarfs him as he looks out imperial and ravenous. Many of the significant men in my life have those qualities. Raul Vega clings to my wealth while betraying me between the sheets. The ceiling fan inside the house whispers an apology. A small green lizard laces with edgy speed the stone wall of the courtyard. Defying gravity, it seeks an Escher sketch to inhabit. This life of mine in Colombia, it presents me an alternate reality to which I cling defying gravity in my own way.

I am a New Yorker by affinity. Artistically and intellectually I am definitively a New Yorker. But my insecurities are a product of Buffalo where I grew up in industrial waste and rust. Chicken wings and football. That's Buffalo. But it was never me. I have brought with me to Colombia the filing-cabinet soul of an artist intellectual, the brittle and yellowed identity papers of self-interest. I have tried to make friends and to become less self-involved. But I am fighting my nature to do so. It's maybe the habit of outlawry to have surrendered away that part of the self that cares less for the self than for others. And I have tried to forgive myself for my wrongdoing. I have tried to reclaim my innocence and love for the word. I have tried to see myself inhabiting Henri Rousseau's whimsical jungle scene, emptying out conscience by dreaming away the complications as a curious tiger leans over my sleep. I want to surrender my dreams to the tiger. But I can't sleep. I have anxiety. I worry Raul will leave me. I worry the tiger will eat my dreams.

I come to realize I am one of Edward Hopper's nighthawks, wings clipped, dreams broken. In New York, in my final days there, I soared and dove. I was strong and bold, sure of myself. Andy Warhol nearly made me otherwise. But now that I have secured my place as an artist, the air in Bogota becomes far too heavy for flight. I move about like an old gray dinosaur. This teeming green of Bogota lichen and mold that invades the tiniest breach of veneer, hairline brachia, this exhalation contagion, these everywhere microscopic forests, no one cares to beat them back. I sicken breathing this shit, but … it can't be helped. I try my best to assimilate. My cock, at least, I think, has transitioned to edible mushroom. If only Raul would care to sample.

I am no revolutionary though I helped murder John Lennon. In South America there is always beneath politeness and a bouquet of smiles a seething old-world discontent. No government is ever really accepted because it's all just too personal. Revolt is a single bullet in the chamber of a single gun. The Latins will tell you that.

Passion is pure. Ideas stink. But of course that's an idea. In Colombia, if you take a life as vendetta, that's a passion. Death is sublime if born of passion.

John Lennon's death was not sublime. I was there. I know. Lennon was no sympathetic martyr. And there was no seething vendetta squirming in the coils of the brain of the one that murdered him, the one that pulled the trigger. It was death by committee. Mark Chapman had a parley of men in his head telling him to pull the trigger. And then, of course, I was there to encourage him. So were my friends. But it was a cold death. There was no agony on the cross beyond Lennon's own self-torture before Chapman pulled the trigger. Plenty of that if the tabloids got it right. Plenty of that if you believe my paintings, the dead Lennon series, the ones that have made me famous. And Mark David Chapman, he killed for an idea. No one that I knew while living in New York City ever died from passion, not even love. The hard, cold idea kills. It killed Lennon. And then the idea itself rolled belly-up, shriveled, died from disuse. In New York, Lennon's murder was but a brief sensation.

Can life happen between parentheses? Some French philosopher grammarian asked this. That Frenchman died in 1980, a month before John Lennon, big funeral in Paris, mourners like sewer rats pouring into Rue Something-or-Other, following the scent of the body's final exhalations (the stink of ideas). Before the death of Lennon I was living in the between space of an Andy Warhol painting. I was an artist then too, a painter, but not a famous one. I was at that moment, and in the prime of my life, stuck, infertile, dry as dung, unsure where next to trend, what next to say after my paintings had stripped the nude of its skin to expose its disease. Andy Warhol knew my work and had placed me on the outer fringes of his Factory of trendsetters. I had done the apprentice phase, night classes at the Manhattan Institute of Art, bending knees in gawkish reverence, copy sketching and all that: insinuating soul in the geometries of Cezanne, splashing pigment pasty and garish as Pollock, gushing biography like a Diebenkorn, pissing on canvas like Warhol.

I was back then in 1980 between phases, cold as the moon in transition. I was also strikingly handsome, chubby though solid with muscle, hair close cropped and a skull perfectly rounded that mirrored a perpetual two-day growth of beard on broad, smiling cheeks. I had back then a giddy smile and devilish twinkling eyes that assured forgiveness for all minor wrongdoing. But I had been reduced to the status of museum guard to make my living. My only anchor was a Warhol silkscreen of multiple Marilyns beaming red, blue, pink and yellow pinned to the museum walls I patrolled. It was the dreamy weight of commercial things. A perfect blend of art and commerce. Like four TV screens oscillating on that museum wall in overwrought, jarring, unfocused splashes of Technicolor. These were mass-produced Marilyns. But each was legitimate as a Marilyn icon of martyrdom – the jilted lover, the abandoned daughter, the inept wife, the seducer, brazen because insecure, haunted by suicide. I caressed that painting with my eyes. I wanted to embrace it, make love to it.

I was into women then. But it was my job to repel adoring hands, my own especially, eight hours a day policing in perma-press museum wear. Odd that this painting should have more security than the artist. Odd that the most likely offender would be its hired guard. Because the imperfections startled me: slips of the screen, uneven inking, graininess. It said to me, eight eyes on a white wall, it said, "Why bother? What you do as an artist is nowhere. I have redrawn the map entirely. I don't care about the imperfections." That Warhol Marilyn pulled at my ego like gravity. Crash and burn. How much self-negation can you take? Where does the artist exist without the ego? Still, I loved that painting. "Destroy the thing you most love" is what my friend Rowan Murray will say in that velvety way the English have in the café where I met with my friends to plot our iconoclast gesture. Yes, and I will destroy the thing I most love. I will betray Andy Warhol and I will kill John Lennon. I am scum. And it has been vapors in the guts ever since, ulcers, dyspepsia and insomnia besides.

As the day fades in Bogota, I withdraw into the house. I look outside a window that opens onto a bruised sky. I anticipate a zephyr. I get a storm. Because I have become famous for my art while living in Bogota, because I have publicly defaced Warhol and helped murder John Lennon, I go off for cocktails in the heavy night air. I agitate to see a stretch limo open its doors for me like some vanity mausoleum. It's a snug fit, this trendy, successful artist thing.

When I bite into a ripe mango I still expect to taste a crabbed apple. Everything here tastes sweet. I have to call this luck, that lawlessness can pay so well. Call it luck if you prefer a fattened Peggy Lee with a shaky voice and mustache rather than a for-ever-young Jane Fonda with an aerobics plan. Have I become a woman? Not hardly. And I am no man's fancy man. But I am the passive one in the relationship. On those rare occasions when we make love, Raul drives me as rough as his taxi through the barrios of Bogota – while in New York, I couldn't get enough female booty.

I got plenty. Some as pudgy as the nudes framed at the Metropolitan Museum of Art where I gumshoed my best glissando to pay the rent. I will have worked two years as a museum guard before doing that dreadful thing, that simple gesture.

I was technically criminal back in 1980. But I wasn't the only one. So were each of my three friends, café habituals, a society of closet radicals collected together by Rowan Murray. Rowan was then a British expatriate, a composer and a professor of music at Columbia University. He wanted this gathering to equal Samuel Johnson's Literary Club of prominent artists and thinkers from three-hundred years ago. Savvy, renowned, and influential. Now very much dead. Still very much influential if you ask Rowan. They met once a week at the Turk's Head Inn on Gerrard Street in Soho, London. That's what Rowan said. He never let us forget what a rich history we participated in. But Rowan had confused his Johnsons. He had a thing for the other Johnson, Ben Johnson the playwright, the one not stalked by Boswell. Rowan didn't always look too deep in his researches. For him a Johnson is a Johnson. Which maybe explains why everything went so wrong for us back in 1980. Rowan wanted more from us than engaging conversation. He wanted action.

Rowan's plan was for me and my friends each to despoil an icon of our choosing. Four icons effaced in the same operation on the same day. I had my sights on Warhol's four Marilyns. That painting still hangs on the halls I once patrolled, cleverly repaired, though imperfect to begin with, so what's the point – the point is the gesture itself. The gesture is all. That's what Rowan said. And the painting, a complex testimony to image overload, it's a work I loved, which makes all the difference if you're an earnest iconoclast. Otherwise, why bother? That's what Rowan said. It was all his idea, and he was right. He was, yes, unfortunately.

The day we chose, December 8th, 1980, was especially good for me, as the museum closes to the public on Mondays, which has become an occasions day for the museum to court big money: dignitaries and a bunch of who's who get the PR spin from special projects curators who cried in their champagne when the damage to Warhol was found, while the artist himself in platinum wig dined among invited guests at the Chanel opening of Diana Vreeland's costume institute. They went panicky with "synchronicity," that's a Mark David Chapman term, when the Lennon shooting happened concurrently a short distance the other side of Central Park. There was damage. That's for sure. And the iconoclasts, we broke something inside ourselves too, most of us. That son of a bitch Chapman, he was already busted up inside, and he did the most harm. He pulled the trigger on John Lennon. Five times. That's more than Warhol got from Valerie Solanas.

I knew intimately the fag that serviced Warhol at the Factory, diminished as it was in heat-seeking sycophants once the 70's pop flag had set and the neos and the isms had arisen (neo-realism, neo-expressionism), among whom I now number as an artist of some repute. But it must have been embarrassing for Andy to have to unwind the ace bandage and butterfly clamps of the girdle he wore to hold together his guts because in 1968 that SCUM Valerie Solanas pressed the trigger three times and lacerated the bowels of her benefactor and chief masculine influence.

The Society for Cutting Up Men. Can you imagine? Valerie – founding member, only member. But why Andy? I suppose his insatiable will to thrive is masculine (even plants do this) or his silence unto stone, an Easter Island deity at whose feet disciples await the next aphorism (they wait 15 minutes). Or changing hair color with various wigs. Or lying on one's back while a man services your needs. The man with trumpet lips, the one who starred anonymously in the 16 frames per second of fellatio in a famous Warhol film. Even ageing unto AARP the blower is said by those that know to have been the best. Imagine the implacable, unmoving face of Andy Warhol, which is all he registers of ecstasy. See a brick wall background. There is no sound. Stillness and Endurance are key. Structuralism. Minimalism. When you break into the isms, you have become the rock upon which ideas are built.

I have become an ism. It has taken some time and some damage to get here: Iconoplasticism. Can you believe? Can you say it without a sprain? Some wag of a New York critic coined the phrase. He applied it to my in-fame and notoriety at the time shortly following that awful deed, the murder of Lennon. (*Newsweek* listed me, Mason Fisher, one of the ten most happening criminals of 1980.) Iconoplasticism means iconoclastic in theme and plastic in the arts, which is a reference to my John Lennon series with material implants in oils. I have become an artist of a singular style. The deviant knows not to deviate.

We called our gathering place "the shop," a coffee and pastry hangout on Amsterdam Avenue a block south from Columbia University and facing the Cathedral. We will have met there nearly every weekend night for a year back in 1980, partly because we liked the way waitresses call names to locate customers and deliver orders – first names only, which is a kind of unofficial introduction that turns heads, a good way to meet girls (back in my hetero days), but which puzzled us when Mark David Chapman lifted his head to the page "Holden Caulfield." The kid has some balls and some smooth. You have to admit. It will have taken convincing to get a patronymic out of the waitress. They're pretty churlish, uncooperative in every way, and they're not thought to be literate. Their accents are Hungarian. They never smile. But their ill humor is half the fun.

Customers get equal doses of personal disinterest from the waitresses and an enthusiastic tossing of Napoleons and fruit torts and cream puffs down those lengthy tables like shuttle bowling with a chrome disk in some smoky bar, an explosion of food and drink if you don't know to protect your morsels and liquids in that tight compress of limited seating. Twelve tables, long and narrow, jammed with chairs. We gnawed our neighbors' elbows at the shop, picked crumbs and meringue off our sleeves from stuff we didn't order, planted our noses firmly in our neighbors' business – read over their shoulders, suggested metaphors to poets, got all obfuscated in conversation fragments. Wonderful!

"The shop" was a happening place in 1980. We café habitués, we four friends, we were all in our late twenties, armchair reactionaries who watched Sesame Street in the 60's, grew pimples through the 70's and awoke in the 80's to poke our hardons at whatever gave insignificant resistance. We were trying real hard to show how pissed off we were at the world; we were having one hell of a lot of fun at the world's expense. New York City! It was a fucking playground in 1980!

Say I'm walking Broadway, no particular destination. It's a sunny day. Even the street trash is smiling. And there's Dustin Hoffman walking toward me. He's walking in the sunlight, his limo following slow behind. He's dressed in a dark blue pea coat and faded jeans and black loafers and he's all alone walking the street, smiling. "Hey, Dusty," I say, "how are you!" / "I'm good," he says. "Thanks for asking." / "Hey, Dusty," I say channeling the movie *Midnight Cowboy*, "who's walking here?" / "You know who's walking here," he says, "I'm walking here. That's who! Thanks for asking." New York City! It's the great equalizer. A movie star in New York is just another man on a street angling for sidewalk room. We all breathe the same air. Once you take a lungful of that sooty air, it's ballast for the soul; once you breathe a ripe, homeless night rider down in the subway, it's proof against all disease know to man. You are nigh to invincible if you survive the first twenty-four hours of street-side New York.

Dustin Hoffman knows this. Ratso Rizzo knows this, although he became his own idea, which you can't inoculate against. Before he dried up on those streets like an old turd, he escaped to Florida. I may have got the idea to escape to Colombia from Ratso. But it's what's going on street side that makes New York. And street side makes us all the same. Everybody in New York is working a scam: it's understood, it's de rigueur, it's pulling the same string together off one big ball of twine and expecting to have more than the next guy. It's feeling we're all in this together even when we're fucking each other over. That's why so many celebrities live in New York. That's why John Lennon lived here. Why he died here is another thing.

Chapter Two:
Radicals at the coffee shop

Saturday, December 6, 1980
6:00 p.m.
(50 hrs/45 min. before John Lennon's murder)

All those secrets Raul keeps from me in Bogota – who he does it with and where they meet and why *that* one – that's bad enough. But it's not knowing when he will leave that unhinges me. Raul has never threatened leaving. But I know he plans to. So I embrace forgetfulness which has led to idleness. And so the income has dried up. I no longer paint. And I don't answer the phone. Invitations from galleries and commissions from collectors wither and fade like the gifts of love from prodigal children.

But it's not the money I miss. What I lack is the benefit of correction, that small degree of apportioned forgiveness bestowed on my blighted soul for each canvas I paint. Raul's intention to leave has so badly gnawed at my nerves that I sit drunkenly with sangria under the cashew trees rather than paint in the studio. You see, I paint in the day as Raul sleeps on the trundle bed in the shed that adjoins the kitchen. He likes to hear the rain on the tin roof. I used to paint all day as he slept and then at night, when his cab slips between rendezvous trysts, I would fall paint-bespattered and spent onto the sofa in my studio and sleep there with our calico cat curled upon my stomach as long as I could but almost always would awake with the advent of birdsong and the screen door banging shut as Raul returns in one of his bad moods. Now it's sangria and idleness.

Then, bless me! The phone rings and I answer, and the voice is buoyant and American, a young lady's voice almost flattering in its uncertainty as to protocol – how do you ask a favor of an internationally recognized criminal? Someone's executive assistant with a radical idea and told go ahead and try for all the good it will do you. Well, I agree! What a coup for her. And an icebreaker for me. I'm back in the studio. This time with a secret kept from Raul.

Time magazine will commission cover art to commemorate the 20th anniversary of John Lennon's martyrdom. What better man for the job than me, Mason Fisher. I am, of course, too famous already to take this too seriously, but I accept the commission and I design an exposé in oils and in implants that some criminal psychologists call a revelation. I effect a kind of last supper of the disciples of mayhem with Chapman a transfigured Holden Caulfield in Pencey Prep letter sweater and scuffed loafers beneath London Fog rain coat and Russian fur hat. His blushes signal an insincere humility. He has just announced into a meditative knot of locked fingers his intention to kill John Lennon and Dennis Zamora's intention to betray his gesture for payment in gold. Yes, and Dennis' intention to betray me.

I place all in the coffee shop on Amsterdam Avenue. On the foreground, seated at table, five dark torsos evanesce verging on strobe in the viewer's shuttering adjustment to these zeroes of color value that anchor the eye's temptation to ride the linear hooks of lighted cigarettes deep into backspace, orthogonals webbing out of tightly packed cones of fovea viewing like tracer bullets over a night sky. On the foreground, this critical mass of intellectuals generates a kind of black hole that sucks away the light of enlightened thinking. There is, overall, a dimpled shadow of chiaroscuro, what the Italians call *sfumato* – smoky soft edges, the veils of shadow.

Perspective is camera obscura. Like the room's image has been projected directly onto my canvas and sketched there in fine detail. Behind the transecting head table of Chapman and company, where the room foreshortens into background, ancillary characters fill the space more fauve in high value color than the foreground. Here the wannabe Ginzbergs posture (every beard a bard). The mottled and harlequin flit and spark in squirms applied over sepia. They identify as neighborhood Romeos, Lesbos, and thespians. There are day-old beards and food dancing on the tongues of laughter. There are chocolate-skinned Hungarian waitresses lifting trays in short T's and tight skirts, leg muscle glistening, hair below navels thick as ants in caravan. There is no place for the eye to rest. I have never tolerated lazy viewers.

My material implants catalogue the implements of trade – embossed bits of metal and china suggesting espresso machines, battered coffee cups, a stamped and rusted tin ceiling, tubular chairs designed to discomfit customers.

We four of the "consequence five" (as the media names us in the attendant article), we four reside upon the foreground. There's me the artist Mason Fisher, the writer Dennis Zamora, the musician Rowan Murray, and the psychologist Leon Rozen. For us the Hungarian Pastry Shop was our therapy group, our sin and redemption, our political caucus, our alter ego, our congregate personality making plans no right-minded individual would consider on his own. Like Chapman, each of us four will find ourselves leveraged to action by an idea that made sense in all but the doing. When the fine art of theory comes to practice, few will remain behind to clean up the damage. One that will is Dennis Zamora. But he won't so much tidy as rearrange the facts.

Dennis will see the advantage of rearranging the littered remains to mislead conclusions. Dennis is a shit. Dennis sits left of center in the composition, the Judas seat. He is a Yaley and back then an assistant editor and an aspiring writer slaving for a big publishing house in New York City. His thinning blond hair contoured by the comb into lush rows of wheat straw is enhanced with commercial volumizers. His shoulders are round though solidly powerful, as if Dennis were eternally leaning into the scrum of an idea, as if ideas need to be engaged physically. His eyes are gentian blue, often mistaken for empathetic. They will have, in my painting, lost their appealing luster as they have sunk deeper beneath the porches of a brow over weighted in self-importance. His teeth are small and pointy, animalistic, hidden behind a cool grin that commands the ironies he believes spin our world.

Alongside Dennis and close beside Chapman sits long-time friend Leon Rozen, a Brooklyn Jew with black wavy hair, eyeglasses with frames thick as the undercarriage of a Cadillac, a sculpted beard, and a guileless smile that signals his trust in the benign influence of universal truths. Leon grew up in Brooklyn Heights where the harp strings of the Brooklyn Bridge have sung to him the kabbalistic mysteries despite his being the first-born son of an almost secular household, the first-born son of an Israelite so in need of redemption because Aaron preferred his own God (the

Golden Calf) and because no one has ever paid five shekels to the Kohen for him to say while holding money over Leon's head: "This instead of that, this in commutation for that, this in remission for that." An oversight that may explain why Leon has wandered Brooklyn an unredeemed Jew, never having left the five boroughs. Like the Jew that ran afoul of Jesus, Leon has always thought it would take personal apocalypse to end the restlessness. He was right. Leon has studied the dimensions of the Torah while shifting from one sukkah residence to the next: abandoned factory lofts, decommissioned ironworks rusting beside the river, the prolapsed lintels of a one-time jewelry store behind metal grating fronting Hasidic bookies. Only when Leon decides to study Freud rather than Moses and takes classes at Columbia University will his mail catch up with him.

"So," says Leon, "a Jew goes to a bar with a parrot on his shoulder. The bartender says, 'Where did you get him?' 'In Brooklyn,' says the parrot." Leon is at home in Brooklyn. He is the Leopold Bloom of Brooklyn, a familiar peripatetic in black turtle neck sweater and gray Scandinavian cardigan with brass buttons embossed in runic geometrics, hands clasped behind his back, leaning toward Jerusalem on skinny legs pushing wool checked pants. Leon's disregard for fashion confirms a life dedicated to the passions of intellect. His one vanity is facial hair, which he trims carefully after a restless sleep and trusts that whatever drapery lies beneath his chin will little offend. Leon tosses in bed, his dreams a vivid nightmare of Heaven's gates barred, his fists pounding the headboard, a trauma to sleep mates who will cradle his sweat-rimed and heaving body. None will successfully quell the barrage, though Leon is perpetually affianced, as he will be at the time of this history, and which will be his last.

Leon is a slob and a blubberer with a saint's obsessions. In my painting for *Time* an almond shaped, nimbus-like yarmulke appears to shimmer dimly above his head in the shock of an overhead lamp. When in the grip of a new compulsion, Leon will operate in strict observance of this new principle despite the inconvenience to his fiancée of the moment and his friends who run away, and then Leon will cry it out and come to his senses and find another girl, usually one of his fiancée's girlfriends, and retrieve what friends he has left. Dennis always forgives Leon. Those two go back many fiancées. Leon brought the iconoclasts to the "shop" originally. Chapman will happen upon this intellectual enclave by accident. The Hungarian coffee shop is Leon's off-campus meditation cell. Leon studies religion and psychology at Columbia University. "I can tell you how big a dick God is in five religions!" is what he says when asked where this advanced education is leading. Now and in my advanced stage of life, I want to know how big a dick God *has*. One who professes to know is Roman Murray.

In the painting, Rowan sits across from Leon and close beside Chapman. Rowan is English. He still wears his university scarf, London School of Economics. But he took a vow of poverty when he found himself tuneful, intimate with a Japanese piano, moved to New York City to insert himself into the artsy set of the theatre district, took a PhD in musicology, then got knocked up by the muse from which came an opera score derivative of Glass and Wilson's *Einstein on the Beach*. But in this case Paul Tillich, a WWII émigré and theologian, meets on a beach somewhere east of Boston a disaffected Roman Catholic priest who puts Tillich's new-world religion to practice burning churches. *Radical! A tumescent brain gives birth to vertical opera,"* said Joseph Papp, who boldly sponsored

Rowan's opera after his effectual campaign of name dropping and schmoozing. *Very much borrowed genius* is what Papp will say of Rowan's opera to *Newsweek* once Chapman's notorious deeds are done and they, "the consequence five," are suddenly worth the ink. Mason's response to Papp's comment will come a week later in a letter from Scotland to the editor: "Borrowed genius? Is there any other kind?"

"Too advanced for the colonies," Rowan says with a thin smile. You see the hurt. Rowan picks crumbs off plates at the "shop," never orders his own, flings over his shoulder a tangle of red hair like a shawl. He agitates over everything, freckles on his skin as dizzy and complex as henna stains, but so positively sure of himself even if flightier than Leon, not likely to perch long when he lands. A passionate Brit. Out of character. Spooky as hell.

Rowan and Leon met one night Rowan played improv jazz to a small gathering in an intimate chamber of walnut burls and stained glass at Columbia University, stitching dark motifs to a lengthy nocturne in a single key so changes would shock. And they did. Leon told Rowan he was blown away by the guy's intensity, which inserted Leon into the thick of that evening's soiree (piano music, poets reciting, political debate, pillow talk in the corners of Rowan's basement apartment). There was scant furniture, mostly pillows and throw rugs and bulky potted fronds that somehow thrived without sunlight and in cigarette and marijuana smoke thick as cumulus. The smoke was getting to Leon. And of course there was that ebony Japanese piano, severe profile and sharp teeth, snapping at Leon when he got too near. A one-owner piano is what Rowan said.

Leon asked Rowan to "transition" with him to the pastry shop, transition being a Rowan word that Leon had adopted as his own. Leon described the attributes of a writer friend and an artist friend, me before the advent of Raul, whom he was to meet there after which Rowan said, "I'd like to. I shall reassert the corporeal among you chaps." Yes, he talks like that, and he said this while looking condescendingly upon his salon guests going languid in smoky circlets of body heat and lungs aspirating. Rowan is never keen on his own parties. He has a habit of ditching friends. We all got cranked on espresso at the shop, which very much asserted the corporeal.

It was instant chemistry with the brotherhood of the café klatch. For one thing, Rowan already knew Dennis Zamora, Leon's writer friend. He knew him from London, and had a couple years later met him again in New York in a bookstore. There was between them, at the coffee shop, boisterous glad reunion, and much discussion of the intersections of destiny, after which Dennis reasserted his superior smirk and observant ways, thinking he will put this all in a novel someday.

But in this novel, things will go like this: Rowan will supply the romantic, impractical impulse to tear at the fabric of convention that the brotherhood needs for engaging reluctant leaps of faith. Leon Rozen, besides Rowan, will have the most gumption/slash/tenacity/slash/grit, what have you. But he won't let go where Rowan won't hang on. Rowan will always be looking for another principle to ride. And me, well, will you be surprised to know I played the fool? I embody a crude and plodding earthiness that Rowan's musical, Platonist abstractions lack. Rowan seemed to want me around for grounding. And Dennis will observe with dispassionate intellectual intensity the folly and the genius of our experiments in applied assertion. We four will establish a habit of coffee shop rendezvous, after which, many months later Chapman will arrive, the obligatory mad man, number five in the iconoclast brotherhood. But first, Claudia Fontaine.

About Claudia, it's like this: by the time Claudia Fontaine and I attend Saturday night at the "shop," December 6th, 1980, fifty hours and forty-five minutes before the John Lennon murder, the other café habitués are already seismic with plans. Rowan has been tight with the boys for several months. I had just met Claudia at the Metropolitan Museum of Art where I worked as a security guard. She had vogued into European paintings, my usual guard station, and had bent in genuflect to inspect the lower shelves of a glass case of miniatures. I was into women then.

And what I saw from behind, my, my – up the skirt a tight package and a herringbone curve of backbone as the sweater slid off hips. That's all I needed. Long legs in knee-high leather boots, black stockings, a black leather mini-skirt foundation to an out-sized designer sweater. Her hair fell to the 12th vertebra. Cleopatra hair, opaque skin and pale-blue eyes. Stunning! And while I recognized her garb as designer elite, runway knockoffs for the well-to-do, out of my league, this didn't put me off.

She sat quietly at table, once I had made introductions, her first time among the café brotherhood. And when the waitress called her name, did she get looks! The place was excited as hell to have Madison Avenue chic among them. When she removed her knobby Italian Krizia sweater, pink and gray with metallic threads glinting, and the shock of her skin emerged in generous, Huxley would say "pneumatic" domes, a *Doors of Perception* tee shirt with Aldous peering out from those Coke-bottle eyes (this guy, more than Leon, was *really* blind), it looked like Leon would shit himself. I sat Claudia directly across from myself, and reached under the table to caress her knee, which she pinched (delicious) and swatted away, never giving sign of the tiny drama going on sub-tableau. Dennis gave one of his best understated performances, waiting until asked to reveal beguiling details of his envious and important life to Claudia. She worked for Sotheby's. She had studied art history at Vassar and was between degrees, "learning to spot forgeries," she said, and gave Dennis a pointed look. I laughed. This might have been the only time I have ever seen Dennis embarrassed.

Rowan launched directly into a tangle of disastrous ideas that would in three days cancel the life of John Lennon: "Are you aware of Immanuel Kant's theory of deontology?" he said. "Are you chaps enlightened as to the what-have-you of its implications?"

He seemed to be looking at me.

"Voodoo. Demons. The west coast of Africa? Am I right?" I said and looked to Claudia for confirmation of my moment of wit, but she was entranced by the violence of Rowan's delicate fingers twisting errant strands of red hair behind his ears, thumping the table to rhythms playing behind his eyes, those eyes bright with passion, a hurdy-gurdy man's resolve to crank out the noise in his head, an exhibitionist that needs a crowd to keep his performance sharp and meaningful. I had forgotten the impact of Rowan's performance upon the uninitiated.

"No, the antinomies? You mean the antinomies," said Dennis in that aren't-you-impressed orbicular tone he puts on in public. "Opposing forces, necessary tensions."

"No, that's Antilles! Voodoo and volcanism. Am I right?" I said with increasing suspicions of having been outmaneuvered by Dennis. I looked again to Claudia. She nodded vacantly, occupied still with Rowan's display of motion at rest.

"Walk tall in a dark continent. Beat drums in the antipodes. A lesson to be learned," said Leon.

Leon is far too obscure, but likeable because his emotions color everything. You know where you stand with Leon, even though his mind is chameleon. Leon has studied the science of metabolic control. He goes so deep into inactivity sometimes that his heart takes a half day off, like the fat-bellied Buddha that sucks in his glands and floats off the ground. Leon can do that. He's been known to disappear entirely during a conversation – watch his eyes, they roll back inside his skull like marbles spinning and he's gone. A whole conversation can go on around him while he's meditating, but he's there with you too. He's keeping track on some level. He comes back from wherever he's been and offers treasures of observation. He'll say he's been swimming in the "collective unconscious," which is a Carl Jung term although Leon's a Freudian and those two shrinks did not get along. Leon thinks he may have lived another life in Atlantis and met Carl Jung there and been influenced by him.

"What lesson, Leon? Beat drums when the flashlight dims? Have your eyes got worse?" said Dennis scuttling Leon's emphatics with a joke. But Leon had predetermined an explanation. He has a talent, or maybe it's a disability, for ignoring the currents at play of bantered ideas. He goes tight as a walnut, disappears into the meat of process, then squiggles and squints as prelude to his next gush of epiphany over some idea already left behind. Leon is always somewhere aslant proportionally as a conversationalist.

"We Jews keep to the shadows, Dennis," said Leon. "'Hold day with the Antipodes' is what we say; 'walk in absence of the sun.' That's Shakespeare. *Hamlet*, I think."

"*Merchant of Venice*," said Dennis.

"Bardic victory!" I said. Claudia responded with a wince and a wrinkle at the flange of her nostrils, a fleeting, not so complimentary glance.

"Pyrrhic," said Dennis.

"Yeah, whatever," I said in complete intellectual rout, sensing that nothing I say will impress Claudia. But I could maybe get her to *SEE* me. I am an artist after all. What I have to say usually messages best from canvas. Must get her to the studio is what I began to think. Which as a cliché of behavior does not place me in the best light. But to be fair, this appraisal of 1980s Mason Fisher does not reflect the man I have become, all the deep reading I have done, the self-reflection, the astute assessment of culture and the art of which I am now capable as a middle-aged homosexual, as opposed to this misguided and callow hetero. My IQ will have increased substantially with man love.

"No, no ... (Rowan won't be out-lectured) it's this," he said: "You must walk in the sun, Leon! So shall we all. Let justice be done though the heavens should fall. That is to say, in deontology, a right action requires no justification in consequence. If we are men, and it is my contention that we are, we must act in the right as we perceive that to be without first charting the consequences. To act only after prognosticating results is to live our lives as aspic shaking upon a plate of garnish."

"Or Mason shaking his jelly on the Coney Island rollercoaster..."

"It's called the Cyclone, Dennis. It's a metaphor of life. The heights, the depths," I said defending my corpulence and my fondness for the Coney Island rollercoaster. Dennis likes to assert my bulk as contradiction to the concept of starving artist.

"Gyres within gyres, my friend," said Dennis. "The center cannot hold."

Which of course will explain my medical problems twenty years hence. As the earth spins and the body ages, all sorts of shit breaks loose – retinas, bowels, aortas, all that defining muscle and flesh. It's the ageing process that's a bitch, not me.

"We all fall down!" I said in haste to derail Dennis' penchant to out-Brit the British, and because I have heard Dennis recite that Yeats' poem a hundred times, and I have suffered the lecture, touched the "purple twilight," and couldn't care less. But Rowan likes that Yeats anchored his poetry in politics, a kind of philosopher king, oracular and lovelorn, so Dennis feels encouraged to expound Yeats. I hate all this romantic, artist as mystic shit.

"Yes, that's right, Mason," said Dennis in his man-of-letters patter we all know to patronize or risk aphorisms blooming into essays. "No need to force heroics. Yeats is right. Giambattista Vico is right. We're slipping into a period of spiritual correction. The 60s will rise again."

"Yes, the Irish," said Rowan in not much of a Yeats mood, maybe feeling upstaged. "Bellies and blarney, Guinness and mysticism, Madam Blavatsky and the like, chasing the muse of history with whips and scourges…"

"Naked! Wouldn't she be … *naked*?" I said winking at Claudia. "The muse, right? Has to be. Always is. Wouldn't inspire otherwise."

"William Blake meditated naked. Like a bird," said Claudia, then hesitated. No one answered. Then nervously began again. "Naked up a tree in his back yard. In London," said Claudia seemingly amused, finally, with my foolish patter. "His wife stood the watch. Also naked."

"What's that? I don't understand," said Rowan going deeper inside his own three pounds of universe.

"William Blake," said Dennis. "The lady has asserted William Blake. Implied fidelity as muse." Dennis nodded at Claudia to assure that he is simpatico, that they have made a Blake connection. She wasn't connecting, not with Dennis. She was, in fact, beginning to accept my hand rubbing her knee. I had been planning ahead, getting headachy from a permanent squint looking through those Coke-bottle Huxley glasses on her tee shirt to the objects of my desire. Doors of perception, yes indeed.

"Barbarella!" I said apropos to absolutely nothing but my perversities and Claudia's renewed interest. "Barbarella over conjugal nudity."

"Yes," said Leon, "de-crucify the angel!"

"And so, the brotherhood welcomes chaos as a friend," said Dennis.

"What? No. Listen, gentlemen, and lady," said Rowan in a fit of pique, disliking interruption, taking himself *so* seriously, typically Brit in this case. "More than chaos, deontology is foundation shaking. Or let's say, so many assertions acted upon may topple civilization as we know it, the exertion of such stresses…"

"Did you say tresses? My lady has the most lovely tresses," I said smiling at Claudia. She smiled back. Instant boner.

"Holden Caulfield!" said the waitress in Slavic diphthongs, tipped at the hip like a broken toy, skinny legs splayed in a Picasso disarray of parts out from a tight black skirt but centered somehow, balancing a tray burdened with coffees and pastry. A cherubic, sandy-haired man-boy said, "Yes, here!" but kept his head low and his eyes lower, contemplated the interior space of latticed fingers on the table in front of him. He wasn't praying. We knew this. His thoughts made too much noise. They whirled like fragments of indecision inside that tangle of hands. "Where?" said the waitress. We looked at Holden. Dennis raised an arm and pointed with the authority of a ventriloquist. Holden spoke again in a whisper: "Here."

A slice of Dutch chocolate cake slathered in fudge frosting and a demitasse of espresso with lemon slice floated to the table. The kid had taken the unpopular head-of-table seat where waitresses bump with hips and slice head space with John-the-Baptist trays. Holden had been monitoring our conversation for some time. We hadn't noticed. He is the kind you don't notice until he shoots someone.

Rowan sensed a void and rushed to fill it: "I was saying," he said, "that society can only be validated, sanctioned as it were, when challenges of equal proportion arise in opposition. Complacency is the death of civilization, wouldn't you say? Change is another matter."

"Don't worry. It'll be decided soon. Your friend is right. They're coming together, history and time," said Holden Caulfield.

"What's that?" said Claudia, more polite than any of us would have thought to be.

"Isn't it obvious? It's New York City, almost Christmas, approaching Monday and Holden is falling. It's synchronicity! That's what it is," Chapman said. There was chocolate on his chin, which he smiled away disarmingly and wiped with the back of a hand, then lifted an espresso to the lips that had advanced this spare but pregnant, well-timed interruption. He smiled again. A long silence ensued.

"Caesura," said Dennis, never comfortable with the unsaid.

"Not to be mistaken for the gap in Mason's front teeth."

"What the fuck?" I said with more vehemence than I intended which Holden took to be a response to his comment – maybe because I had turned my eyes on him in frustration, as Claudia had slapped me off her thigh. Holden effected that doughy wounded look we would see a lot in the next few days. He's the kind of kid you want to kick around the block, know it's wrong, but can't help yourself. But if you ever did, he would come at your back with a hatchet in a pique of blind temper.

"I'm saying," Holden said to Rowan, a hand covering his chocolate mouth, shaking a finger at Rowan and eyes at me, "I'm saying you're right. Something's gotta give. Watching the wheels go round goes nowhere, man."

"Ah," said, Rowan, "a companion in sensibility – a man of foresight, a modern among pagans. Shakespeare and Yeats, indeed! Quote me a little Beatles to keep us forward looking. May I ask your name, sir?"

"Mark David Chapman," said Mark David Chapman, blushing purple and beating to airy thinness with his spoon crumbs of chocolate cake.

"Well," said Rowan, "may I on behalf of my friends here welcome you to the café brotherhood."

In celebration of which, and by way of apology, I held up upon a fork the remains of my cheese Danish and snapped the crust into my mouth which had been recently chewing my foot.

"You were saying, Mark. Something must give," said Dennis.

"Yes," said Mark. "Change is coming. We all have doors to walk though. Doors for change." Chapman looked for the longest time at each who shared the table, spooky, before he spoke. "You want the king-maker's door (he said to Rowan), the visionary's door for you (shaking a finger at Claudia's Huxley tee shirt), the door to the tablets of law for you (Dennis smiled self-consciously), and for you the door to the secret garden (he said to me). I'm not sure about you – root cellars and insect larva, I think (he said to Leon, which was agreeable to all but Leon and elicited chuckles from all but Leon). And for me," he said, "I will open a door into the soul of John Lennon."

He had a little red book buried deep in a jacket pocket which he slapped on the table, which we mistook for the Communist Manifesto, companion to that ridiculous Russian fur hat pulled down to his eyes and long-tailed London Fog raincoat draping his pudginess in a fashion which regressive Moscow, in the voice of Pravda, would have condemned as cosmopolitanism.

"Do you mean icons?" said Rowan, pointing to the red book. "Icons of philosophy, religion, law, pop music? Is this your angle, Mr. Chapman? I don't follow exactly." But Mark didn't seem to care who followed. He had lowered his head and was ignoring us while playing with his smear of chocolate fudge on the plate. He removed his winter hat and ruffled his hair in agitation. We were getting a little freaked.

"Well," I said, "if there is no conclusion to this confusion, Claudia and I will bid you toodle-oo. We're off to see my sketches." This I said with some trepidation, but Claudia said nothing back, which I took for affirmation. "Later at Francine's?"

"Sure," said Rowan, "but conclude we must."

"Please," said Dennis," put a nail in the coffin."

"All right then, chaps, it is thus. We must in all conscience and in aid of our planet's reconstitution ... "

I just hate this too, too seriousness bullshit of Rowan's.

"We must all," said Rowan, "and I concede the point to our friend Holden Caulfield, we must each of us design a plan to pressure icons, to crack the veneer if not entirely destroy and reform that which defines us, because you see, what evolves will be more who we must be. We must do what's right and disregard the consequences. Because to do so will ensure a more valid world. Evolution through a modification of ideals."

"Yes. I feel that too," said Leon quietly but with a dark intensity.

"Good!" said Mark David Chapman. "I'm in for John Lennon. The phonies will fall."

Chapter Three:
Claudia Fontaine views Mason's anatomies

Saturday, December 6, 1980
9:00 p.m.
(47 hrs/45 min. before John Lennon's murder)

"You say you want a revo-*loo*-shun, *un* ...," Claudia throbbed basso profundo in my yellow Toyota. "Well hell you *know-o*," she crooned bel canto, "the phonies gonna fall." She collapsed from the effort, arms splayed, palms raised, underarms florid with pheromone. My senses inflamed. I had intuited turns on the road from Manhattan to Brooklyn, fogged on cannabis, following like a blazed trail familiar commercial signage – Sanka, ESSO, Nabisco, Purina – looming billboards, the gods of commerce leading me God knows where. I had convinced Claudia to view my art, stacks of canvas rejected by New York galleries, glamorous intentions of self-definition and self-introduction, now like business cards gone to where business cards go to die. They littered the floor and leaned in abjection against apartment walls. Yes, I was bitter.

"What in hell does that mean, Mason? The phonies will fall," said Claudia. She gestured gracefully an arabesque of long arms sweeping a trail of cannabis through delicately structured questions, so she imagined, the Huxley tee shirt expanding, doors opening wider.

"I don't know. He wants attention. He … Chapman… he has … ungracious urges," I said gazing at the tee shirt, pleased with my tidy little summary, deferring my habit of complication beyond assessing Claudia's urges like interpreting a cubist rendering of a female nude in multiple planes suggesting parallel lives, one of which I thought I might seduce.

"Creepy. But Mason, defacing a painting at the museum? You would do that?"

"Andy won't mind. He might be flattered."

With that statement, I shocked even myself. At the shop conversation had ended by summoning icons of personal significance. Rowan had said make it spontaneous. What do you love most? Something that would mean something if you were to destroy it. To me, Warhol is the master, the profound theorist, a celebrity intellectual. I wanted Warhol's mentorship back then, and I had already been introduced, but I found myself vying with Jean-Michel Basquiat for Andy's attentions. Jean-Michel is the Puerto Rican/ Haitian graffiti artist Andy had offered Factory sponsorship after the Colab exhibition that June at Times Square. My paintings were there too, but Basquiat was given the Factory attention I wanted. I had been relegated to lurking at the edges, shamelessly voyeuristic and star-struck. I wanted to fall into orbit around Warhol but found Basquiat eclipsing my talent. Maybe in my case, the act of destroying one of Warhol's paintings was Oedipal, an impulse to replace the patriarch. Who knows? I did stupid often enough back then without rattling the windows of the thought police. I had opportunity and access. I could deface, literally, and with ease, Andy's Marilyn Monroe silkscreen.

"How can I be mixed up with anything so foolish? Here, toke

for you," said Claudia. We had idled at a traffic light through cycles of green, yellow, red. Traffic had diverted around us. I snagged the joint, stroked Claudia's thigh. My as yet intact hetero-motor generating, I liked to think, intimations of a climactic resolution. I will discover she is one of those who can't turn off the brain, who cipher through sex like tallying the phone bill. Very frustrating when navigating a love canal hopelessly toxic in static and chatter. But this revelation will come later for me, in the dull and sticky afterglow beyond partnering in sex, and in crime.

"Listen, Mason, you notice Leon staring? Stared at me but said hardly a word."

"Notice *me* staring at you, Claudia? You are an object of some worth."

"How sweet, Mason. An object."

"Yes. You are … seriously. You are… oh, shit! Claudia, look at you! You have taken glorious shape … and walked out the gallery. I *found* you in a gallery. Did you forget?"

"Pygmalion."

"You know that one."

"Couldn't be an object of worth if I didn't."

"Art is leaving the gallery, Claudia. You notice? The artist is leaving the gallery. They might as well for all the good public adoration does that stuff. It's flies in amber in those museums. The living, breathing, buyable, sellable object … it's leaving the gallery. Art makes life, Claudia. Or is it life makes art?"

"You just want me naked on a pedestal."

"Nice thought. Do you know Duchamp? His collage paintings and constructions?

"Fingernail clippings, bottles of urine, cigarette ash – Merzbau.

A shoe left on a gallery floor. Crap!" said Claudia.

"An artist selects his materials, Claudia. That shoe in the gallery … maybe the janitor's, maybe Duchamp's, maybe the mistress'. Those materials become art when the artist surrenders his ego and embraces what's given by chance. Chance placed you in *my* gallery, Claudia. In this urban garden… you grace the paths. I am an artist, Claudia, and I have accepted this gift. You *are* an object of worth, Claudia."

"Touching, Mason, but disingenuous."

"Disingenuous? Who talks like that?"

"Pardon the sins of Westport. You going to *do* me, Mason?"

"What?"

"Destroy what you most love. That's it, right? Destroy me, Mason. Project what you see us doing the next two hours, Mason – oh, shit! watch that cab! (I palmed the horn and cussed Jesus, nosed the Toyota aggressively into traffic. I intended for Claudia to feel secure in the testosterone flush of my response). So, Mason, you have asked me to see your etchings. Very cliché."

"Yes, but they're oils, Claudia. I paint. I don't etch."

"I thought you guard."

"What I paint, I guard with my life. For the rest … I sell a service."

"What does Leon do?"

Notice what was going on. I may be right to swear off women. Notice me provoking intimate while Claudia potentializes my friends. It's the partnering instinct, the female neolith calculating cave rent potential, comparing the single eyebrow scraping antelope hide beneath a full moon to the romantic, slack-muscled guy painting cave walls by flambeaux. Who do you think inspires more vaginal effluvia? As to pre-provider flings, these go to the silent, brooding loners, the Leon types. I knew well enough Leon's attraction potential, having lost to him already a love interest or two. The Leon types get all the action from women that think. But it's the Dennis types that march them down the aisle. It's all that arrogance and self-assurance. I was around for the entertainment. I knew. I had no qualms about that.

"Listen, Claudia, you could maybe nab a little Leon attention between fiancés. Stay with me tonight and make a play before vows, if you like, if they happen. He's my housemate – eternally affianced, eternally single. He'll be here before daybreak to change clothes because he works on Sunday. We can wait out the party. Stay overnight! If you'd like. If that's not against your principles."

"My principles, Mason, are beyond your approach."

"Look, Claudia (holding back the rush, handing back the joint), I'll show my paintings another day. Let me be your roustabout. We'll stay toasted … run wheels off this circus wagon … circumnavigate the island … smoke more joints … play the radio … sing Beatles … maybe go to Coney Island … groove on the winter ghost of Cyclone's mighty arcs. After I'll drive you home like I promised."

"That's just silly, Mason. We can be more adult than that."

"What's wrong with silly … silly has its place. And what's so silly about Coney Island? We can walk the beach under the stars. It'll be romantic. No one else there. All those working-class bodies glistening with sweat and salt water, they're at home watching TV. In the summer I do my anatomy studies in the shadow of the Cyclone. It's a magic place."

These conventional date plans evaporated all pretense of my taking control which cozied Claudia in her seat. Huxley's doors of perception opening just a bit wider.

"Mason," she said, "I'll let you, if you want … you can have me. But I won't love you for it. And after, I want to see this party."

"Why not love me? I'm eminently loveable. I'm lonely and deep. Far deeper than Leon."

"The last man I let myself love, Mason … he was an artist … another fucking artist … had the… what you say… critical eye. Sardonic. Weary of the world before he even found his place in it. Critical of *everything*… I don't sense that in you, Mason … he was a cartoonist … selling cheap to the alternative tabloids. Those ones with shocker headlines, those ones dropped outside bars and coffee houses. You know those ones I mean, Mason (she took another drag off the joint): those ones with personals group sex, used cars, used roommates (giggles), punk band desires amphetamine drummer, that kind of shit … his cartoons, they were … yes … they were ads too: ADmonishments: tiny cynicisms upon which a reader might suspend a life, like we're all sets of empty clothes looking for a hanger (giggles). Oh, shit, I should smoke this stuff more often! My old boyfriend, did he have answers! Oh yes, so many answers, oh *God*, he had answers … (Claudia dropped her feet on the dash, scooched lower in the seat, cranked the window and tossed the nubby joint) well, there was one fucking answer he didn't have, but I won't go there … it was like … Mason … it was like cozying with a consumer guide… making love to Ralph Nader… do you see?"

"I pretend no answers," I said with conviction.

"What does that mean?"

"I mean … Oh, shit. I'm stoned. How can your brain still be working?"

"Your mind doesn't quit when it gets a little smoky, Mason."

"Mine does. Hell I haven't had an idea since sixth grade."

"And you're a revolutionary?" she laughed.

"No. I'm a reactionary. I don't think I think at all. I react. Most often walk away. I'm wired that way."

I received a lovely smile and a pensive, dreamy silence after that all the way to the house at Sheepshead Bay. I had somehow triangulated the way home by a casual design of untoward lefts and deviant rights, which is the post-modern way to get there. Leon and I had thrown in together for the ground-floor rent of a granite facade townhouse with turrets and bay windows. It lies a hefty distance from the towers of Manhattan so was affordable in an Orthodox Jewish neighborhood. We could park cars on the street, buy dinner on the cheap at kosher delis or gentile pizzerias, decorate the apartment at will, make all the noise we wanted. We could even delay the rent because the agoraphobic landlord worked nights and slept days in the basement. The woman upstairs, a writer she said, had usurped the landlord's authority, copped a gig as rental agent. So Leon and I got the place cheap under condition the rental agent's nympho daughter share a bathroom and inhabit our summer porch. What the heck. It worked, despite the routine sexual ambush of nympho lounging naked in our bathroom, and strange men habituating the alley path to the backyard sun porch. But I didn't tell Claudia about all this. I didn't think she'd stay around long enough to give a shit. She was too classy for me.

So we crossed the threshold of the weathered oak door with etched and beveled glass some bourgeois, gentile family had installed in the 1920s, before the gangs, the pizza parlors under raised train platforms, the liquor stores, the widened lanes of all-night traffic, the Hasidic Jews, the homeless laid out on sidewalks as obstacles for pedestrians. Claudia said, "What can he mean, Chapman? What can he mean 'be with me, people'? Did you hear him say that? He was talking to himself like there was somebody there inside that head of his beside himself? Crazy person. What about you, mister. You crazy too? You crazy for *me*?"

Claudia draped her arm through mine and leaned on me as I jiggled the key to trip the latch. She rubbed affectionately the toe of a Versace boot across the arch of my sneaker. I got a lot more of this kittenish kneading once we had gone through the preliminary tour of my artist's studio/slash/bedroom. After we flipped through canvases stacked in a corner, drained a half bottle of scotch, I said, opening the frig door, which held little promise of a cure for the munchies, "Dine?" then pointed to the bedroom, "Or recline?" We fell between the sheets.

It was a little awkward at first. Guessing what the other one likes, elbows planted in the wrong places, those stray attentions you get that do nothing for you but you're too polite to say. But we were high enough and drunk enough to let ourselves play, to allow ourselves to discover what was needed. And after, there was no false modesty, no draping of sheets or hasty gathering of doffed clothes. Claudia had no problem being in her skin. She walked directly and proudly in her nakedness back toward that stack of canvases, her breasts swaying like a jungle goddess, said, "You know, Mason, I've been thinking about your work." Of course, *thinking* while screwing. "How you can be so warm in bed, so much passion, yet these..." she said fingering the stack. "Somehow, in your painting, distant emotionally."

This was not the first time I had hear that complaint. Before artistic fame attended my connection to the death of Lennon, one

New York critic had carped, the same one that made Basquiat an instant buzz: "Mason Fisher's style is Campbell's noodle soup poured into porno cookie molds." This critic will also be first in line to drop the guillotine on Mapplethorpe's dick. While in Bogota where I will escape murder charges and capitalize on notoriety, the critics will say: "Kinetic outlines of human form, stripped of fat but supple in contoured knots of muscle and genitals and red nerves, snakes jumping in an electric matrix. Fascinating!" This is what the critics say where the sun shines eternal. I will become famous in Bogota for my honesty and for my brutality as a stylist. Well, and something more, which I'm not too proud of, which will plant me solidly in the winners' circle – the John Lennon series, the invisible man in paint with all his internal trauma from various sources exposed, including Chapman's hollow points.

But here in New York, before the death of Lennon, I was just one more voice among five million others, every one of them in your face and howling like an Edvard Munch, just another artist contemplating suicide off any one of the five borough bridges. And who gave a shit! What I wanted most was for a viewer to imagine what is inside himself and to feel compelled to poke and rub hands on the canvas, strum the gut of sinew and squeeze the internal organs that blossom into cancers, examine the suture scars, jam fingers against plastic and metal inserts, smear the blood. Everything God and medico and chance and preference have done to the human body, all those enlarged breasts and penile implants and face lifts and nose croppings, I wanted us to see, up close and personal. And, yes, I get emotional about it. Even as my canvases come out cold and forbidding. But they should. It's the way we have allowed the sciences to manipulate how we perceive ourselves – our flesh cold as fish laid out on the operating table in a room cold as hell with tubes in our arms and masked strangers leaning over gauges. The body is our temple for fuck sake! My paintings show the clinical corruption of disease and the hidden results of our tamperings for fuck sake! That's why I want fingers on my canvas. I want to get human fat back on those stripped-down torsos. I want the grease of fingerprints. My canvases say, "Touch me, please!" Museum security guards be warned.

So I told this to Claudia, and darned if she didn't sit cross-legged, buck-naked still, and begin to trace with fingers those details of our blighted anatomy, and right away the stuff began to glow. The pigments I had deliberately thrown down un-stabilized began to blend and blur and soften. She pricked her finger on a shard of tin and placed a fingerprint in blood on canvas which she smeared then sucked off the excess. She was enthralled. She called me genius. I guess she must have still been drunk/slash/stoned, because I was. But I couldn't help feel that someone here on this planet gets it. Gets me. And that's powerful stuff. I could have fallen in love with that feeling.

Chapter Four:
Leon Rozen an item in Francine Carlton's trousseau

Saturday, December 6, 1980
8:00 p.m. – 10:00 p.m.
(46 hrs/45 min. before John Lennon's murder)

We must now consider Leon Rozen, true innocence. He is the most sympathetic victim of John Lennon's murder. Why he participated in the death of Lennon is one of the mysteries of Leon. He already carried with him the shame of complicity. Lives have been snatched away over the years within his reach, within his compass, all points of the compass, suddenly, for no justifiable reason – There was *Auntie Shelby, to his left, with the brain aneurism spazzing, blowing lunch at the Temple retreat of Rosh HaShanah, defibrillating and flopping, splinters in her arms from the weathered picnic table, slamming her head on the plank wood, groaning, and baby Leon strapped in his carrier seat beside her, gap-mouthed in wonder; then Stuey Jenkins, to his right, struck by lightning with aluminum bat swinging at the red laces of a giggly hardball at Jaycees Little League with Leon chewing gum in the batter's box; then Ranger, who ran ahead, the blintz-white Saint Barnard with black fetlocks ambling off a cliff in the Catskill Range with Leon yodeling his goodbyes* – and now, coming from behind is justifiable reason.

And now, the murder of Lennon, engaging in gesture, is coming from behind.

Only Leon, besides me, will experience debilitating pangs of conscience over the death of Lennon. And sadly, there will be, despite a parade of fiancées, no marriage, and no child born to Leon. And there will be no life for him in the healing arts or in translating God's words to man – no *public* life anyway. When all is done, Leon will abide sallow and pasty in the basement of his parents' house in Brooklyn Heights among worn books and empty pizza boxes, the fruit of which pre-paid by Dennis Zamora and delivered by prescription outside the front door. Some will petrify inside their boxes. Dennis' concern for an old friend's well-being hardly suggests nobility of gesture, but we, the narrative and I, must endorse this rare moment of kindness. Dennis knows Leon tends to neglect nourishment. He knows Leon is likely to disappear again into the labors of an obsession – this time medieval and occult, manuscript-strewn, candle-lit, cheap-wine and stale-bread induced.

Leon will become a neurotic compulsive. He will tack with adhesive across the perimeter of those damp cement walls a ribbon of scroll upon which to inscribe research documenting Old Testament views of Jewish identity. He will consider himself a betrayer of Freud. He will as a consequence attempt to reconcile his two gods (Freud & Moses) by showing definitively that Freud's preoccupation with the id was Kabbalistic in inspiration and a good thing for psychoanalysis. The paper he will publish in a reputable university press and then in the magazine *Psychology Today* will suggest as much but will go only so far. He will need to go further in his researches and in his understanding.

Like Gershom Scholem, the Jewish mystic, Leon believes in the power of language to invoke supernatural phenomena. He will want to unlock the power of the id through the symbolic words of the Kabbala. He will ignore the progression of seasons through window wells at ground level. Cracks in the foundation will emit salamander ooze and generate mushroom spores. Leon will become Dostoevsky's unnamed, navel-gazing hermit when by nature he is most suited as wandering Jew – telling the story of the murder of Lennon rather than hiding behind doors with the oracle that foretold it.

He will place his face against cracks in the foundation cement and breathe deep the gasses of decay he believes the oracle has released to open the primal consciousness of the Kabbalistic id. However abhorrent the image, we must imagine Leon feverish with expectation, his rubbery lips sucking a cavity of spores in the basement wall of his parents' home, infecting his blood with the decay of New York City. But Leon will never trust his interpretation of the sublime message from the inchoate. Self-doubt will deal the death blow to discovery. And Leon, make no mistake, he is a discoverer. Or should have been. Another Ulysses steering home, obstacles and oracles be damned. But Leon will lose his homing instinct from never again leaving home. He will spend his final days a blind man in a cave. Leon will live entirely upon the ethers of a theory, like sucking exhaust off expended energies from the machine that compels this drama.

So laugh if you must at frowzy Leon in his brown wool coat with the synthetic fox collar. After our first meeting with Chapman at the pastry shop, he maneuvered gears of his vintage Buick at curbside, belts screaming, kissing bumpers each end of his 88 Special outside his girl's apartment in Queens. He drove like a queen, hands on the wheel at 9 and 3. He pushed with his shoulder and all his squirrelly weight the sprung door of his tan and rust Buick with the shredded faux canvas top, hinges groaning like the gates of Hell. There is too a pungent residue throughout of vegetable matter, because Leon used the Buick to rid himself of garbage. He wrapped it in neat packages of brown paper sack secured with twine and that endearing Francine touch, a tape-on bow. Garbage then went onto the back seat of Leon's 88 and was stolen come dawn, the garbage not the car. We had taken to calling his vehicle "city garbage" but for different reasons. It's because some enterprising young turk with spray can became inspired. Could be that broad expanse of trunk said "billboard," could be the artist was a victim of garbage snatch, but whichever, the 88 got sprayed in Art Crumb/slash/Peter Max/ slash subway bravado with swirls and curly-Q's and multiples of primary color: city garbage it said. Divine! Leon loved it.

What needs to be said about Leon is that he had Claudia Fontaine on his mind even as he was shtupping Franny, his latest in a long line of fiancées (Francine Carlton: like the cigarette, long, slim, designer classy, dangerous to your health). On the sofa he was shtupping her. His teeth grinding, secretly intoning the Torah to elevate his thoughts. Sublimating the animal in himself with mediation.

Franny lived in a boxy glass and steel high-rise excreted from realty indulgences when the 1964 World's Fair had burgeoned across the Van Wyck Expressway. That's where Warhol painted his 20 by 20 mural of the thirteen most wanted which were, big surprise, all Italian. Governor Rockefeller thought this might insult his constituents, so made Andy whitewash it to oblivion. But the chrome globe unisphere with gyro rings remains intact. It floats even now in Franny's window. Back then it added three hundred to the rent. It evoked for Francine a selection of wedding rings, but that's Franny – aesthetics applied to commerce. She and Andrew Warhola would have got along perfectly. But this is a New York thing, art as commerce. No blaming her as originator. Nothing original about her, unless a fiercer than most audacity to consume. She pinned curtains mid-sash to suggest an unveiling – the globe constructed for her, set upon her plate, served up raw to a generous appetite.

The apartment's interior decoration suggested a sensitivity to a cultural ideal Francine doesn't share. She used Islamic design to imply the infinite, a dissolution of matter lost within ornate patterns, while her view of life is really quite limited. Franny's personal aesthetic positively claustrophobic. There were dense tangles of mandala rugs, Kasbah lamps of cobalt blue in wrought iron sconces, prints in gold frame of sultans and viziers in a pinchbeck, Klimt-like mosaics of battle regalia (pointy helmet diadems, impossible feathers, lion robes). Decidedly heretical, thought Leon, as Allah forbids human representation in art. But Leon knew Francine well enough to judge any awareness we might think she has of religious practice as imagined.

There were also sandalwood screens of carved acanthus and lotus intimating labyrinth in an apartment that was structurally one large box filled with things. This Islamic "architecture of the veil" was meant to separate a complex meditation sanctum from a desert landscape, in this case the one-dimensional, brassy Van Wyck Expressway. Islamic aesthetics had been further compromised by Sears dish stoneware in coronet ivy pattern and matching silverware etched with vine and wine glasses that flare invitingly like tulips. Francine's soul may be divined within this room, catalogued as contents, a 600 square-foot hope chest waiting for a man.

Poor Leon. She had been laying for this guy. But you can't blame Leon for being attracted. She has a lovely shape, tall and lean, well toned, curves in proportion. She has Nordic ice blues and natural white-blonde hair and the translucent skin of an Andrew Wyeth Helga painting, before Wyeth's obsession cloyed and clouded tinting Helga's complexion gray. Francine is sexy as hell so long as you like your women squeaky clean, sun-bruised, submissive in coitus, and complicated. She had yet to achieve orgasm.

Francine won't do the monkey unless she has a box of tissue near. She won't smoke a joint unless ash has its tray and smoke its ventilation. Potheads are asked to please lean over the kitchen stove and exhale out the fan exhaust. She serves white wine because of white shag beneath the dining table. Surfaces gleam severely dusted to primer. But you can't take eyes off Franny. She is most often draped low cut and shimmering like silver lamé, a throwback to silent movies film starlets, an echo motif of the armored warriors that gallop in contest upon her walls. The dress moves upon her like a force field. When she leans to tidy, her male guests bob and tip drawn irresistibly to that force field. And despite tweaking substantial income from book keeping at a property investment bank, to people that think, she's dumb as dirt.

As Leon took his fantasies of the raven-haired beauty Claudia Fontaine to the Lethe arms of Francine Carlton, the white princess, once he had shuddered his load of ego into her cold repository, he was less infatuated with Claudia, for the moment.

Leon had made the mistake of mentioning to me as a permanent condition Claudia's inability to climax. The antidote I had then frequently whispered to Franny out of self-interest, so as to get a second glance as potential back-door action. I'm not proud of this. But you see what I was like back then. How many ways had I enticed her to transgress with descriptions of a woman's orgasm? I tempted her with a libation from the fountain of youth; with kingdom come in her own personal big bang; with the rush of an unlimited charge on VISA; with a key to the door behind which Daddy awaits with an erection. I tried them all on Francine, but all she ever did was squeeze my wrist and grin at me and say, "Don't worry, Mason. It's a temporary condition." And I think she meant my condition, not hers. And even if she meant her condition, she would have been implying it won't be me that breaks through. She had stumbled onto the perfect response. Pure luck. Which is another of Francine's qualities. Everything she does is from self-interest. And everything she does works out perfectly, for her.

So there was Leon spent, trembly and numb while Franny bothered him for shoptalk of who among the café habitués will be in what mood for the party that night? What new alliances? What potential separations in relations? What new additions to the rotation of influences? With Claudia Fontaine coming guiltily to the forefront of his memory, Leon sidetracked to Rowan via Mark David Chapman:

"It's messy," Leon said. "Masada hopeless (a favorite phrase of Leon's). Beyond that, heretical. Crack the tablets and run. Regressive. Little boys in the bushes winging snowballs. It's little boys winging snowballs at police cars from the bushes. More screwy than what Rowan has got us into ever before."

"Will this make sense anytime soon, Leon?" said Francine, practical down to the inscription on her toe ring –*lick here* (which

Leon had tried, as have others, but to no effect). She lay beneath Leon still, rubbing her foot along his ribs while mopping with Kleenex.

"Rowan! Man! He's gone too far. His needs. He says he *needs* from me heresy! Can you see me a heretic?"

"Doesn't sound like you, Leon."

"No. Not me at all. And that Chapman. He says he's going to do it."

"Do what, Leon?"

"Kill Lennon."

"What Chapman, Leon? You must know Lenin is dead, Leon. Khrushchev killed him. You have got to get out of the Torah and read some *modern* history."

"No, the Beatle Lennon. He's serious. Chapman. He has expressed the constricted affect of de-realization. That's what we say at the clinic. He's going to run amok on the world. From docile to homicidal. He wants too much to please. He is sublimation of the will, turn the other cheek, a good little Christian, but if you strike that cheek it's grandiose delusion and mood-congruent psychosis. He *will* kill. Some part of him will. Enough of a part of him will. But Rowan … My god! He's clueless. Gone way too far this time. He says – Just another dance to step to, lads."

Leon pushed himself off Francine. Gripped the hair above his ears like pulling on wings, like taking flight in answer to his stress.

"I've been there for Cesar Chavez. Unsatisfying. Very. A whole week lost. Rowan could have lost his job. Beat garbage can lids outside the chancellor's office. Divest university stock in Florida citrus or something. Whatever. Then hands in the lap, boys. Twiddly dee, twiddly dumb. Abstinence in New Orleans. Purification begins in the loins, boys. And it's Mardi Gras, the whole world half-naked and crazy with lust. We make our point. Stay sober and unsullied. Drive back home with Bible Belt on the radio. Ah-Men. Are we not men! All the way back home dry humping on God vibes. Thought I would have permanent heart burn. Then, back in New York, Rowan brings *Hustler* to the shop. Says ... read letters to the editor! Some article on purification of the libido through wham-bam sex. After that, Rowan's insistence of course, whatever, the bars, the hangovers, and we're fucking girls in alleys – oh, unimportant, Francine, believe me, momentary – a ritual of opposing tensions is Rowan's plan all along, a counterbalance, the agapé of our New Orleans abstinence, the eros of our fuck rut in the alleys of New York. But this new thing Rowan is onto, this cultural iconoclast thing, it's thanatos ... goofy, dangerous. Conjure the daemon! Dance the whirligig! he says. Rowan says we all have genius. But he means himself. Says this every time. But now. He wants the one thing we love most, pillars of high culture and a higher self, shattered. Why damage what makes the most sense? Rowan, jeeze, sip the hemlock. Take the slow death like the rest of us. Mithridates, he died old. Respect the large things! Is what I say."

"You've been in school too long, Leon. It's not healthy for you. And if I'd known of you in those alleys, mister, well, let's say your blood would have been tested to the last drop before I would have considered a merger between the two of us. If you can't do it in the light of day, it is not proper doing. That's what my mother says, and she has a very, very solid marriage, Leon. You should get out of that coffee shop, Leon, meet some nice people. Well, soon enough. Once you're out working for a living among respectable people. Oh, that reminds me. Leon, you need to go out for wine. If Rowan brings that anorexic film directoress ...

"Director."

"She's a man?"

"No," Leon said, shaking his head, and bemused said further, "She dislikes female gender tags."

"Well, her loss. Will Rowan be joining us tonight, Leon? I'd love to find him a nice girl. That Chinky bitch drinks all my wine and won't say a word to me. *Never* sends thank-you notes. She's very arrogant, Leon. I have invited someone Rowan could bring home to mother. This one has a season's pass at the opera and is good, American stock. I need more wine, Leon. A nice Zinfandel will do."

"Yes, okay, yes. I'll go. But if Rowan is right – I should end your life right here."

"What's that?"

"Destroy the thing you love most, lads, he says."

"How will you do that, Leon? Sounds kinky."

Leon, naked still, walked behind and massaged Francine's throat like muting the stops of a flute, pressed the arterial vein to feel her heartbeat, the blue vein of a frozen shrimp. She melted into his thigh, wriggled. She has a lot of moves for being so frigid. Leon kissed her on the neck, patted her fanny, shook into his clothes and set off for wine. The moment she heard the door close Francine fingered herself in case there was latent heat there. But there wasn't.

"Heresy!" Leon said to the cars speeding past alongside, as he drove two-fisted the lane to A & P in a wavy state of agitation, ten miles below the posted limit, entirely unawares, reflexes like guide wires, thinking maybe he shouldn't be sorry at all as regards his proposed iconoclastic gesture – redesigning the argument in

Freudian/Judean bickering. "Intriguing idea," is what Rowan had said. Take God's favored, Moses, and Freud, the father of psycho-analysis, and shrink them down to comprehensible size. Rowan seemed to like the idea. Freud and Moses on the couch, give them a session. Who is the most fucked up? Who has the answers? Leon raised both hands off the wheel and banged them twice saying "Shit! Shit!" with each gesture. "The closer to permanence, the more flux I become. What am I doing? Attacking sacred scripture? Demeaning Freud? Getting married and wanting Claudia Fontaine? I'm a low coward. That's all. Say my theories make the pages of *Psychology*. What kind of stir? Intra-office buzz, footnote in a scholarship journal, at best a tremor of one of the seven pillars of wisdom. So what? I am no Luther. I won't be nailing the results on a temple door. I can't. And I won't de-Freud psychometrics. And I can't not have someone in my bed. Fuck me! I'm lost."

He loves Francine. He thought. Or maybe he just wanted to fuck her brains out and place his own thoughts there. Easily done since there was not much up there but *things* which a vigorous probing would dislodge. He wanted to open Francine to a fraternity of sexuality: coupling should mean a coming together of two rather than a "coming" of one. But she regarded him a dildo minus the batteries. And even worse she regarded him a money clip: Doctor Rozen's practice bankrolling the decorating seasons. He was two payments into an engagement ring best suited to nostril piercing, Francine urging him along on a leash, her man-monster. Their kids would need Daedalus to design a playground so as not to frighten the neighborhood. Bully for Leon! Franny was six payments into the honeymoon (a group tour a là *Love Boat* where high seas romance requires audience). Francine loves an audience.

She was planning this big party, her official engagement announcement, all of Leon's friends. Well, sure. She doesn't have any. And all Leon could think about was Claudia and lightning bolts from God because he was spilling seed into a petri dish and about to shrink God's number one go-to prophet and defame Freud and present the bad news to the world all because of his need to please the café brotherhood. Where was the ballsy, pushy Brooklyn Jew? Maybe he should have gone into African diamonds with Uncle Josiah and let his soul fend for itself.

Francine hung up the phone. Dennis again. She assembled props and reviewed the guest list. She had cleared a space for presents, assembled finger trays of exotics, set ashtrays beside the cook stove for pot smokers. And she had laid out the photo album of Hawaii to establish a credible pursuit and surrender history, though in the photos she is lobster red on the beach and suffering while Leon, swarthy as a native, is barely recognizable over the binding of his tome-sized beach read. Francine was serious about unseating Rowan's girlfriend, a punk-rock screamer Rowan called his spiritual doppelganger. Francine intended to replace her with Sharon Demey from the office, an affectionate red haired Irish girl with no pretensions, no fashion sense either, but family oriented and a violin player in high school so someone who will preen Rowan's musician's ego, and hover on the flickering wings of tenderness, do his bidding with a light touch.

Which, thought Franny, *is all a man wants anyway.* Francine took a seat, offered herself a glass of wine and an interior monologue: *Although, Mason Fischer,* she mused – *he's another type of the same type. He likes a challenge, thinks every woman accessible. Thinks abracadabra, open sesame those golden brown legs! is what he thinks.* Francine laughed. *But Dennis Zamora* (Franny's old friend and lover from before Leon), *who would think he would prove a frequency below malleable – what a surprise! Who would think Leon, a man with one foot in rabbinical robes and another in a tweed suit, who would think Leon would be much of a one to review silverware patterns. But he will. He does. When not running errands. More likely ever than Dennis to homebody. Dennis is an easy read – his need to be a girl's phone buddy after sex, like sex is preliminary and after-chatter the main thing. Comparing notes. An intellectual gossip. A hairy one. A round teddy bear in bed, tickling and squirming, asking this way or that way? So you just want to scream, "Do it <u>any</u> way, but <u>do</u> it and shut up about it!" because you have a hard enough time getting lost in the moment. But you don't. Because he's there for you. He lets go nothing from his past, especially women, his women. Like we're a stable and he's the bowlegged mare buster. He wants references, testaments to his virility. We're a kind of walking, talking, fuck resume. But he will call with timely informa-tion. And he knows who needs to hear what, and he doesn't judge so much as put all on the scale and negotiate a balance. Dennis is very balanced. That's his best quality, his only best quality.*

Francine had arranged the chairs for Monopoly. "I'll take Man-hattan!" her opening gambit. She centered a punch bowl of spar-kling wine blended in orange juice on the glass top of the rattan dining table, stacked the bottom rack in the frig with Heineken. The music selection was next, but that required consideration, and she was having too much fun reviewing the guest list at present.

So onto whom? Oh, yes, she decided, *Mason. What makes him think he can bring me to orgasm? What's in his pants twenty others, give or take, have not yet come up with? Can't wait to hear the latest* *in his assessment of female orgasmic potential. He must be jealous. Talk about your reverse penis envy. Call it clitoris envy; he calls it my tiny football. "I've always loved football," he says. "Forward pass is the way of the game. None of that lateral bullshit." He's one of those men that must experience <u>everything</u>. He's frustrated by impasse. Well, maybe he's worth a toss. They say artists have a different perspective. Hah! That's funny. But Leon could never know. And Mason is just too obvious. Always. Which could maybe work to mask the event if ever it were to happen, should I accede to this experiment. Because who will believe Mason has had <u>me</u> – in his wildest dreams is what they'll think. Yes. But this Claudia. From what Dennis says, she's quite the cultivated lady, dark and serious, artsy, a scholar of obscure poets, an antiques expert, all that lovely contact with old money. What in Hell can Mason be doing with her? She's not his type. She is obviously Dennis' type, the subliminal message of his phone call. Dennis says she has a lively mind, which is what Dennis is really into: the mind fuck. That's Dennis. Although, he's got a point. Once you get beyond the face, it's all about getting inside the head. If you stay interested.*

Dennis also had some spooky things to say about Chapman, the new guy, new to the shop. Those boys … still talking revolution? Yuck. How childishly self-important. Boys still and ever shall be – boys. A-Men. They should be more stingy with the rope ladder to their tree house. They never grow up. That's why Chapman. That's how he got into the club. Leon says he's serious about killing whom? One of the Beatles I think he said. Why would they want anyone in their club who even pretends to want to kill? That's just sick. Dennis has no really bad feeling about this guy though. But he said Chapman's a little "odd," that he might be coming to the apartment tonight be-

When Leon returned with the wine, Sharon Demey shared the white leather divan drinking punch with Francine. The hostess was forecasting the event. She is a master of summarizing her guests in introduction, each to the other. That's what she was doing with Sharon, running down the list and summarizing, especially as it involved Rowan and his love interest of the moment: "He's so cute and so talented a musician. His hair flies all over when he's at the piano, it's the most lustrous deep red, and he leans into the piano like making love. (Sharon blushed with intrigue. Francine asserted the trump.) And he's sensitive, very sensitive, and the girl he's with doesn't recognize that. And he dresses, well, sort of bohemian with scarves and pointy black boots. But that can be changed."

Sharon is, from a guy's perspective, the kind of girl you'd like to have at home naked behind an apron in your kitchen. She is kittenish and chunky in a deliciously squeezable way. She is solicitous, angling for a man who will provide but drawn to the ones that need taming first, which was probably why she and Francine got along so well. There is three feet of sugar icing to get through before finding the real Sharon, the one that chose a high school stud with biker boots to take her virginity, the girl that lost her father to Haight-Ashbury in the sixties after her mom got knocked up at some all-night vigil protest for some long-forgotten cause. Sharon's mom was too busy working minimum wage to put much into mothering. Sharon spent most of her teen years alone in the apartment after school, surrounded by girly dolls and soda pop and nachos with the sitcom laugh track for company (her laugh, as a result, had developed hair-triggered and prolonged and plastic).

"Rowan's only flaw is gullibility," said Francine. "Wouldn't you say, Leon?"

"Can't hear you," Leon said from the bathroom staring fiercely into the mirror, an often-attempted exercise in discerning metempsychosis, other selves that calve away from the main like disavowing responsibility for the life currently in play.

"Here's an example," said Francine. "Rowan comes to New York, four years ago, far into disco, gaudy poinsettia collars in synthetic, you know, one of Dennis' old friends he'd met in London, said he found Rowan stowage on a banana boat in New York Harbor, funny guy – you should know this – and what happens is Rowan takes dance lessons, the Travolta craze, you know, and Rowan gets studly at disco, all the girls in his study group want a piece – Columbia University, that's why Rowan's here, plays piano, teaches some still, I think, PhD eventually in music theory or something – you should know – so Rowan he falls for his dissertation advisor, the department chair I think, she's married, of course, right? But he thinks he can't miss. He's so cute and British and all that, right? But she won't give him the time of day. Rowan, he falls hard as a perm in Paris. Well, not that I would know really. But I have read the weather there is quite thick. Anyway, Rowan is a teaching assistant back then, reads Schopenhauer for fun, which if you don't know is damn boring! And won't teach his students only but John Cage tunes, which you and I know is not appropriate for a boy with a bruised mind. And so what happens is Rowan goes far moody, permanent eye shadow, nothing even a lap dance would cure, right? – well, that's not my sense of humor; it's Mason; he's rubbing off on me. Oh, that's not good either. (giggles) Well, never mind. So Rowan gets a gun, he says to himself, 'Get a gun, Rowan!' and he brings that gun he's bought off some alley hoodlum straight to class, oh, a lot of things going on in that alley, I could tell you, but never mind, and he puts that gun to his head, all those children stressing because clueless on performance art, skinny arms hugging brass instruments, or was it a chamber group, yes, I think so, strings then, hugging violins and violas and whatever else, and he puts that gun to his head and he says play *Misty* for me and if you don't I'll pull the trigger and if you do and you stop, I'll pull the trigger, is what he says, wants to create some kind of crisis for his students to pour into their music, 'tuning the spirit through tension' is what he tells Dennis, whatever that means, and which is okay if they, any of them, had known Rowan is nuts about art films, he gets off on *Blowup* and *Taxi Driver*, and when he came to New York he toured midnight cabbies looking for Travis Bickle, which is maybe why he likes that man Chapman, but anyway, this misty, if you don't know, is a 77 Sunset Strip, Kookie lend me-your-comb kind of movie, Clint Eastwood's hair greased and teased and his deep sexy voice deejaying somewhere California where all the bitches are nuts, their tans orange with vitamin C, more flake out there than a Betty Crocker piecrust, and so Rowan, he is so gullible, has no mind for commodity assessment, he whim-whams these gals and guys their tiny brains lost in bar scales, he overestimates the shelf life of their life experience, as if they ever waste time at art movies, and they all freak, I mean *freak*! pee themselves and blubber and faint is what I hear which leads to Rowan's saying to the Dean at Columbia University they all made this up, every last one of them, that they all have it in for him because of grades or something or – get this – because he's seduced them like he has every girl in his study group which of course is true, but of course not a bad thing because you want an experienced man. Oh, yes, of course you do. Take my word. But as to Rowan, I understand he ..."

"Francine!"

"Yes, Leon?"

"What are you telling? My God! This can't be who you are!"

"How long have you been standing there, Leon? In that towel, *dripping* on the oriental!"

"O, very long enough. This can't be you!"

"That is an existential question," said Sharon. "Isn't it? I've been reading Sartre (*especially* for this party, she neglected to say, as Francine had said "prepare yourself for a room full of randy philosophers"). You imply that Francine has an empty soul."

"It's not empty, Sharon," said Francine. "If anything, it's chock full and very shapely."

"Yes, stuffed with *things*," said Leon

"That's right, Leon. All designer!" said Francine with a small laugh and placing a hand on Sharon's knee said further, "Let's give Leon a chance to make himself presentable and go into the bedroom and look at photo albums. I think I have some early Rowan shots in there. Rowan and Leon and the boys together in Little Havana, some two, no, three years ago. They were such infants. Can you imagine!"

Yes, Leon could imagine. Leon closed the door to the bathroom, rubbed steam off the mirror with a towel, rubbed steam off his glasses and looked into the mirror directly into his eyes long enough to get that disconnected, back-and-forth ricochet. He liked the feeling – weightless and timeless. With his face objectified as beard and hair matted in dripping wet ringlets, he time traveled, became a Roman soldier of the first century bullying Judea, rooting out a Jesus sect of cult radicals with the help of Jews, this soldier and his fat-necked indifference reflected in the mirror and back off the retina to the mirror again to the retina, in quickening strokes, strobing back and forth through time until Leon began to off-load qualms of heresy should he commit to this iconoclast gesture. This was not just Leon he was carrying around with him. It was three thousand years of humanity. Leon was not specifically a Jew. He could as well be a Christian, a Hindu, a Druid, anything but an atheist. Leon could live off the wispy edges of a dream. He was, so he felt, destined a mystic, a tribal shaman, a sojourner of the human psyche. He knew he needed grounding in cause and effect. That was why he and Francine were suitable. The physical world meant nothing to him beyond the standpoint of its malleability, which to his thinking was different from manipulation. That was what Franny did, she manipulated, lives especially. She should have stuck with decor.

And Leon was bothered by Rowan's latest game, though intrigued – damage the thing you most love. A proposition serious in the undertaking were Leon to undertake the proposition. It is easy enough for the others to get cute and schemey with ideals, thought Leon, because they're cynics, every last one. It's a gentile thing. All they have is this renegade Jesus martyred from imagining himself the Son of God. Make a bold statement, turn the cheek and dangle all day from a crucifix until you're dried out to beef jerky. What kind of philosophy is this? How useful is this? If you believe in something, you don't give your life away. You cling to every vestige of this miserable consciousness, you survive in the face of the insurmountable, and if the end is coming despite your tenaciousness, you go out in triumph, a torch of consuming righteousness. Leave the enemy nothing of yourself to gloat over. No whimpering on the cross abandoned and scoffed by criminals. This is not humility. This is humiliation. What kind of Son of God is this?

No. Gentiles have nothing of the strength of Jews. And they have nothing of our torment either, thought Leon. Because we believe in something. We are not cynics except so far as we perceive the material world. Sure, I'll admit. We do understand how the world works, what can be done and must be done in slipping a coin into the palm of a hand. There is nothing mystical about securing a nest in a hostile world. How many times must Jews be shaken from the tree, plucked and roasted on the spit before gentiles understand that we *are* the gold we secret in foreign banks in all available compass points in preparation for the next pogrom, the next hegira. We *are* the gold beat to airy thinness fanning out in widening circles but from no discernible center. Warsaw is no center. New York City is no center. Not Dachau. Not Jerusalem. Yes, I'll admit. We are cynical about the material world. But the spiritual! That's altogether otherwise. That's where we are centered.

I have made of my heart a citadel, Leon continued lecturing to himself in the mirror. And as I have been taught to do, and to please Rowan – damn him! – to please Rowan, and some ugly need of my own, a mighty leveling force of doubt must assemble in the dark recesses of my soul and shake its foundations. Rowan asks me to toy with these beliefs of mine as if they were mutable, insubstantial icons of false gods. I will need to weigh the strength of my beliefs, that which *is* my love, weigh against the weakness of my doubts and see what follows. I will place both the chosen Moses and the secular god Freud upon the couch and psychoanalyze. My God, the Old Testament God, he *will* be a better god or he will shatter like a votary of base metal. And Freud will stand up to the scrutiny of his own theories or fall back to the dark shadows of the cave from which he emerged.

"Leon! Sugar! Won't you come out and be a host? I need to get in there before our guests arrive. Not that you're not a guest, Sharon. Will you come out here and entertain Sharon?"

Leon pulled on a ribbed black turtle neck sweater and white painter pants with straps for hanging hammers that catch on door knobs when he rounded corners, though Leon hardly noticed, and a pair of Birkenstocks over rag wool socks. This is about as party togged as Leon gets. And all at the instigation of Francine who had thrown into the wash his several pairs of checked paints and all his cardigan sweaters. His beard and hair glistened with faux Mediterranean olive extract, which Francine had found in a bottle of conditioner. Leon tried his smile in the mirror but disengaged before a repeat of meditative time travel. He passed through the door into the material world as Franny entered the bathroom perfectly coiffed and superfluously self-adjusting, giving his bottom a tweak and winking flirtatiously for Sharon's sake. Leon walked his smile into the living room where Sharon had crossed her legs and gone from invitingly plump to seductively El Greco, lean and fleshy. Her thigh sneaked into view beneath a forest green pleated skirt of wide-wale corduroy. Leon kept his eyes trained on the far wall so as to avoid a cheap thrill and settled into a white leather chair matching the sectional divan.

"You said empty soul?"

"What's that?"

"You said that I said Franny has an empty soul."

"No, no," said Sharon after a fit of nervous laughter, "not really." She placed the goblet of punch carefully on the arabesques of an inlaid wood table. "I don't mean Francine has anything missing. Really just the opposite. She has it all. She does. Well, it's a long story, but I have been reading Sartre and I guess I got caught up in your relationship a bit. I'm sorry. Really. I spoke inappropriately."

"No. It's nothing. I mean I don't mean it's *nothing*."

"No, you're right. It's nothing. I have projected – that's the right word? Projected? Well, I have looked to you and Francine as Sartre and Simone de Beauvoir, his lover. I have imagined you two that way, that is, endless debates on your relationship, your state of being. I'm not saying this very well. I mean where existence precedes essence, which I think means there is no truth to life beyond living it. Is that right?"

"Yes, that's right. Where else but in Paris? Aesthetics everywhere. Fuck and argue philosophy, brains and glands served together on a silver plate, all out there in public. Makes me shiver."

"Yes, I guess. Different in New York do you think?"

"No, not so much," said Leon, finding himself sympathetically drawn to this ingénue of philosophy, her pudgy and inoffensive face, her soft voice, her self-effacing postulations, and her willingness to see in Leon the depth of knowledge he had so assiduously cultivated through twenty years of formal education.

"Will you tell me what Franny said of my friends? I want … I want to correct miss-impressions."

"Oh, well, there's nothing really. Just that …

"Yes, just what?"

"Just that Rowan will be the perfect man for me. Do you think so?"

"Oh, God! Franny's matchmaking. Her pat summaries. Tiny explosions of insight. Dig, dig dig. Kaboom! goes the petard. Down go the walls. The emperor exposed. Can't you see the emperor's clothes? And so on. Damn! Do you see?"

"No, I'm not sure I understand."

"Not important. Go on. Franny says?"

"Oh, well, as I said, Rowan will be my most passionate lover ever. He will tune me and then pluck my strings."

"Beautiful. Francine said that? I'm glad for you. And you will do what for Rowan?"

"I will keep some part of him firmly planted in the material world."

"How so?"

"I will bake him bread, make the comforting white noise of girl talk, I will keep him on a long lead, yank his chain when the little girlies in his classes inflate his ego and he begins to float away. I will be the weight of love."

"Again, most beautiful. But this does not sound like Francine."

"Well, some is. The Harlequin Romance part is me."

"Charming. And you have heard what about Mason Fischer?"

"Yes, Mason. He's going to sniff my tail all night looking for a sign I will meet him secretly in the bathroom or bedroom or whichever is less frequented by guests."

"Not far off. And Dennis Zamora?" Here Leon wanted there to be serious character assassination, as he too was getting headachy from squinting in the bright light of Dennis.

"Complicated," said Sharon. "He will expect me to fall into his orbit but when I do he will take me only half the way there and yet never let me go."

"Yes, very good. I won't ask what you've been told of me."

"Won't tell if you do."

Chapter Five:
Dennis Zamora reviews his options

Saturday, December 6, 1980
8:30 p.m. – 10:30 p.m.
(46 hrs/15 min. before John Lennon's murder)

As I take you a distance into the psyche of Dennis Zamora, don't be dazzled by his balancing act. He manipulates the scales to tip in his favor. When caught doing so, he simply thinks others will accede to the weight of his superior argument. And, well, mostly we do. We did. It was Dennis that ended Rowan's dizzying, intoxicating plan to seduce strange women in the back alleys of New York. This in contrast to our New Orleans abstinence during Mardi Gras. Dennis said, one Saturday at the shop following two weeks of back-alley experiment, he said, "My friends ..." (which you notice already takes liberties with what I feel about him), he said, "this romancing in the alleys, I suppose carelessness is the point, but nobody wants to invite STD's to the party, and we could find better dental plans." Which was decidedly not appropriate shop talk and elicited from Leon a look of disbelief, while I said, stupid me, "Why not simply forego oral, or upgrade the source?" But no one wanted to pay ten bucks for a beer and fifty to get in the door. So that was the end of that. No more randy nights in the neighborhood bars. So, when Rowan began to promote the iconoclast gesture, Dennis felt the mood would blow over. Unless, Dennis considered, this new guy Chapman does something freaky. The café brotherhood should have listened to Dennis, is what he thought with some pique in the cab ride home remembering saying while squeezing into camel hair jacket as the evening at the pastry shop broke up, "Apologies to the newcomer," Dennis had said, "but he's not really one of us. Why involve him?" Rowan invited Chapman to Leon's engagement party anyway which made Dennis uncomfortable but then he reminded himself, a passing phase, simply a passing phase.

The taxi delivered Dennis into the high numbers East side. The brick there rising not above five stories, a neighborhood stooped with age and fading significance. Unsuitable as Dennis digs. In New York "high rise" means pay-for-view, nosebleed sumptuousness, but also expectations of self, and tall enough to repel the slings and arrows those you have betrayed will launch against your coronation. Dennis expected to cozy his ego behind the polished steel and tinted glass of the tall back rows that lean over their flattopped, tar-roofed elders in disdain of a squatter's claim to a river view they have largely ignored. Dennis expected to ascend within elevators piloted by servile courtesy. At night he anticipated laying his head to rest upon the leaden clouds of industrial waste, and in the morning ascending similar towers into the counting houses.

But for now, Dennis grudgingly paced stairs toward a studio apartment in a brick and mortar Bartleby hovel facing identical 19th century sweatshop rehabs rather than the river. Dennis will tell you his apartment had a Roosevelt Island overlook. And it does, from the backside, from one sooty alley window, something like the smoked lens of a solar observatory. While inviting his guests to have a look, Dennis himself ignored the neck strain necessary to effect the correct angle for that view – stretching toes to level chin with top of frig to access the top four panes of a rattle-wind twelve-on-twelve.

His building was an 1890s textile plant, its one grace note a fan brick motif arching a row of windows at the roofline defining attic storage, unless you count as sculpture an iron zigzag fire escape bedecking the street-side facade with dipsy-doodle curls and knobby blandishments anonymously fired and banged and fitted by blacksmiths in a back-alley pony barn long ago burned down. Call it utilitarian art. But once the last doting rent-control hold-out falls permanently asleep, all will upgrade to condo, the fire escape will become scrap and its modern ancestor, an aluminum alloy with retracting ladders on springs, will have moved to alley space, and that attic will make a cathedral loft which Dennis cannot afford. He will however and shortly, as a consequence of his ambitions, move to better digs in Jackson Heights. This will be the fall-out/slash /fall-up from his involvement as an iconoclast in the latest of Rowan's coordinated gestures.

Meantime, Dennis had risen only four stories tall in the industry of words. He would want to impress you anyway with his view of the river, so you would have been asked to stretch over the top of the frig, twist the cords of your neck and expand vertebrae to get a slant-angle gleam of river. You would probably ask yourself, why bother? Like you'd see girls on the beach and not another cityscape brick and mortar construction on another island that is impossible to define as island unless you're 2,000 feet above this mess peering down a clear sky from strong winds having blown poison emissions out to sea, in which case your plane will fly so far above the turbulence you won't see anything but cloud vapor and indistinct geography anyway.

It's human nature to find irritation in a succeeding Dennis Zamora game plan. It's not just me. I stumbled into fame and wealth. Dennis planned it. As this narrative draws attention to Dennis' slick manipulation, it could be accused of going hog-wild butchering character. But all narrative is subjective, all character projective. The reader will need to place Dennis in an orbit appropriate to her/his own observations of human ethics. Frankly, Dennis doesn't give a shit what we think of him. His focus is sharp enough to exclude twittering complaint from the dim edges beyond his reach. Dennis counts life an intellectual proving ground. He will play against the house until he *becomes* the house. And stupid us, the café brotherhood, we lined up to spin the wheel, took the challenge, because there was plenty you're-no-better-than-me in every giddy one of us, and because we went moon mad with expectation when we walked into Dennis' apartment, like all things were possible, because that's the Dennis projection, and so we went straight to the window over the frig and contorted as Dennis goaded us to spot the tram gliding on cables to Roosevelt Island. Like star-light, star-bright – a brief jag of red carapace floating at the edge of a square of window glass should you get the timing right. A beetle crawling down a clothesline would make similar drama if it weren't for Dennis' infectious gamesmanship. Many have looked for the tram from that slice of window, mostly women. And most women would think that if it appeared so infrequently, and if they did see it, it was there to bless them, so make a wish. But it was hard to get the timing right in Dennis' apartment. Franny would have said so, but she was probably talking about something else. Maybe Dennis imagined he had a room at a chichi Swiss ski resort. That would be like him – excellent views of gondolas up the Matterhorn. That sort of thing.

Dennis' apartment was two blocks from the tastefully appointed home office of the *Prague Review*, which is *the* place to get published as a novice writer Dennis used to say. Its senior editor once wrote books but now lends his name to spin-off anthologies of stuff he never wrote but reserves first serial rights or some such legalese. Dennis complained about this guy, maybe because he'd love to have been anthologized, though *Prague Review* interns had routinely pink-slipped him (that's a rejection slip writers get in the mail from inferior submissions – make a note, Dennis, those slips mean to say *inferior submission*). Dennis would tell you he wanted to be close enough to the *Prague Review* transom to hear its British editor says in those affected, fat vowels, "Puurfect for us, don't chu say, Haaaley dear, must haaave this story!" (Halley was an editor's assistant, youthful, elegant, a Kentucky blue blood with aspirations of her own). Dennis wanted to be within hailing distance. Accessibility and such – all the double-c, "ak-sounding" words are what Dennis is about: "accessorize" (for obvious reasons), "account" (not as in "on account of" but as in what's "in" the account), "accelerate" (because he was in a hurry to break loose), "acrimony" (which is deficient in double-c's but applies to Dennis through his detractors, including this narrative), "actuary" (because it's a money word applied to risk, and well, yes, dropping more c's but etc. and etc. and so on). These are cold words, arid words. Burs in your throat. Nothing like a spoonful of British editor's vowels that go down like honeyed lemon. Rowan kept telling Dennis, get an accent and you'll get published there. Dennis never listened. Dennis must have thought the editor would eventually notice Dennis' address was too near his own to reject him eternally. Like the gesture would one day boomerang back.

Dennis did not give up. He kept writing and submitting his work and receiving rejections. He collected voyeuristic observations for short stories off the dark lives of his complex neighbors. For two hours, exactly, after dinner, Dennis wrote. He removed his camel hair coat (the mauve sheen a perfect match to his delicate, thinning hair), folded his tie and returned it to the box from whence it came, showered and shaved away lupine growth. Then a regimen of pull-ups and sit-ups as prelude to a shower and dinner. (Dennis worried over his tendency toward corpulence.) Then a stingy repast of angel hair pasta spattered with cheese, steamed broccoli, a half glass of red wine and home-brewed espresso to motorize the enzymes. The apartment was small but neat and shiny with varnished woods. Dennis liked the Scandinavian look, and had taken it so far as to strip away wall-to-wall carpet, sand and varnish the hardwoods. He would glide in socks between rooms like down a bowling lane, never a sliver, the boards glowing warm and shiny as the galley of a yacht.

Dennis sat at his work desk naked inside a worsted housecoat, legs crossed to pinch off drafts. Hot water from the old boiler of his building cycling through pipes banged the walls. Roosevelt Island floated in the distance, the tram inched along groaning cables. His desk faced the only window street side with neighbors across the way he could see between the stairs of fire escape, though not without some neck twisting. Must be some significance to all the contortion it took to see outside the walls of that apartment. Most of his neighbors' windows were un-curtained and back-lit like small TV screens stacked in rows in the dark. He voyeured shamelessly. There was plenty to see and more to imagine. City folk bare all as a natural consequence of environment. Like fish in a tank, they feed and fight and copulate in the altogether density of desensitized community.

Dennis typed on a Smith-Corona a taut string of sharp observation. He paused frequently, daubed with white-out and huffed minty breath. Food never fumed in the pleats of his mouth. He blew on his mistakes to dry liquid corrections, paused, typed black indentions onto painted tracks. Dennis was a slow writer. Call him a bleeder. He had a precise thing to say in each story and a single design in narrative, like a bobsled he would tell you, a slow start and then irresistible momentum and explosion at the end of the track – cross the finish-line a winner, wreck and die. Contrived irony, but Dennis provided a slick ride. Jarring modifiers and errant metaphors, he purged them nimbly, niggardly, decreasing friction, increasing probability. He was good with words. Given his commitment to routine, the work got done, the words piled up, the characters of his stories stepped half awake out from their dreams (or Dennis' dreams) and ran like hell from the realities he imposed upon them in their waking hours, and ended their lives invariably in disaster while reaching beyond their means for a last, great triumph. Victims of ego. Makes you wonder how self-assured Dennis really is about his own prospects.

Dennis was a master chronicler of doomed intention: Modigliani excesses, Lolita obsessions, uncompromising Coriolanuses. But he did all this on a small scale. He shrank it all down. He manipulated a coterie of studio apartment waitresses with Broadway aspirations, homo wannabe ballet dancers giving Tango lessons, deli sandwich architects aspiring to franchise. He observed parties that ignited tiny rooms like Christmas lights, brief trysts passing down halls in telling window flash. Then there were the flannel suit guys like Dennis that keep a measured life, that dropped the arty stuff by nine o'clock, chatted with friends by phone until ten, read in bed until eleven, and disappeared next morning into Wall Street arenas or Publishing House slush piles or Hotel Marketing offices, ascending the ladder of improved circumstance. Dennis' short stories came from his observations of these tiny dramas played out on that endless bank of TV screens. But his characters don't so much pull the reader into sympathy as keep him at a distance even when looking close up: how close can you get to a specimen with your insight/outsight pressed against the eyecup of a microscope. Oddly, the same can be said (has been said) of my own paintings. But if you recall, I invite you to touch my paintings. Dennis won't ever want you that close. His words fall where he wants them. Let them lie.

On that particular Saturday night in December of 1980, forty-six hours and fifteen minutes before the murder of John Lennon, Dennis typed a few dozen serious words in the two prescribed hours he had set aside for the task, lines that he changed and changed again (picture Sisyphus pushing words up a hill, tiny fingers all bleedy – yes, small hands and small feet and you can guess the rest). He poured a second burgundy, no make that a 1/2 glass, as he was planning ahead to the night's festivities at Franny's so avoiding premature buzz. It's all about control.

He relocated to the futon sofa of Norwegian skeletal blonde wood that expands into a bed, like sleeping on a ladder with pillows, Spartan self-torture a temporary Dennis trait, justification for the four-poster he could not yet afford to house. He swirled the red wine warming in his hand, reached for the phone, hesitated, rose from the sofa and pulled together the robe lapels and cinched the belt, ambled to the bookshelf.

He ran fingers down spines, a wall of books alphabetized by author. Dennis never forgets a name. He pulled down the collected poems of William Blake. He opened the book while thinking of Claudia Fontaine who was currently in bed rubbing with her hand my ovoid tummy. I had not yet heard a good reason not to grow stout. Consider by contrast the skinny chimney sweeps of London. Dennis read:

When my mother died I was very young

And my father sold me while yet my tongue

Could scarcely cry weep, weep, weep.

So your chimneys I sweep & in soot I sleep.

Did Dennis shed a tear? Not hardly. But he thought Claudia might. He will recite these lines then pretend sympathy, tell of those four-year-old boys sold by parents into indenture, twenty shillings profit, prodded with poles into 7" widths of twisting pipe, deformed of spine and retarded in growth, no closer than 3'7" to Heaven but sought at weddings, a foul spectacle of sooty warts, cancer of the scrotum, crippled limbs, hair like porcupine. Kiss the bride! Symbols of fecundity! All that hot work in the black tunnel, you know. Another example of Dennis spinning advantage off the suffering of others. Do you see? Dennis couldn't give a shit. He wanted Blake for Claudia. Sing a line of poetry, lay a lady.

Dennis checked his watch – one hour and thirteen minutes before the cab arrived. He lifted the phone and dialed Francine the moment Leon had gone for wine. Impeccable timing.

"Franny!"

"Oh, Dennis. Listen, I'm very busy."

"Just need a minute."

"Only for you, Dennis."

"Leon say anything about Claudia Fontaine?"

"Yes, some."

"That's what I thought. He was agog, as were we all."

"Oh, I see. Competition."

"No, nothing like that, Francine. Did he say anything about a Mark Chapman?"

"Some. I can make him say more."

"Nice distinction, Francine. So, who first?"

"Let's talk about the diva," said Francine settling deep into the throw pillows of her white leather divan, a glass of Chardonnay in her hand.

"Mason brought her to the shop. Not at all suitable for Mason. Far too refined, a Blake scholar."

"Well, no threat from my perspective. Academics have such a blind side to the more practical concerns of life."

"Which are?"

"You should know, Dennis: it's all about the money, and its derivatives."

"Which are?"

"Well, interior design, first impressions, a selective wardrobe, and, well, landing a man."

"With money."

"Exactly."

"Franny, this girl has class, even in a funked-out tee shirt."

"Does she have a man?"

"No, but Mason thinks she does."

"How so?"

"Well you know Mason. He's just met Claudia and already he's feeling her up under the table. I counted two light slaps and twice that in exasperated sighs. She stayed in the conversation though. Spoke impressively compact zingers. No waste. And a versatile physicality."

"Meaning what?"

"Meaning she could accommodate a stranger in a subway as comfortably as a husband in mission. She could draw the perverse and the mundane into another sphere altogether. Bless it to Heaven with her ministrations."

"Lovely sentiment, Dennis. What the hell ever it means."

"Sorry. I've been reading poetry."

"Yes, you and Leon talk the same nonsense. No wonder you're buddies. But this girl. She's a novelty, Dennis. Wait until she's kept our company a month. If she lasts that long. We'll compare notes after a month."

"Yes, but let's compare notes after the party. Whoever heals first calls first. And speaking of Mason ... he still trying to get into your pants?"

"Old news, Dennis. Have to go. Bye now!"

The line died. Dennis dialed without hesitation Rowan Murray's number, which rang five times before Dennis hung up, checked his watch and dialed a Jersey number (Rowan having gone to the Village to meet his girlfriend).

"Mom."

"Dennis, how are you, son?"

"I'm fine. How's Dad?"

"Same. Can't get him out of bed unless there's ball games on TV."

"There *are* things can be done about depression, Mom. Counseling, drug therapy. He doesn't have to be like that. *You* don't have to live like that. Don't let the son-of-a-bitch bring you down, Mom."

"I'm fine, Dennis. Your Dad is hurting. And he's so proud. I love his pride. I love yours too, but I can't have you talking about him like that. You two are just too much alike."

"Scary thought. But all right. Sorry."

"He still won't admit he's depressed. He says it's a blood infection from Korea. He's even written the State Department. That's what he tells the boys at the Legion. He's missed the council meetings at the Legion. Can you imagine! That place is his life. It's a good thing he's retired. That's all I can think. Good thing he's ... (she weeps quietly, sets the receiver on the kitchen counter, clears her sinus with a tissue). Sorry."

"That's okay, Mom. New topic?"

"Yes, good."

"How's the BMer?"

"Your Dad has it in the garage now, Dennis. He didn't like to leave it outdoors, such a fancy car, not even with the tarp you bought for it. Oh, and he washed and waxed it last week when we had that spell of Indian summer."

"I wish he wouldn't do that."

"No, he *wants* to, Dennis. He wants so much for you.

"From me."

"What?"

"Never mind."

"He says that all the time. He says, Dennis will ..."

"I know, write the next great American novel. Well, maybe. Anyway, just wanted to see how you're doing. See if there's any change in Dad. Listen, promise me you'll tell me if things get worse."

"Yes, all right."

Dennis disconnected and reached for a stack of manuscripts he was supposed to read and assess for his two type-A bosses at Holmes and Stout Literary, or "lit wits" as Dennis called them: Chief literary agent Pulte Holmes, a beaked and scrawny malcontent from the 50s baby boom, a frustrated dysfunctional writer wannabe; and Chief literary agent Winona Stout, a Wife of Bathe lookalike, gat-toothed and oversexed, gray haired and chapfallen, foul breathing and hateful. Dennis would have liked to chop these two into pieces and scatter them in the East River. But he knew his best revenge was to find the *real* next great American novel and take it with him in a breakaway literary agency of his own. He thumbed the first ten pages of a manuscript top of the pile of the usual garbage, his mind cleansing itself of all but the patter of words that had begun to insinuate into his consciousness. And then he realized. He was captivated.

It was the first manuscript top of the pile of countless piles he had sifted with growing assurance of the eventual and complete ill-idiot-cy of America. But he was *not* happy. He was agitated. He had read the first twenty pages in short time. He was hooked and carried away on the rhythm of its cadence and by the depth of its atmosphere. He found himself immersed in an era he would never have thought as anything but cliché and un-compelling –the wild West – with characters emoting at him. What an upper! What a downer! He began to appreciate the implications of Rowan's theory of iconoclasm. Find something you love and destroy it! He was jealous as hell. He wondered what it would feel like to destroy something he would have been proud to have written himself.

What better way to effect meaningful gesture in a publishing business drawn to the bottom dollar than to find the next great American novel and trash this book to his bosses and write a nasty letter of rejection to the writer. Why? Maybe because the American readership doesn't deserve this gem. Rowan will be pleased. And this book would otherwise make it *big*: large numbers in cash and in print editions. And the movie rights. Well, the bigger they are the harder they ... no, the tree that falls in the woods that nobody ... the clichés that ruin a life. But, Dennis had to remind himself, this guy, this writer, he was already a nobody. Dennis read carefully the writer's letter of introduction. It was brief. He was an Oregonian with no friends among the literati (the obligatory name dropping noticeably absent), no contacts in publishing, no previous publications, no education beyond community college (delivers the mail he said, on back roads), and no residencies in trendy retreat colonies.

The plot synopsis went like this: Sheriff Wyatt Earp busted to civilian, chased out of the territories by bankruptcy and disrepute after his vendetta ride against the McLaury gang, abandons his laudanum-addicted wife and takes up with an actress/dancer/prostitute, Josephine Marcus. He makes a life with her in San Francisco where her actress colleagues are being murdered, one after the other, placing her in fear of her own life. Wyatt is drawn into a detective's role after he had thought to have hung up his guns. The culprit will be a ruthless land speculator intending to buy and tear down the theatre and adjoining saloons to build a warehouse and extend the wharf for shipping.

Dennis read another two chapters then set down the manuscript, sipped wine, considered the appeal of this work, that it came from its contrast of natural characters inhabiting an unnatural setting, or not so much unnatural as exotic – fog spilling down the streets of a pungent, polyglot, and dangerous dock-side San Francisco, shadowy damp saloons, black market cut throats, prostitutes and johns in the streets, raucous dance theatres where Shakespearean drama is lampooned as artfully as Clemens's *Huck Finn* but to a darker purpose, blood and steins spilling prodigally, gaslight beatings at night. And through all this Wyatt Earp loomed large, dangerous and aristocratic.

There was a theatre of the streets, a babble of languages and costume and odd behavior, and Wyatt stepping confidently throughout in mauve suede suit with wide-brimmed cowboy hat and pointy boots. Josephine was sexy and earthy, brave and engaging, devoted to Wyatt but otherwise extreme in independence. These were wonderful characters with evolving morality and pulsating emotion. Very modern in its way. A clear enticement to the recent desire in publishing for "real" people fictionalized. And an easy 88-milimeter adaptation with vivid scenes all but scripted in stage direction: Gene Hackman as Wyatt; Meryl Streep as his wife (she would need to lose a few pounds); and Robert De Niro as the evil developer. Beyond that, the way it was written –positively visionary in oddities of phrase that jar but ring with a loopy kind of syntactic logic. Surprises everywhere! The kind of writing uninhibited first timers do, self-learners like Joseph Conrad coming to English from Polish/Russian and the British merchant marine. Dennis never had that advantage. He was simply too well educated. Oh, hell! Call it what it is: Imagination. Balls! Vision!

Jealousy stung Dennis, a poison in the veins. He tossed the manuscript onto the floor but resisted further demonstrations of emotion beyond downing his glass of wine in one tip of the stem and pouring another.

He felt mean. He phoned Rowan's girlfriend, Suki Miyushi, a Japanese NYU film student with a punk/grunge influence whose father has Samurai ancestry which he had to sublimate in his work as ambassador to Germany. Or maybe it was on account of his warrior tendencies he had been assigned to Germany – beat swords to ploughshares but keep a spare one polished and hung over the fireplace, on the ready, which the Teutons would understand very well. Dennis had smoothed his way into Suki Miyushi's confidence. He had finessed her phone number in the interest of cultural "synchronicity," a word we of the café brotherhood had adopted as our own.

Dennis got Suki on the phone. She was reluctant, sensed Dennis was one upping her date, and Rowan just minutes from her apartment, if she were lucky. She tried not to give way to her cultural programming, her polite geisha tendencies: the man will insist on having his way, the woman will put him first as an affirmation of her grace and breeding. Consequently Suki tried over-hard to do the tough punk girl routine on Dennis. Maybe Dennis was too like her ambassador father. Dennis wanted to discuss Rowan's theories of the iconoclast. He wanted her candid opinion, needed some direction before it was too late is what he said. He wanted to know, Will Rowan follow-through? What is his real motivation? This could be trouble. What has he told her about Chapman? She is about to meet him. Rowan is bringing him to Francine's party. Does she know about Rowan's teaching scandal at Columbia? The histrionics and the near self-destruction? Maybe she put him up to it? All those weepy coeds and the Dean's office in a fury, the countless hours of counseling given his students, the generous scholarship bribes and Dennis nearly terminated. What could Rowan be planning now? What is his gesture?

"Listen, Suki," said Dennis, "you do know Rowan is going to bring us all down with this one, this iconoclast gesture, if he's serious. I'm not sure I can go along."

"But Dennis, Rowan is fucking artist. Rowan make fucking music is all, fucking opera, *Nōgaku.*"

"Yes, agreed. It's all high drama with Rowan."

"*Fuon* we say in Japan, fucking turbulent of emotion. Rowan want storm of emotion but also idea, big fucking idea. Do you see? What is fucking idea word in opera …?"

"Well, Suki, and I mean this in the best possible way, speaking to you is much like recitativo, but the term you're looking for is, I think, coda. That's where one final idea is put forward in the performance."

"Yes, is so. Dennis wants make one fucking final American coda. Do you know in Japanese *nemawashi*?"

"Not the least."

"I know of students Rowan make hysterical to Deans. Rowan make newmawashi. He prepare soil for moving tree."

"Transplant."

"Yes, move plant. For which fucking soil must be prepared to thrive tree. He tell me he wish prepare students for life. But he must do so with warrior heart."

"Rowan the samurai!"

"You make joke?"

"Yes, sorry, but the idea of Rowan in a kimono with diapers and a sword ..."

"You make joke."

"Oh, shit. Look, Suki, I'm sorry. Please go on."

"Rowan sensitive fucking man but maybe overmuch *tsuwamono kokoro* ... maybe overmuch warrior heart. Columbia University not understand *nagoyaka* tsuwamono. Students not understand. But Rowan not need Columbia University to justify. He carry warrior heart. He carry all else in small valise. Piano gone too. Yes, sat is so. Rowan has no more need of Columbia University nor you, Dennis, nor me too. He is fucking compact being. Sat is so."

"Rowan packed to leave? Is this what you're saying, Suki? Where to? This iconoclast scheme – he's serious?"

"Yes, serious. Is fucking coda."

It was easy to end a conversation with Suki. She wasted no time getting to the point. She spoke as though a conversation were going to end in a moment. She explained with no hesitation nor prick of conscience in having broken a trust that Rowan had recently emptied his basement apartment, given away his piano, and secured passage aboard an airplane bound for Scotland. He told Suki he was eager to engage a people deeply wounded by the politics of treachery and spiritually moved by the harmonics of their natural environment.

Dennis had met Rowan years ago at the Tate Gallery in London while on the "grand tour" after graduating Princeton where he studied the Irish Renaissance with a brilliant if eccentric English department. Rowan put Dennis up in his flat for a week, shared his wine, food, girlfriend. Then Rowan came to Columbia University where Leon reintroduced them and they have been tight since. He knew Rowan had grown sick of America and its "tolerances," which to Rowan's mind was another word for complacency – minorities absorbed into the mainstream from lack of interest rather than compassion, cathedrals gone to the malls, preachers with comb-overs emoting neon Jesus on late-night TV, and an impotent prevalent anger on the highways whose source cannot be isolated. But once an American gets his finger in the pie, he sits back on his haunch and licks that finger contentedly forever after. The Vietnam era hippy, the punk, the grunge had all sold out for two-car garages in the suburbs. Their complaints had evolved to indictments of gasoline shortages forcing lines at service stations for petrol half the price everyone else pays. Fast food and fast ideals. Rowan had had enough. Yes, apparently so. If the piano were gone, Rowan would soon follow. That piano was Rowan's only anchor to the continent.

Then Dennis thought about his writing and the manuscript he had found in the slush pile and wondered how an artist could possibly destroy the work of another artist. He thought of me, Mason Fisher. He decided to phone as I was warming up for round two in bed with Claudia Fontaine so ignored the phone which Claudia couldn't resist. I knew who was calling. Dennis was the only one on the planet that called me anymore.

"Claudia?"

"Yes, this is she. And this is ..."

"Dennis Zamora. We met at ..."

"Oh, yes. Do you want to speak to Mason?"

"Only if he has his clothes on."

"He does not."

"Is Mason painting in the nude? What I mean to say is I'd rather not disturb him if he's working. He's been blocked lately. Can't break through to where he wants to go as a new direction in his art. But maybe you know that by now."

"Well, Dennis, there is no evidence of blockage that I can see."

Claudia had switched on the lamp that sat on the floor beside the mattress that also sat on the floor. The lamp was shaped whimsically as a candy-red crayon standing on end, sharpened tip pointing above the shade. I had drawn a fuzzy vagina on the shade. She giggled and ripped back the covers, discovered me playing with myself and threw the covers back over me. She returned to her conversation with Dennis.

"But, yes, I know what you mean, if you mean his pallet. He has paint on his chest and thighs – and such. (She winked at me.) He seems to want the human body his canvas as well as his subject. This boy is … unusual."

Dennis had no immediate response. He quoted Blake:

"'O why was [he] born with a different face?/ Why was [he] not born like the rest of [his] race?' … May I speak to the human canvas?"

"Was that Blake?"

"Yes, Blake."

"I'm impressed!"

"You're supposed to be."

I got on the phone with Dennis. "Shit!" I said, "What's so damn important, Dennis? I'm working here."

"Yes, I get that. But I'm worried about Rowan."

"You should worry more about yourself, Dennis. This iconoclast thing is high stakes. Someone could get busted. Hurt bad. Don't worry about Rowan. His getaways are famous. Never a scratch. How does he do it? Must be the smoke screen. That's us,

Dennis. We're the smoke screen to whatever he really has in that limey scheming brain of his."

"Listen, Mason, is Rowan leaving town? I'm told his bags are packed, his piano sold."

"Did you say Rowan sold his piano? Now I'm interested. Where did you hear that?"

"I can't say, Mason. This seems to be a big secret. But I thought it was an important factor in our proceeding with this iconoclast thing. Don't you?"

"Hell yes! Fearless leader makes quiet exit. The gang rounded up and executed.

"Isn't that always the way? The revolution preserves its leaders. Sacrifices the foot soldiers."

"Yes. The limousines keep rolling along, a change of chauffeurs is all."

"Drivers, start your engines!"

We laughed. We could sometimes get on a roll like that, like a mind meld, Spock's antenna fingers joining us at the temple. Some metaphor would catch our imagination and evolve playfully, synchronously. That's when I liked Dennis best. I can't stand the son of a bitch otherwise, and I was not real happy Dennis was aware I was bedding Claudia. Because Dennis would wrangle her phone number as if to impart meaningful info about me she couldn't do without. That's how he works. He wouldn't ask me how it was to make love to Claudia. He would ask her how it was with Mason because that way he would find out about her.

"Listen, Dennis. I don't know a damn thing about Rowan's plans," I said. "You're his good friend, not me. I don't know why you expect me to know anything. But I do think we need to rethink this iconoclast moment. If Rowan is playing us, if we're his little experiment in social psychology – and he's staged this kind of theatre before, you know he has – I'm going to beat the shit out of him."

"You hold his arms," said Claudia. "I'll work him over."

"What did she say?" said Dennis.

"Nothing," I said pushing Claudia back down in bed, open palm to forehead. She giggled. "Look," I said, "I need to go back to work. I'm doing my art."

"I'm glad you think so."

I hung up. Dennis took no umbrage though regretted the disconnect with Claudia. He thumbed Vasari's *Lives* to load up on learned artsy anecdotes for the night's revels. He grinned at the reference to Giotto's "O," the Tuscan word "tondo" meaning both a geometric circle and a stupid person. My blossoming gut came to mind as tondo, a conversational insert with satiric overtones he bookmarked as rejoinder material – of its own too aggressive a platitude. Would not endear him to Claudia. He returned to Blake, read bio material to get a fix on the man's preference in women. He read a distance. Took vigorous notes. Wondered that Blake may really have avoided landscape in his painting because of its association with the female, the fleshy sensual. But Dennis thought he remembered landscape in Blake. It was a masculine landscape, crags and blasted dead trees and the like. Yes, maybe so. A master plan evolved as ink spilled from his twiddling fingers onto the blank, back pages of the book where Dennis kept notes. No conquest without preparation, he thought, and then segued to a challenge more meaningful than rubbing skin in bed. Dennis read another ten pages of the authentic great American novel, greased the collar of his robe with the sweat of perturbation. A rime of conscience? No. Vestigial in Dennis. Deadweight to Dennis' forward motion. He had evolved beyond compassion for others. He smiled a pointy teeth smile and ejected whatever tiny bubbles of principle may have surfaced in the mux of his intestinal juices. He squeezed butt cheeks together, loosened the sphincter and farted away temporary discomfort.

Dennis wondered how Chapman could have impacted so quickly the dynamic of the café klatch. He knew Rowan likes periods of disorder, but he did feel that his own filters of proportion might counterbalance potential disaster. Had it come to freakish lawlessness for the sake of impact? Were they so bored? Dennis included? Was Rowan's current culture jarring meant to send each off in different orbits? Was this Rowan's plan? Drive the wedge of establishment reprisal deep into the quick of their avant-garde souls? Test their resolve, their true relevance as culture impact against the status quo? Dennis pulled on khakis and draped a gray herringbone sport jacket with leather elbow patches over a starched white collared shirt unbuttoned at the top to assert the casual. Dennis sank into his one cushy chair, a leather recliner that belonged to his father before retirement, before his depression and symptomatic inactivity.

Dennis considered the chair's résumé: twenty years experience supporting gluttonous, ulcerated, corpulent, TV induced somnolence, as evidenced in beer spills and stretch marks as prominent as a woman's stomach after birthing twins, symptomatic of having birthed two new lives: in its absence, intended to prevent afternoon slumbers and promote the previous user's industry post-retirement (woodworking in the garage in this case); and in its presence, pulling Dennis deeper into the Xanadu pleasure dome of his measureless intellect, spot lit in this case beneath a spindly, chrome standing lamp.

Dennis dressed his feet in oxfords from a collection of boxes. Chapman wore Adidas, Dennis remembered. No depth of character as Dennis saw it. In twenty-five minutes the cabbie would arrive curbside. Dennis locked fingers in his lap, closed his eyes to weigh the significance of Leon and Francine's engagement party. What are the advantages in partnering? He conjured the lives of the famously accomplished whom he had studied for guidance. These were their habits of partnering:

First, the spiritual – marriage as access to the certifiably holy. St. Augustine then, to wallow in the extreme. Two mistresses, one illegitimate son, and an arranged marriage for privilege. Gains political and ecclesiastical prominence and ascends to the summum bonum. But he must eject a loving mistress, mother to his only son, to finagle a marriage of connection, to advance beyond professor of rhetoric to the Roman court. Then another mistress before his child bride is of age to marry. A smorgasbord of partnering. His Persian Manichean tendencies perhaps? Maybe. He leaves behind the academic life, his wife dies, he becomes a Christian, does a lot of God work, preaching and teaching. Held in high regard for that. Augustine dies a spent and diseased Bishop writhing in bed as Vandals gather outside the gates of Carthage. We build that others may rend asunder. The partnering of his youth, the marriage for advancement catapulted him the furthest into significance.

Science next. A woman this time. Madame Currie gave her health, by degrees, but gained what ... the Nobel Prize, twice I think. She married once. Had one illicit affair that nearly ruined her. Here's

*a woman eluded the Czar's police to self-educate and to fill a profes-
sor's chair at the Sorbonne. Easy enough back then you'd think. Submit a paper for a PhD back then. But she – the first among women
to do so. And before the accolades and all those radioactive materials sniffed out, she marries her lab partner, ten years her senior. He
grounds her, supports her. Both irradiate the blood and the organs
before the ox cart squashes his head when he slips on paving stones.
Another cow that makes history. But her husband's death doesn't
stop her. Too much momentum that one. The second Nobel follows
soon after. But before his death, they are partners in every sense of
the word, in the lab especially, working from uranium, shaking out
plutonium and radium. Okay, she carries her husband's surname,
but who remembers her Christian name? She goes a great distance
beyond his capabilities on what he has given. The way to science is
through partnering someone of capacity and taking everything from
him – his work, his life, his name.*

*Politics next – Marat. The French again. Vive la Revolution!
Marat gave his life, blood bubbles in the bath. He married for maid
service. His mistress was Revolution herself. There's Marat's* <u>Philo-
sophical Essay on Man,</u> *Voltaire's invective after that. It takes a science of the body to understand its connection to soul, says Marat,
court doctor to the aristocracy before he incites reasons to lop off
their heads. Nice! And political intrigue. In favor, out of favor, rejected by the Academy of Science. Ah, the French. How they foment.
And then Marat's final occupation – newsman, writer and publisher,
provocateur, hiding for his life in the catacombs, from whence came
the scrofula – pruritic, blistering, emaciating – and after that, soak-
ing in the bath, and voila! he takes a wife, a waif, some poor young
thing to service his medical needs while he composes a death list of*

*political criminals until one absent from the list, Charlotte Corday,
stabs him as he lay in the tub. He should have known. No list is complete. But here's a man who marries for maid service. She opens the
door. In walks death. Partnering during revolution is unwise. And
Revolution is an ungracious mistress.*

*All dead, but all forever remembered. Assertions of prominent
selves, even through marriage, marriage to some degree. What of the
common man, the common woman. Marriage for the sake of family.
Sublimation of the self. What of my own family? Let's see. Mother's
definition of self: peacekeeper. Father's: nihilist, armchair quarterback. (Dennis beats with his fists the arm rests of father's chair.)
What, Father, have you sacrificed? You do and have done much
whatever you want. Cranky, imposing, ignorant you. Unless – did
you give your dreams away to keep a job? To raise a family? I wonder if you dream? Can you dream after a thirty-year grind taking
the edge off pipe fittings? How much of yourself have you ground to
dust? Married to your job. That's clear. That's where you sublimated.
Mother and I were just in the way. Well, I kept out of your way. Isn't
that what you wanted? We have nothing in common anyway. You
brag of my Princeton degree but introduce me to nobody. Imagine
me at the Elks Club, the VFW. I suppose I didn't help much. There's
Little League out there rolling in the dirt to make fathers proud and
there's clean little me at home with a book.*

*And Leon soon to marry, maybe. What will he sacrifice for
Francine? Everything!*

Imagine Gustave Aschenbach married? Never happens! <u>Death in
Venice</u>. *Remarkable book! Epitome of the writer as aesthete. Aschenbach would have pissed away his art if he had married! Imagine him
in Venice at the Hotel Excelsior without the solitude and leisure to*

drink the image of Tadzio in that blue sailor suit with those blond ringlets of hair, skin the spotless bloom of Persian marble. Imagine Aschenbach weaving his thoughts through a wife's chatter, assuaging her headaches, bankrolling her gewgaw obsessions, inserting beneath her derriere pillows like she is some Queen's Terrier. But the bachelor Aschenbach, he sacrifices much in Venice. He surrenders his life. He breathes the cholera so he may breathe the same air as Tadzio. And why not? As an aesthete, as a writer with adamantine standards, how could he hope to achieve more in his art than the physical perfection of Tadzio, this Adonis grown in the flesh more glowingly than what Praxiteles might have carved. Tadzio, the apotheosis of proportion in divine creation. Aschenbach died in Venice. But he lived more substantively, more passionately in those few weeks than ever in his books, with all his fame. And there was no wife. So will this be the way to aestheticism! Perhaps, if indeed aestheticism should be the priority.

Poor Leon. He might as well grind pipes as repair human psyches for all the peace Francine will give him in making a spiritual life of his work.

Outside the cabbie lay on his horn. Dennis turned off the light but couldn't resist a peek out his window where rows of shut-ins back-lit and oscillating in the filthy air had downgraded their expectations of another Saturday night.

Chapter Six:
Rowan Murray neglects Suki Miyushi,
favors the company of Mason Fisher's future lover

Saturday, December 6, 1980
7:45 p.m. – 11:00 p.m.
(47 hrs/45 min. before John Lennon's murder)

Rowan flagged a taxi from the "shop." He intended a beeline to Suki's apartment in Greenwich Village but found himself instead negotiating the blind turns of human complication. He made a friend of Raul Vega, the taxi driver, the man I have come to love, who is what Dennis calls "fraternal." Rowan used to tell anyone in New York with a foreign accent the story of his first gift from America. He told Raul. He had disembarked off the aluminum projectile that carried him to LaGuardia from Heathrow. He had a letter from Columbia University confirming his status as doctoral candidate, which facilitated his release from Customs. He was the first of his flight to appear at the luggage carousel. He found his cheap, over-stuffed bag burst at the seams, his worn and pedestrian clothes spilling out like seed from a weed pod.

As it happened, a gorgeous set of leather bags that looked male enough lay beside his own on the carousel. Rowan lifted the leather bags and by this equipped himself in executive garb of excellent quality tailored to his dimensions. Rowan had never stolen before. He was even inclined to return miss-counted change at kiosk transactions. But somehow here, in the land of opportunity, stealing felt appropriate. And the clothes perfectly matching his dimensions suggested the virtue of his first capitalist gesture. Consequently, this gift endowed him with expectations of great things from America. Rowan felt compelled to share this story anywhere belts convey American goods for others asserting the boundaries of gift capitalism. When for example groceries glide the conveyer of a cashier's line, he would regale with his suitcase lore the blue-haired lady with food stamps feeding cats, or the teenager with fake ID sweating over six Buds. The cashier warily presented the charges.

Rowan asked polite questions of Raul to identify his accent and got a castaway's gripe of hard knocks corrupting his particular American dream: ineligible for a visa of both varieties which insinuated his otherness, said he; rolling the miles of a gypsy cab for cash, said he. And sleeping nights in floating residences in abandoned housing suitable to drug runners (one of whom he once happened to be). This forestalled extradition but placed him uncomfortably in a den of Jamaicans in Hell's Kitchen who bragged ceaselessly of, and tested to the limits, mail and pizza delivery. Miracles of American commerce, said he. Rowan nodded his head agreeably. Yet Raul found no percentage in Americanization, which brings, as he explained, bad air, mean people, factory foods, cramped spaces, dead landscapes ("la vista muy muerto," he said of the steel and glass), and no tolerance for gay men. (Rowan felt his eyebrows rise.) But mostly, no joy.

Of course Rowan was beginning to feel the same, or affected as much. He had come to America with his red hair pulled tight in a pony tail, his eyes tactfully indirect, his voice calm, declaring only his "genius" at customs, which he soon applied to a PhD dissertation at Columbia University and, more significantly, to a score with libretto intended to popularize avant-garde opera. He was thinking something irreverent and compellingly offensive, but with intellectual vigor. He called it *Tillich and the Burning Church*. Something like what Glass and Wilson had done with Einstein. He conceived a fusion of soprano sax, organ, flute, bass clarinet, chorus, dance and recitation in two parts, each 3 and a 1/4 hours long and each running concurrently in two adjacent theatres. One ticket. Simultaneous admission. The libretto would be episodic, similar to the Glass opera, depending less on plot and more on intimations, shades of meaning, allusions, and an imposing musical score in Hindustani sargam. This would, of course, require two complete and separate casts as well as musicians, and he wanted two elaborate sets – one of water crashing on a beach and one of a burning church. There would be no intermissions, since the effects on the audience were meant to be abstract and cumulative, nothing linear like narrative. Theatre goers would simply wander at will and whim between the two productions – the beach and the burning church.

Rowan anticipated theatre goers of New York City would lose their weary, glassy-eyed, "I've-seen-it-all" complacency and generate waves of enthusiasm for his twin operas, eager pedestrians pacing the sidewalks between these two Rowan Murray productions. Singing his praises down the avenue. Here's to the new, hip Wagner of song! He had his moment. Joseph Papp produced the thing, this conceptual art happening. But what opera devotees received paled beside the zeitgeist of another Brit. importation simultaneously invading New York after Texas – "new wave," the true wave of enthusiasm. Nothing abstract there, very direct and in your face. The Sex Pistols touring, their offensive behavior, final throes of a nearly disbanded band, they generated an overwhelming buzz, dominated the tabloids, the music reviews, the TV talkies, even the arts sections of the uptown papers. All of which had de-tuned a now de-sensitized audience to the comparative subtleties of Rowan's cutting edges.

Vasoconstriction of the gray matter is to blame, or so Rowan said. Which, he explained to his sympathizers, occurs in violence stimulation and produces a kind of dumbing down to mad-dog sensibilities. Rowan's audience was expecting Rowan's opera to change its views on art, on religion, on the world at large. But after the Sex Pistols, Rowan's material seemed far too tame. The critics ripped it to shreds, raw meat thrown in a cage. They may, in fact, have been frothing. One said, "Gilbert ditches Sullivan, drops acid and wants to convince us Paul Tillich is burning churches to universalize religion. Can this be serious art? Has Joseph Papp gained religion and lost his soul?" Another *Rolling Stone* review.

Rowan's Broadway hopes moved farther off-Broadway with each demeaning review, until a high school tour in the Midwest with a trimmed-down, sanitized production seemed the only likely venue. He considered. But instead retreated to Columbia University where he received clumps of uptight grad students worried over grades, clawing for a hold on that rare vacant symphony chair by the ends of their bleeding finger nubs and vying for hottest newcomer at the Tanglewood summer music festival. He found himself not caring about much of anything – his students, his music, the subtle and profound verities of the universe.

Raul, too, felt numb. Then abandoned self-interest became a kind of automation of street survival. He had worked at first for a legitimate cab company and made good money doing the La Guardia run but night clubbed his tips away. The rest he mailed to Colombia. But more on this later. He thought he had found the ghost of tango in the spotlit glitter of the disco mirror ball. This made him feel somewhat at home. He had, perhaps, been grooving to the rhythm of the Bee Gees the same time as Rowan, maybe in the same clubs. But then, disco had died, and techno rock, punk, and grunge had plunged the elastic grace of synchronous motion into the dark body slams of untouchables in a spiritless, punishing dervish. This held no meaning for him.

◆◆◆

The two night riders enjoyed sharing their pangs of personal effrontery, their nightmares of expatriation. Rowan suggested beer and conversation in a warm space that wasn't moving through space. Together their eyes appeared in the rear view mirror like planets, un-tethered, free of gravity, they touched and repelled, jounced uncertainly in that prescribed universe of cold glass: Raul's Aquarian water planets and Rowan's rust-brown Martian orbs. Limitations are an unhappy condition. They agreed. The universe is known to be expanding after all, said Rowan. "First round on me!" said Rowan as Suki Miyushi bit green nails anticipating his arrival, but which failed to produce enough calcium in her diet to delay the osteoporosis that will eventually, in her post-menopausal years, lock her hip and send her spinning down the Spanish Stairs of Rome (a bruised Vatican pilgrim who will have touched the capstone of all but this last of the four *isms* of spirituality). Her young lover will be appalled. She will wonder who is to sign the hotel bill as she leaves Suki keening there on those famous stairs. Suki has issues of abandonment. Rowan will not have helped much.

Rowan is incapable of arriving anywhere on time. Though he will say the opposite. Rowan refuses to keep a watch, argues time is an artificial construct, so why should he? Maybe this is his response to the Deist theory of an indifferent God winding the clock after creation and walking away as time runs down. Rowan did, however, participate in astral cycles which he said he could intuit as well as any animal in the wild. It's easy, he said. Anyone can do this once attuned to the meridians and the axial angles of sun slanting across the glass canyons of New York. If he were to arrive within a 1/2 hour either end of anticipation, Rowan considered this confirmation of a well-tuned internal clock. He explained as much to Raul, who said, sneaking a look at the Timex watch taped to the Chevy console, "*Si, tiempo est morte.* (But he meant here in New York, where there can be no stargazing at night apart from what is artificially rendered upon the rotunda ceiling of Grand Central Station.) We two shall kill a time together, *si?* We shall do this at the Club Beau Geste." Raul had referenced, perhaps knowingly, perhaps not, a classic movie of beautiful French brothers (a beautiful brotherhood) who disaffected to the French Foreign Legion, who broke with societal norms and embraced death upon the lance of the tribes of Ishmael, a most graceful gesture.

Club Beau Geste resides below street level. As they walked down ill-lit stairs, Raul pointed to an Arabian proverb painted upon the lintel above the door: *The love of a man for a woman waxes and wanes like the moon...but the love of brother for brother is steadfast as the stars, and endures like the word of the prophet.*

Rowan guessed he was in for more than a casual introduction to the brothers Geste. Patrons occupied bar stools and side tables floating upon the sinuous music of a reed flute as evocative as adhan, the early-morning call to prayer. Men by pairs had gathered there, hands rubbing china cups and crystal wine glasses like warming talismans, whispers sulky and thick, or clear as bells with metronome phrasing, emotions surging in tidal eyes. Only one man prone to self-love felt the need to make a scene. "I am, you see," he said leaning back in his chair, arms sweeping wide to appropriate attentions, "I am especially graced because free of TV. I am, as you will observe, conversant above ten minutes, because you see, I come without commercials." Tiny worlds, perfect little O's affixed like cartoon dialogue floated in the air above each table, or the Yin and Yang of compatibility, heads nibbling tails, the joys of fellating 69s. Raul ordered a Dos Equis and Rowan a Scotch neat. The frothy insouciance of New World beers still eluded him as acquired taste. The place was a tangle of accents. Even the bar tender spoke English as if under water, what Rowan took as French vowels soaked in Berber. Raul said that Akhmed, dark hair flecked with gray, a goatee of same, acne blemishes and gaunt cheeks but clear blackberry eyes and a massive physic, he was the owner. Akhmed smiled warmly. Drinks were on the house.

Rowan felt nothing of the sting of an outsider, straight man in a gay bar, although he knew instantly that he didn't belong and yet maybe so. All patrons, as Raul explained, are like Rowan – expatriates. There was nothing showy as alternative life style going on. The only disquieting moment attended curious stares at their blustery entrance, at their loud street voices before recalibrating to blend with the tenders of confession. If ever ambassadors were appointed to the gay nation, this place would have provided suitable candidates. Rowan was impressed.

"So, Raul, you must tell me. What ever can a life of man-to-man sexuality offer that a man-to-woman relationship cannot. I *am* curious."

"Ah, *si*, the man-virgin – this is what we say of you – the man-virgin will have no knowledge what will make a man to love a man. And you, a Nordic, you especially cannot know. A man of the equator will know."

"But you can't be sure of this, can you? What of David Herbert Lawrence? He of the coal mines and the abusive father and the chilblains of Nottinghamshire. That's in the north of England. But yes, up north where Hadrian built his wall. How will you explain David Herbert Lawrence? This very Nordic man whose final assumption relegates living with a woman to incompletion. Oh yes. And this he asserts in the shadow of the wall Hadrian built, Hadrian of the equator tribes, indeed yes, he that built the wall to safe keep his sunshine legions from the Scots, that most Nordic of tribes. As a wall, in Lawrence's view, it stands as some kind of chastity belt between north and south. Do you see? Lawrence wanted north and south to embrace passionately."

"I have no schooling for this, señor."

"Well, no matter, my point is this – Lawrence, Nordic or no, he had this theory of 'blood consciousness,' but yes, this idea that only a man can truly know another man. Not through his reason. Rather through drum signals coursing the veins or some such rot. Do you see? He wrote of naked men, Nordics, sweating and wrestling in the glow of firelight. Which would be a Greek ideal, do you see? Nude wrestling, the Olympics and what all. Oh yes. But I take

your point. We English have managed to make of the Greeks a dispassionate race. All those Doric columns, brainy Aristotle, Spartan
boot heels. And Greek mottoes for what all anybody does or hopes
to do taken so very seriously and, yes, all that wonky rot. But I have
a yen to know in practical terms what makes a man so desirable,
beyond the sexual, I mean. Once the sexual relation has been established. You must have me understand what occurs beyond the
sexual. How deep a man can go in knowing another man?"

" *Pero es esto. Si.* Regard: You wish to know more than whisker
burn on thigh, señor? You wish to know *this*," Raul said sweeping
his hand across the room.

"Oh yes, I see … what do I see? Well-mannered, well-dressed.
But there is something more here that I miss. "

"*Si*."

Rowan looked around. He divided the room into tableau like
intaglio upon a ring to make a "jeweler's eye" inspection of detail.
He saw breakout sessions in the board room: middle-aged homos,
pin-striped and balding, graying mustaches neatly trimmed. There
was no machismo of glistening muscular arm nor tight jeans with
pronounced pelvic bulge. These were advertising execs and Wall
Street speculators, lawyers and college professors. These were suits
and appropriately so. Were any one of these patrons liquefied and
emptied out from his pin-striped suit, any of the others might have
been poured in without stirring a stripe. Faces and hands were
tanned, relaxed, Bahamian warmed beneath shade umbrellas;
drinks were warm and fiery; eyes wandered but voices telescoped,
a learned contraction of attentions perhaps whittled to a point
by the invectives of a hetero world. The accents were prevalently
French. Ah, he thought, the French … they have a way of making

the commonplace distinctive, ceremonial.

Rowan assessed more carefully Akhmed, who was dip-washing glasses in a double sink, bending over with stiff arms and pumping his legs like, well, Rowan didn't want to think about like what. And did the man wink? That was a bit cheeky! And, yes, now that he noticed, the place was a decorator's theme of film noir, antique theatre posters like parchment framed in plexiglass. Rowan felt blanched to sepia, grainy, relegated to the dubious translations of subtitles in this whispery bar with the only Americans being Gary Cooper, Bogart and Bacall in garishly yellow hues with black gothic lettering and splashes of red to effect danger. These posters were the only wall decoration to the only lighting – a row of swag amber globes pulsing over the bar, bouncing on their stems like over-heavy flowers. Rowan felt overwhelmed by atmosphere and at this moment more alien than he had thought possible.

"I must say," said Rowan turning a thigh and twisting a shoulder to indicate tables behind, "I must confess, Raul, that I cannot imagine these conversations between these ... gentlemen ... so earnest."

"I tell you. They make the grocery list, they say about the weather. You must think they say what insolence dare make of you a misery, my love? I kiss your eyes in service of our love. No, señor. They make the sound of after day. Because the footpaths of New York they hammer so hard the spine. Concrete, señor. Even the dead beneath they cannot make a small wind."

"Do you mean breathe? Do the dead breathe?"

"*Si.* In Cartegna the dead make small wind."

"Yes, but Raul, you imply break wind, which I can tell you takes a recent meal and an unhappy collection of gasses."

"Ah si, yes," Raul said as he laughed, the pirate blue of his eyes opening like spring flowers. "Or but we may say *huelepedos.*"

"Brilliant word! Perhaps too lovely a word for breaking wind."

"It means farties that carry turistas in the town in carriage. It means horse's ass that feed on green oats."

"Oh, I see. I think I like rather more *the sounds of after day.* Oh yes, that phrase, beautifully done! Oscar Wilde types then if you will. But no, sadly, a misconception by me to be sure. I am, well, don't please make of this an invitation – but oh yes, so sadly un-initiated that I would have expected Oscar Wilde types. My God! That's awful. It is as if I have relegated all gay sensibilities to characters of literature, banished them altogether from the corporeal world," said Rowan with no small embarrassment.

"Wild, *si.* That is what straight men will say of us. But sensitive too, much as Lorca in New York City. Do you know Lorca?"

"Yes, of course, but still literature. Do you see? I thought you said you were unschooled?"

"I read Lorca. I read because he is Spanish. And he writes of New York. I come to New York by Lorca. *Pero*, I am no poet myself. I find no love of New York."

"I see. But what I am asking is how can you fall in love with a man? I can see the sex part. But yes, indeed I can. I'm no Victorian. There are many ways to satisfy the flesh aren't there? Flesh-on-flesh of any sort preferred, of course, to mechanical means. But agape, true love of a spiritual nature ... I cannot comprehend. Unless, and don't mistake me, Raul. I don't mean to offend. But can this be self-love? Narcissism? A marriage of minds and all that rot is so easy when there is but one mind to enthrall. Do you see?"

Raul's mustache quavered, his cheeks reddened, his breathing staggered and his hands gripped palm down the table as if exerting the power to levitate. Rowan wondered if somewhere near trees were falling, buildings collapsing, tides reversing, clouds scudding violently, but all gradually subsided. Raul raised his head and smiled, his eyes radiant. He shook his dark gleaming hair like a dog shaking off a swim, said almost whimsically, "Señor, you make a great insult. I forgive. But, señor … a great insult."

"Oh dear, unintentional. I assure you."

"*Si, si.* I am sure. I forgive. But you make for me much pique, *señor.*"

"A very good word, 'pique.' I shall try not to make pique again. I assure you."

"I have not the knowledge of all you say, but to me it does seem, so much … assuming."

"Oh yes, I see. Stereotypes again. My apologies … again. But you see, Raul, we must all of us labor in the dimness of our subjective selves, but yes, yoked as we are to assumptions. Do you see? You must be the emotional Spaniard and I the impassive Brit. You the emotive Segovia and I the restrained Handel. Wounded bloody fingers pricking the strings of a sinuous guitar, and silk cuffs brushing the cold ivory of a scrupulously tuned piano. There we are. Can't you see us? Raul, you must tell me. Why cannot I appreciate a man as you do? I mean, beyond the sex. Why am I so limited?"

"Because, señor, you are very much *cachacos.* Such are my countrymen that live upon the dry highland of Bogota. I am myself *costeños.* From pirates and black slaves I count my ancestors. Much passion from Caribbean lowland and a little bit of dangerous. I tell you of my life. You judge as you wish."

"Oh, no. I promise. No judging."

"I have woman and child, señor. In Colombia," said Raul then told of halcyon indiscretions, living as a child with his family in a

barrio of Cartagena, ten children and he the elder. At fifteen the
first sibling to kiss the ring of Escobar, so running drugs to the
border of Panama on his motorcycle through dense jungles of the
Darien Gap, banana plantations, swamp, palm plantations, camp-
ing among sandstone block ruins of prehistory Ciudad Peridida
where the coca-chewing Kogis live. He was small time, living off
the only livable wage offered by Escobar to the dispensable poor.
He did his job well. Made notable impact as the undeterred, black-
masked, mystery Norton courier, escaping armed banditos, whom
even the police knew to avoid, ripping through mud paths, a flash
of chrome natives called lightning, the Norton growling like thun-
der for lack of a muffler, villages cheering and chickens scattering.

One time he took a bad spill, the Norton's back tire spinning
laterally off the wet-slick of a rib of log laid out to stop erosion,
donkey carts being the chief transport of the region. He broke an
arm and bruised himself purple. A Kogi girl of maybe seventeen
on her way to plantation, already plumping, breasts heaving like a
fertility charm, a plum complexion and the brown stains of coca
on her teeth and lower lip, speaking a dialect he could not fathom,
she had seen him go down, removed the black ski mask and fell instantly lovable. Nights there even in the Caribbean tropical dense-
ness are cool from ocean winds, and for Raul intolerably chill. He
went into fever. He availed himself of the girl's warming flesh. But
it was the girl's brother, her younger brother, that most intrigued
him. Raul spent his nights with the girl, and only one afternoon
beneath the fronds beside the river with the young boy. But it was
the boy's attentions that spoke to him most endearingly. He had
felt, for the first time ever, at peace.

"The *peace*, señor. La paz. And with this, I find my way to manlove. It is a quiet room, señor. The door to this room opens for only some ones of us. For some ones of us, no. But I am father of a child and to the child's madre I send America dollars to buy Toyota truck. The child's madre now brings produce to market in Cartegena. No longer to suffer the cruel plantation. This make of her a rich woman, provide for child."

"Oh yes, I see. And the child is what gender?"

"*Como?*"

"Boy or girl?"

"*Chico.*"

"Oh yes, thought so. The ironies were unavoidable. And the room you speak of, it is much like the room we currently inhabit, is it not?'

"*Qué es?*

"Much like *this* room," Rowan said sweeping his hand across the view.

"Ah, *si.* Yes, yes."

"Yes, well, fascinating (there was no irony in his voice), but I am afraid we must finish our talk another time. Suki Miyushi will have my head for this delay, although I must say she should be used to my casual timeliness by now. Listen, Raul, would you care to accompany me to a gathering of friends later this evening? You will find them excellent company, and I must say I like the idea of altering the dynamic with your rather colorful personality."

"*Si.* I am honored! I will make of you a great friend. This night, I have no heart for commerce. This night will be friendship," said Raul thinking reset the cab's meter to zero; erase all debt when friendship weighs more heavily upon the scale.

"Done!"

The two raced Adams' apples tippling dregs and left a generous tip for Akhmed. They walked away arm-in-arm like lovers into the jangly streets of New York where street lights bruised their eyes and newspapers sucked down alleys attached to their shins and car horns ricocheted off the sharp edges of stacked and insulated cubicles. Raul removed the taxi marquee from off the roof and keyed the ignition of his gray Chevy Caprice inviting Rowan to share a bench seat beside him. Together they swayed down the pocked streets of Manhattan on soft springs comfortably ensconced like sharing a living room couch as smaller cars beside them fell away soundlessly into bottomless potholes where the Chinese Dragon sleeps his papier-mâché dreams deep in some sulfurous cavern.

◆◆◆

Rowan had felt no inclination toward male-to-male sinsuality, but he had felt an expatriate's kinship and even more, connections of circumstance. Raul had left Colombia because of a woman, or so Rowan had assumed – from the shock of finding himself a father – or repulsed by learning more about himself sexually than he was ready for, or from wanting to provide for his son. But mostly from the need to transform himself into something other than a drug runner, a short-lived future at best, should the term "future" apply at all. And Rowan had left England because of a woman – not what she did but what she would not do – and from a need to develop artistically beyond the influence of London's Leicester Square.

There was a woman, a beautiful chestnut-haired, milk-faced girl who had studied in the carrel across from his at the London School of Economics library on Portugal Street beside the Waterloo Bridge. Just one stop off the Underground from the theatre district of Leicester, where Rowan had often retreated, or disaffected like a spy changing sides. He had become a disenchanted student of economics, which had come to seem to him an unavoidable, almost predestined cycle of influences and consequences, dull, very dull. He had become by default an intimate of opera and musical variety performance, a back-stage hanger-on. But there in the closeted School of Economics library, in the mote-swirling morning hours of research drudgery, she had smiled at him, routinely, every morning. Had nodded but never spoken. Until, finally, the sky being so blue and the pressures of his studies and the creamy beauty of the woman seated across from him with the pencil in her ear and her gray eyes so earnest in her books, it seemed a crime. He startled her as he stood smiling above her in his gangling height with his Coxwold accent beseeching her to share with him a matinee revival of Inigo Jones and Ben Jonson's *The Masque of Blackness* at the Garrick. He blathered in his nervousness.

"Oh, but," she had said in a whisper, concern twisting her mouth, "but we have not been introduced."

As if *his* people could possibly know *her* people. He was not of her ilk, never would be. And that was her point. His rough, border town gutturals, his over-large hands, his jarring tavern familiarity, his guildsman father peering over his shoulder, wrenches rattling in his jeans (genes?), and his "Oh, but, are we still doing that in Britain?" response to her whispered negation of Rowan's genius, his O-Levels of distinction, his future ambassadorship of world economics. He was a spark on the horizon no less bright than her own. Well, ballocks! to the institutions that serve the Lords and Ladies of this land, inbred, waterlogged wormwood of ancient stock that stuff themselves in excelsior to make a show at substance that any finger could poke through and fill a room in sawdust!

He knew that despite being English, he was very like Raul Vega, a passionate nobody rather than a cold, aristocratic somebody. So Rowan resolved to attend the masque alone. He did so. And from that day he gave himself to the dreamy insecurity of the staged musical. He had made a habit of music and theatre as a way of moderating the strains of graduate study. But music and theatre would from that day be his future. Damn the economics!

If we examine the influences of this intriguing Brit, the "gestures" of the iconoclast five, like the students he threatened with suicide, all participated in "happening art" that goes back to Ben Johnson's 1604 work *The Masque of Blackness.* The author of which, as I have already mentioned, Rowan had confused with Samuel Johnson whose London Literary Club inspired Rowan's café brotherhood. But this particular Johnson, his masque was the first real experiment in audience participation, shock theatre, a happening as rich in substance as anything Yves Klein might have staged. Klein's *Anthropometrics* for instance: twenty musicians playing, three nude females smeared with paint rolling on canvas, the audience and the artist seated in formal wear. Johnson's *Masque of Blackness* was Seventeenth Century social commentary with music, stirring set designs, costumes and special effects by Inigo Jones. Jonson's incomparable scholarship had gone into the libretto. Rowan was smitten, artistically smitten.

What he heard and saw was this: six tritons blowing, wreathed sea-shell trumpets, and sea maids singing, a tenor and two trebles:

Sound, sound aloud
   The welcome of the orient flood,
      Into the west;

Fair Niger, son to great Oceanus,
    Now honored, thus,
  With all his beauteous race:
  Who, though but black in face,
    Yet are they bright,
  And full of life and light.
  To prove that beauty best,
Which, not the color, but the feature
  Assures unto the creature.

... the   Tritons   sounded, and   they   danced on shore,
every couple, as they advanced, severally presenting
their fans : in one of which were inscribed
their mixt names, in the other a mute hieroglyphic,
expressing their mixed qualities. Their own single
dance ended, as they were about to make choice
of their men : one, from the sea, was heard to
call them with this CHARM , sung by a tenor voice.

Come away, come away,
We grow jealous of your stay;
If you do not stop your ear,
We shall have more cause to fear
Syrens of the land, than they
To doubt the Syrens of the sea.

... they danced with their men several measures
and corantos. All which ended, they were again
accited to sea, with a SONG of two trebles, whose

What he saw was gods and goddesses traipsing, which made sense considering the cast and audience of its premier – all nobility. King James requisitioned the work. Queen Anne, the Countess of Bedford, Lady Herbert, the Countess of Derby, Lady Rich, and well, you get the idea. They were the cast. They sang and danced and recited. And considering the nature of masque, they were not so remarkably in the play as of the play, dancing and singing, all painted blackamoors, painted black to intimate the daughters of Niger, and those unmarried all gloriously bare-breasted. Beauty and nobility in black! The antipodes of a world order accepted outright, applauded and embraced because of its outrageousness, its revolutionary message taken at face value, so to speak.

And there was too the Inigo Jones influence, an artist of brash form and color that impressed Rowan as having created the ultimate "happening" experience – his set, costumes and special effects. What Rowan saw at Leicester Square was not so extensive and costly as what King James might have seen, but there were, as in the original, a landscape of woods and ocean, a motion of waves breaking on land, a bright moon shining through the moving cloud, and torchlight upon the shore. And there were tritons singing with blue hair and fish body parts, masquers placed in a large shell of mother-of-pearl, sea monsters swimming, feathers and jewels setting off the black and bared throats of the women. It was a feast to the senses. Maybe overmuch, but it appealed to Rowan, had a powerful effect upon Rowan, a multi-sensual happening on a scale beyond the jarring presentation of blackface and nudity. And as if this were not enough, there were readings from two other Ben Jonson plays occurring simultaneously in sequestered alcoves of the Garrick, audience members encouraged to wander at will between these performances (sound familiar? everything is derivative, some call it tradition, some call it tribute).

Rowan knew genius was rife among commoners despite current claims that Sir Edward de Vere had quilled Shakespeare. Nobility won't easily accept genius from the son of a glover, though Ben Jonson was a favorite at court and a brick layer's son, and Inigo Jones a builder of palaces and the son of a Welsh cloth maker, and then Rowan Murray from Yorkshire whose father plumbs toilets. Rowan had decided, as had Raul, that America was the place to make a new self. So he came to America on a grant to complete his doctorate in music at Columbia University, which was secondary to his operatic aspirations, but cracking the books paid the rent. Grants and scholarships paid the way.

Shortly after completing the doctorate and taking a thumping in the theatre business, Rowan happened to meet again Dennis Zamora at Rizolli's bookstore on Fifth Avenue. Dennis had a Herman Melville beard then and was healthily tanned in a white short-sleeve tee shirt, faded jeans and sandals. Rowan recognized the voice of Dennis asking for a book on trout fishing by Richard Brautigan. Rowan sidled up to Dennis and gave a "Howdy sport! Been fishin?" in his Coxwold accent which generated in Dennis a disquieting look as if anatomizing the moment after which Dennis laughed for so long Rowan wasn't sure if he had misidentified his old friend. Dennis was oddly unimpressed the two should meet by accident in a city of seven million and an ocean apart from their first introduction. He said, "Why not. There are millions in London and we met there five years ago."/"Not the same thing," said

Rowan. /"Right, said Dennis, "Guess not, but this kind of thing happens all the time in New York. It's the world's largest village." They exchanged phone numbers and promised to be in touch, but this won't happen until Leon brings Rowan to the coffee shop a couple years later.

◆◆◆

But we do Suki Miyushi a disservice. She too has a life in arrears and one presently stalled as she awaits Rowan at her studio apartment, chews green nails and froths green tea with a bamboo whisk, a little too brisk in her gesture, but not because Rowan is late. She is used to his un-timeliness in a number of things. It's just his nature. Nerves are hers, or at least a half portion thereof.

Suki likes nothing about herself, though she would not tell anyone this, not even her shrink, though she could read a pay check in the shifting landscape of Suki's pie-round face. Her parents had at first sent her to a Zen Buddhist monk, a friend of the family who was asked to make sense of their rebellious, teen artist daughter. The monk sat her down before him, took her face in his hands and saw clearly the two faces of the Dhamma in contradiction – the soft and pliant side of faith and devotion; and the sharp-featured, hard-headed world-view bent on critical inquiry. He said Suki must understand the guiding purpose of the Dhamma, a path to spiritual emancipation, liberation from the cycle of repeated birth, death and suffering. Then the two sides of Suki will integrate and stresses will be relieved. But Suki had no intention of ending her cycles of rebirth, and she cherished her contradictions as sources of artistic inspiration. She was then sent to an occidental therapist, a Chinese woman with a Princeton degree. The time she spent on a Freudian's couch, two plus years, she had not spent alone. She was by 16 years a wizened, cozened teen.

And now, at age 25, she is in New York City waiting for her lover Rowan Murray, biting nails and reading from a coffee-table collection of her favorite cartoon: George Herriman's *Krazy Kat*. She likes the uncertainty of its dialect (Brooklynese Russian with an intellectual goyim lexicon), a voice as unfixed in proper English as her own. And she likes the love-struck attentions of Krazy affixed as they are upon Ignatz Mouse who bounces bricks off Krazy's head, which Krazy mistakes for love gestures. But mostly she likes the iconoclast attributes of Krazy's persona as compared to Japan's epidemic "culture of cute." Compared to Hello Kitty (Har Kitti), all white and rounded soft, absent a mouth which corresponds to a wordless mind, Suki likes the ink black of Krazy and the sharp detail of feature.

But mostly she likes the ambiguous, cross-gendered nature of the cartoon's heroine (hero?). There has never been in the cartoon's twenty-year run a defining moment of gender. Suki identifies with Krazy. She wondered if she herself is much like Ignatz. Is she a cartoon without an inside? Would it hurt to grow a heart? She has tattooed on her left buttock a portrait of Krazy Kat with red, pointy hair giving itself a hypodermic to effect the starry glaze of its eyes. So much for the culture of cute.

Back to Suki's two faces: one side a Zen plane of quietude, the other sternly murderous, as if planning ritual suicide, seppuku, as if she can already feel the tanto slicing like a hot wire her intestines. She knew death would lower the veil almost before pain could register, so swift is the scouring of the bowels that bleeds out the heart's blood and releases the body's poisons to work against itself. She knew Rowan liked the feeling of being at death's edge, not necessarily his own, but in the company of anyone desperate enough to commit a desperate act. Her relationship with Rowan … Francine would never understand. And she would find it very difficult to sabotage. Suki knew what Francine was about. She was a nester, all round and soft with mundane thoughts. Hello kitty!

Rowan and Suki had met at NYU at a performance of Kabuki. Rowan had attended with his latest squeeze, a cute grad student from Columbia University, but one outside his discipline, history or medicine, so considered a safe liaison, safer at least than his department chair whom he had fallen in love with but knew to avoid. A middle-aged woman expert in identifying and authenticating Henry VIII lute compositions. A woman sick to death of her dusty Victorian Lit. professor husband and wondering why she had spurned Rowan who had hit on her as proof of the kittenish desirability she had maintained over the years.

Suki had attended the Kabuki theatre unescorted and had sat in the front row in black leather, hair dyed purple and spiked, both hands gloved and metal studded. As the onnagata, the female lead played by a male, stepped on stage after a gut throbbing introduction on an odaiko drum (a large brass plate suspended in a massive wooden frame), Suki was the only one of the audience shouting the actor's house, or guild. Kakegoe it's called, the shouting that is, what's expected from an appreciative, informed audience. During the illustrative moments as the actors exaggerate freeze-poses to suggest a narration lost to everyone but the most devout and Suki, as the shomisen plucked and strummed reverberated something like a sitar, Rowan took first notice of Suki. And he watched for her as the audience emptied into the theatre lobby at intermission.

Rowan's date had a face as waxy with make-up as the Kabuki players, a sensible closing of pores to New York City air. As she drifted off to the lady's room to make adjustments in the impression she meant to assert (urbane but flirty, youthful but experienced), Rowan brought his champagne glass to the sofa where Suki sat by herself with arms crossed on her chest and legs crossed at the ankles – the universal sign for no access. That didn't stop Rowan. He had had considerable success meeting women in America after his ego-bruising rejection at the London School of Economics a few years back. So he asked Suki what could be the significance of her chant during the performance, which the players seemed to appreciate if not the oblivious American audience, of whom he had to count himself ingloriously one. The effect upon Suki was an immediate unfolding of limbs, a kind of blooming of flowers when the night has passed and the sun emboldens. Suki's pale face a white flower on a black bough. Suki had been a loner for so long, a film student at NYU with indie sensibilities and, maybe because of her trust fund, no apologies for the brooding, indecipherable, even at times upsetting experiments in film she lay on her class-mates and instructors.

Yoko Ono, as it happens, was a significant influence on Suki. She had met Yoko one summer as their families came together in the foothills of Koyasan, the sacred mount of Koya, at the Miyushi ancestral home nestled in a copse of towering cypress, downwind and wafted by incense and sunrise chants from monks with shaven heads meditating in their Shingon Buddhist temple tottering on a cliff above them.

Yoko was a mother then from her first marriage to Anthony Cox, an American jazz musician, and despite her renegade status in the art world, she took flack humbly and in generous portion from her father, a prominent banker, for deserting her daughter and recently marrying John Lennon and pressing ahead with her career so noisily – the heavy dose of media hype, the billboards and the love-ins and such. Yoko lowered her head, said very little but let the ramparts of her cheek bones and the void of dark glasses and the black clothes deflect these criticisms that she knew her family had to air in the presence of Ambassador Miyushi and his wife in order to "save face." The two families sat around a low table of lacquered wood placed in the okuzashiki, the inner sitting room. Five adults and one girl child sat upon a cedar floor and upon tatami mats, legs crossed, the *ken* of the house. The proportions of the room had been designed in accordance with the number of tatami mats required. The moving walls of mulberry tree paper and bamboo, the fusuma, had been arranged to expose through a series of rooms opening like shadow boxes a change in threshold – a courtyard empty but for one large clay vase and two trees, a crooked pine and a tall bamboo. Symbolic of life's verities as sometimes supportive, sometimes withering.

Suki was impressed with Yoko. Suki was 13 years old. This was in 1969. Yoko Ono was 36. Her film *Rape* had just been released to the art houses in New York, London, and Tokyo. Suki had always looked older than her years. After this brief time with her family and Yoko's family in the hills of Koyasan, and once back in Tokyo, she dressed in black for the first time, applied eye shadow, exposed a portion of burgeoning chest, and brassed herself a ticket at a trendy back-alley movie theatre. Suki watched as the camera pursued its victim through city streets, a young Japanese girl living without English and without legal papers in New York City, ending with her curled into a ball on the floor of her apartment, trembling and weeping. Suki thought of herself as that girl, one of the disenfranchised, one of the "other." But she also knew that Yoko, despite her famous marriage and her gutsy art felt just as vulnerable because Suki had seen Yoko with her family, had seen her take abuse from her father and knew that the occident in her wanted to sever, eviscerate the orient in her, but could not. Suki became a Yoko Ono devotee from that moment.

It was Suki who suggested to Rowan the idea of *iconoclasting* as an art form to counteract what she had seen in Japan as the practice of celebrating kawaii style, a practice that had reached the stage of epidemic: cute people, cute accessories, even cute hand writing (horizontal, stylized, rounded characters with English, katakana and little cartoon pictures of hearts, stars and faces inserted randomly). That which had led the great writer Yukio Mishima to commit ritual suicide, his protest of the westernization of Japan. For good reason Mishima wanted to remain of the orient, Suki thought. He was male.

Suki had explained to Rowan while pulling his long red hair and planting a tongue in his ear (they were in the bathroom of Suki's favorite tea house sexing it up in a toilet stall, their first time doing it), she had said that iconclasting had got started as a popular response to the American export of its pop culture, and that her hero, Yoko Ono, had been debunking custom with her objects and installations, her language works, her film, music, and performance art, together with all her Fluxus buddies of 1960s Manhattan. John Cage and Marcel Duchamp were frequent visitors of Yoko in her Tribeca loft.

"Can you not fucking see? Make it new!" she had said while

riding Rowan's phallus on the porcelain. "Make it new. Make it most *true*."

Rowan found Suki's ideas fascinating, practically coitus interrupting, and he made Suki tell him exactly what she meant once they had returned to their green tea.

"You must," she had said, "disrespect sat which most make who you are. Make deep hole in self which can be filled with oserwise. Do you see? Make better self by disrespect of what you most be."

"Oh yes, of course. The phoenix rising from the ashes. Destroy to make anew. That's an old idea."

"No! You not fucking understand."

"Well, tell me then what it is I have missed!"

"Destroy sat which *make* self, not self itself."

"I don't follow."

"Do you see blemish."

"Yes, of course," said Rowan having to lean over the table to get a close look at a tiny eruption of skin beneath Suki's nose, her complexion slick as onion otherwise, gleaming with vitality.

"I make pressure so," said Suki having caught between two green nails the tiny protrusion sending a spurt of blood and puss onto the table.

"Oh, shite, Suki, that's just awful!"

"No, is make outside pressure of sing sat seem to be me but is not so much me. I am still here, am I fucking not?" said Suki having run a hand under the table and onto Rowan's overworked phallus.

"See," Suki said, "you make tiny leap in hand. I am here most definitively."

"Ah, big idea for little Japany girl," Rowan said effecting Suki's accent, for which he got a kick beneath the table. "But, yes, I begin to see what you mean. Say I were somehow to topple Big Ben, notice my choice of images dear one (another kick). You must stop that, Suki. But say I were to bring down the big cock, as a Londoner I would be forever affected, and yet still the same. This is what you mean, is it not?

"And make big hole for new icon to fill space. You see? And still be Londoner."

"Oh yes, surely. I do, yes. So the trick is to efface these icons as you call them and accept as legitimate what takes their place. Fascinating. Truly. And may I say that I hope sincerely never to accrete enough cachet as a composer to ever become iconic, at least not with you swinging Daddy's bonsai sword from the white steed of righteous art."

This was the last civil conversation Suki and Rowan were ever to have. They were soon thereafter to establish a routine of bickering that seemed always to threaten to be the final argument but that somehow never did amount to that. Per example, Rowan had trouble accepting the Orient as expert so had to sift through the dead letters of the Occident to find Kant's theory of Deontology, which he then used as his path to iconoclastic gesture. Suki saw through Rowan. And maybe it was what got her really mad at him. Everyone but Rowan and Suki expected these two to break up, despite their being together for nearly two years. Still, at that moment, forty-seven hours and forty-five minutes before the murder of John Lennon, Suki awaited Rowan's arrival with a fierceness Rowan had never seen, the end result of a phone conversation with Daddy in Berlin. The warrior princess had emerged hard as tempered steel. Maybe Rowan had become iconic after all. Or maybe it came down to Orient vs Occident. Or maybe the upcoming event, the destruction of international pop idol John Lennon, would be the first meaningful cooperation between Orient and Occident.

Chapter Seven:
Inside the mind of Mark David Chapman

Saturday, December 6, 1980
9:15 p.m. – 11:45 p.m.
(47 hours before John Lennon's murder)

Mark David Chapman married for normalcy. I think most of us do. I would marry Raul if I could. Mark didn't marry for love or for financial convenience, but to be like everyone else. He collected Norman Rockwell paintings funded by his father-in-law and called them investments, but really, to Mark, they are irresistible tableau normalcies which he had hoped to experience and envied, desired and disdained because he had been denied a simple life. And then, to spite normal, he liked to think his otherness had made him superior. This is how people who experience self-loathing mask their vulnerabilities. Mark was always looking for transcendence, confirmation of a destiny beyond the ordinary. He looked for this in LSD, in born-again Christianity, in Tod Rundgren's *Deface the Music* lampoon of John Lennon, and in the murder of John Lennon.

He found intelligent design in discovering a nest of café iconoclasts who accepted him and his intention of ritual murder, a purposeful murder. This was another bit of "synchronicity," confirmation of his gesture and of what he had come to expect of this trip to New York: God and history were cooperating to write a new chapter in *Catcher in the Rye* into which he anticipated merging as a significant character once he had killed Lennon. It was all coming together. The jig-sawed pieces hacked out from Mark's psyche by all the injustices he had suffered were shifting back into place. The final portrait would be a statesman-like Mark David suitable to framing in a founding-fathers gallery, which is what he was explaining to the Chairman of the Board of "little people" that routinely convene in his head as he stepped off a curb at Columbus Avenue and 73rd Street and into traffic.

It was forty-seven hours before he murdered John Lennon. The light changed in a congress of vehicles bending the corner, one driver particularly irate, pumping the horn on seven coats of black lacquer shining in street lamps and December rain, a land yacht with U.N. flags attached to fenders and courtesy lights gleaming between six doors. Very little of this imperial assertion had sifted through the neuron filters of Mark's brain where the board meeting occupied virtual space. The meeting had come to order.

Chapman had as a child invented a civilization of "little people." These are the voices in his head. Chapman has lavish emotional needs. He needs admirers that he can humble and punish. These little people appeared in his bedroom one night, an entire village of diminutive ones going about their businesses on the oval hooked rug at the foot of Mark's bed: shopkeepers, lawyers, parents, teachers, children. They made commerce. They made love. Or as close as a pre-pubescent boy can project the act having to guess at the stifled violences done behind his parents' bedroom door. They broke laws, which Mark corrected. And they died, many of them prematurely due to Mark's tantrums.

They shook with fear at Mark David's tantrums: the hammer of God, Mark David in the sky. Looming above the village and holding in his right hand a burled bedpost like wielding a chieftain's staff, delivering the law. They saw nothing incongruous in their titan dictator appearing to them zipped inside flannel Roy Rogers pajamas (mother kept her son eternally childish while also demanding of him the machismo of an avenger). Mark tried to be fair to the little people, but his mother had programmed an aberrant disregard for fairness by exacting of him protection from her abusive husband. Ten-year-old Mark couldn't protect her, couldn't protect himself. Thus his need to escape deep into his imagination where he rules with a hammer in one hand and self-contempt in the other a tribe of quivering miniature adults.

While stepping off the curb at Columbus Avenue, Mark had been consulting the Board of Town Fathers of little people. This is the fairness committee composed of the best little citizens of whom Mark is protectorate. This committee had discovered Mark's insecurities and had begun to intrude into his life. It had become the governing conscience of this gargantuan child that is Mark David Chapman.

Mark had been telling the Chairman that his extravagance of late (the trip to New York from Hawaii) was inconsequential in the larger scheme of things. The Chairman was easily convinced.

But the Minister of Finance, lean as a hound but with a neck thick from scrofula, he was not easily swayed. Even the Chairman frequently deferred to the Minister of Finance, a model of Mark's father who crunched numbers for an oil company and beat his wife at home and smashed the roast turkey against a wall at family gatherings – the silent, explosive type. The Minister of Finance considered this latest Mark David outing a waste of resources –

round-tripping New York from Hawaii, laying-out cash for a hand gun, the excursion to Georgia from New York to buy hollow tips, plans for extravagant rooming at the Sheraton, and for what? Nothing consequential as commerce goes. His usual summation of Mark David was this: "Old enough to know better; young enough not to care." Particularly as regards money he intended to use to commission a prostitute. Squandering the loan from his father-in-law, strains on the familial creditor/debtor relationship, not to mention the obvious moral decline of stiffing an in-law and stuffing a whore.

The Minister of Defense, mimetic abbreviation of General Peter Sellers in *Doctor Strangelove*, he was most inclined to make a sport of mayhem. He saw most of this Chapman's way. Preening a thin moustache with delicate gestures from a long skinny index finger on hands gnarled and thick as potatoes, a whiplash grin, a V-pattern forelock of deeply receding hair, campaign ribbons gleaming, he pronounced John Lennon as great a threat to Christian values as the vampire Keith Richards. Vampire! he called Richards, perhaps intending allusion to the excesses of rock-star life routinely cleansed in blood transfusions. Mark David agreed with the Minister's assessment of John Lennon. He carried it further. Mark David quoted Tod Rundgren: "John Lennon ain't no fucking revolutionary. He's a fucking idiot, man!' The Minister of Finance brooded silently, ineffectually. "The Beatles more powerful than God! My God!" said the offended defenseman.

The Minister of Morality concurred. He had taken a back seat in the proceedings as was his wont, but this was fast encroaching on his bailiwick and he knew to stir himself to indignation or surrender the small gains he had recently made assuaging Mark David's temper when deliberations didn't always go Mark's way.

The Minister of Public Relations decided to quietly hang fire until the shape of things to come had taken solid form. Besides, he was seldom taken seriously by the others anyway.

The large, black limo klaxoned Armageddon, closed the door on the closet drama in Mark's head, tweaked his focus back to street side which had become a postcard diorama of New York City that shattered and splintered, the slivers of glass of a TV screen, images calving and slipping off screen, each fragment a scene trapped in its distinct geometry on a red backdrop, the deep blood red you see closing eyes against the sun. Same effect. Chapman was blinded. He knelt on a manhole cover middle of the intersection, the ground telescoping, thought for a minute he had found a penny, rubbed his eyes, pedestrians pointing and motorists stepping out from their cars to gawk and fume.

A young Vedic woman, a new convert, a new bride shivering in the rain in an orange sari, a beautiful face shiny in tinak and kum-kum, she had slipped the confines of an overfilled 2nd Avenue Temple. She had tired of chanting her daily dose of the sixteen rounds of the Hare Krishna mantra and deliberately welcomed the pollutants of metropolis. Her rebellion will be brief, as Chapman will scare her back to temple where she will become one of three things a Krishna man can beat: a drum, a dog, a wife. This the supreme guru, Canakya Pandit, has decreed.

When the black limo bullied its way down the street, the female Krishna recognized a symbol of darkness gathering, the shadow beneath the light of life. She saw it would violate this frail man on his knees lost in chant. She responded to her training. Conditioned and aspiring to sati, as Prabhupada had taught, she planned upon the death of her husband to relinquish her soul in ritual suicide and follow him to the next birth or, if they are blessed, back to the godhead. She projected into the moment of sati, raised her arms to include herself in the wrecking path of the black carapace. She knelt before Chapman, closed her eyes for the inevitable. But it did not inevitably come. She rose and asked had he found the path to self-discovery? For she knew, two-thirds of the evil that offends us is caused by ourselves.

"I fell off the curb," Mark said. "I fell and fell … I just kept falling," *falling …*

he said, then fell into his own thoughts:

But I will not fade. I will not fade. I am not like you, he thought and startled her with a cold stare while she tried to coax him to move out from the road. *I am no Krishna incarnation. Before this, you were what? Fish, turtle, pig, dwarf – you fade and fade and fade. And still you are only what you have become, avatar orange, pretense of vibrancy. You will fade. But I will not fade. I am STORY, the final chapter of Holden Caulfield. The flesh shall be made word. I will never fade.*

These New Yorkers … these café revolutionaries, they say, What happens IF? If there is no heart, there is no substance. That's what if. If they are all brain, they have no balls. That's what if. Except maybe Rowan Murray. He could matter, someday. But my day is now. When I merge with STORY, Lennon will fade, these café revolutionaries, they will fade, this Krishna, she will fade. They have no purpose, no story beyond their what if's. What if there's no Heaven? What if there's no Lennon? Warhol will fade. Freud will fade. Even Rundgren will fade. And Norman Rockwell. But especially, LENNON – he will fade.

Lennon is the door through which I secure my destiny. I will remain solid. He will fade. And that waitress at the coffee shop, her saucy rudeness, declassing me a nobody, telling me I am no Holden Caulfield. What does she know? And all these self-righteous, angry, well-dressed, meaningless people on these sidewalks in a hurry to nowhere. They will fade. And she is just a server. She will fade. She will serve and serve and serve until there's nothing left of her. She will give it all away and fade.

She said, "I read that book. What makes you think you're Holden Caulfield anyway? You think you're a fiction? That's just weird."

She won't be here. She doesn't get it. True art has the power to transform. Lennon is pretence. He has not made art. He's a phony. He will fade.

The Krishna, her orange robes glistening wet, she pulled Chapman's arms, urged him farther off the street and repositioned him at the edge of the sidewalk away from traffic. The *Playboy* magazine and the Lennon/Ono album, *Double Fantasy*, were black with tire tracks but having come into the world flat needed little adjustment in their collision with the weight of round. Less certainly than Chapman who went deeper into Holden Caulfield as the Krishna relented and sat patiently beside him.

That curb, it's a long way down. Someone could get hurt. The sidewalks of New York are dangerous. John Lennon will know this. Leonard Bernstein, Rex Reed, Gilda Radner, Lauren Bacall, the Dakota will learn this. Pilgrims will assemble to lap the blood of Lennon off the sidewalk. The gargoyles seated on the Dakota building will fly down and lap his blood. They will smile their pointy teeth and suck their lips to see the carnage. They will come off their stone perches and suck the blood.

And maybe, okay maybe if there is reincarnation, if this Krishna is right, if God has a sense of humor, if my soul does not enter the book of falls with Holden Caulfield, my eyes may soon inhabit the stone sockets of a Dakota gargoyle. Yes, that's me – grotesque, twisted transmigrated soul and twisted limbs and pointy ears and claws. To view New York City from any street corner is to see, eventually, the entire world go by and all its carnival grotesqueries – what passes for love, for hate, for indecency, for reverence, for selflessness, for murder. It will all eventually pass by. The Dakota invites my transformation. As do Lennon worshippers who shall wither and moan in my presence beneath the stone towers and stained glass windows of the Dakota – this fortress, this palace, this church of the devil. Rosemary's Baby was conceived here. John Lennon will die here. The Devil could help me. Father Mayhem, give me strength to pull the trigger. Smile, my gargoyle brethren. Smile your pointy teeth.

The Krishna pulled his arm, desperate, insistent. Chapman's incomprehensible mumbles escalated to vitriolic fragments shouted at passersby, insisting they bear witness. Freaky! He punched her skinny chest, kicked the Krishna into the street, crabbed back from the curb, slammed against a smoked glass pharmacy window, pushed against the black glass facet imbedded in granite façade, as if seeking a door to a parallel universe. The Krishna rubbed her chest, tears welling from the pain or from Chapman's lack of appreciation, maybe both. Chapman collapsed into fetal. His arms gathered together the magazine and the Lennon/Ono record. The Krishna shook her head and walked away. She took her abuses back to the brahmacharini where she knew better the man who beat her. Pedestrians circumscribed an invisible barrier, a bulge in space to encapsulate Chapman's stuttering shakes.

Chapman said aloud to passersby: "Why am I assaulted by this

Krishna? How can she think she is God's avatar? (A delivery man with Coke-bottle eyeglasses paused, shook his head and carried away his load.) She pulled at my arms like she needs to save a soul. (A middle-aged woman said, 'Pardon?' Listened a moment, touched his arm in sympathy, changed direction and walked away.) Does she know how big a fall she is about to take? (Sidewalk pedestrians surrendered proscenium space to Chapman's rant.) But, in truth, there must be a fall before there can be ascendancy. Holden Caulfield knew this. Do you see me leaning against the glass wall that supports this building? How can it? Do you know? How can glass support a building? (A small boy holding a stuffed animal toy paused to listen but was snatched by a matron back into the passing flow.) Because glass is frozen liquid. That's why. When things get cold, they get hard. My heart is still warm. New York is cold, and not even because it's December.

"Beneath this concrete, beneath the pulse of subway trains and miles deep of wires and conduit and iron bracing lies the rock upon which New York is built. The heart of New York is cold rock. I touch this wall of glass with my body's heat. I bring it warmth. I could thaw this glass and send myself to the other side. I could melt this glass altogether and tumble this building. But that's nothing. Anyone can do this, because there is really nothing solid about New York. Can't you see? It's just that everything is moving so fast, or you are yourself, so all this stuff *seems* solid. It's not. Everything here participates in a steady, slow descent. Waves of shoes falling over curbs, and over and over…. I make an effort. I spider the glass wall and steady my feet. I hug Lennon's album. I hug tits and ass. I am a bruised mass of humiliation, but this is *not* the fall I've been worried over. I'm Okay. I am. Really. I'm Okay."

Chapman then walked unsteadily down Columbus Avenue. He walked as if in a dream. He was very near the Dakota. He wouldn't look down. He looked instead into the gray woods of Central Park.

I move onto the horizon, he thought to himself. *I am eye level with the world. Tree limbs bare and chattering, a cold rain falling. Awful December. Honolulu is so lush, so green with life. This place, it welcomes death.*

He gripped the London Fog jacket collar at his throat to block the wind.

How did I get here? I mean this street, this moment? Oh, I re-member... (he stopped, looked up at a black sky, snapped a finger and walked on). *I remember. Yes. I remember. I walked here from the café, and then I saw a poster of Lennon/Ono in a head shop window, their figures in cardboard: she with those dark glasses and Mona Lisa smile, he with granny glasses and a stupid, doting look. <u>Double Fantasy</u>, the album. Looked like single fantasy to me. Poor John. But it's too late for him. And then, serendipitous, synchronous, as I stood in line with cash in hand and passed by a magazine rack I saw, wrapped partially in black plastic so as to protect the children, at least Heffner cares about the children, I saw this <u>Playboy</u> inter-view with Lennon/Ono, the first they've given in many years. I'm blessed! It is all too perfect!*

I told the check-out, some skinny goateed pseudo intellectual with nicotine teeth and an eating disorder or an amphetamine habit... I told the checkout – " I plan to get the record autographed."

"Yeah, well, that's cool," he said. "But Lennon's just a househusband. You get Yoko to sign and you got something. She has dignity. And, hey, man, check this out! Disconnect the belt on your turntable, use a finger to spin back the Ono tune Kiss, Kiss, Kiss. Guess what it says?"

I had no idea what the guy was talking about and I didn't care. But I was polite.

"It says, I shot John Lennon. Says it real distinct. Spooky shit. That girl's some kind of witch. I swear," he said while running a wand over the magazine's bar code which chirped and bleeped. Then he said, "Tits or ass?"

"What?"

"What's your preference, man? Don't tell me you're into this for the articles?"

"Yeah, well, I sort of am, yes. The interview – John and Yoko. You read it?"

"Skimmed it. Jerk off to the centerfold and you'll feel a whole lot better about what you're about to read – that fucking nowhere man."

"Yeah, for sure," I said. Silver coins lay in my hand burning my palm.

The sound of the street brought Mark David back to the present, a flow of pressed suits and perfumed elbows jostling, traffic slinking and gliding and yellow cabs darting into gaps between cars like birds of prey.

I remember feeling, with that purchase, more at ease, more in Holden's element. I stopped beside a mesh basket on a street corner to discard the plastic covers of both purchases. I was about to go down the dark tunnel of Holden's fear of falling. I was shaky. Which is a sign. And something about that shiny, plastic protection, like windows, like condoms, false protection, and that's when I fell.

"Hey, shit, fella, watch where you're going!" said a man with a camera hung around his neck quick stepping out of Mark's way on the sidewalk.

"What?"

"I said, watch where you're going."

"Hey, do I know you?"

"Well, maybe," he said, ego flowering. I'm Martin Arbesh, freelance photographer, familiar to the stars," said Martin Arbesh nodding across the street where a black limo approached a stone gate as a doorman in livery greeted John Lennon dressed in a fur-rimmed leather bombardier jacket and Yoko Ono in black and five-year-old Sean in jammies. They had returned from a party at The Hit Factory where *Double Fantasy* had been recorded, the album named after an orchid, a collaborative album. Yoko had her side/John his, like two sides of a bed, which is maybe why Yoko had recently commissioned a publicity shoot of John and she making love in bed. His dry humping and her cries of passion reminiscent of Yoko's punk, off-tune wailing, grating, perhaps dooming the project. Or maybe it is more accurate to view the album as a top/bottom struggle symptomatic of their marriage. "The vampire woman," as *The Village Voice* called her, having nearly tossed John out of the Dakota and divorced him. From boredom she had said. And John knew of her recent affair with an art dealer friend of Andy Warhol, but John wasn't exactly monogamous himself.

Mark David shook himself wakeful, gripped tightly with one hand the album and the *Playboy* magazine, realized he was at the Dakota building and that John Lennon was across the street. He gripped more tightly the gun in his coat pocket, stepped near the curb to cross the street, hesitated, looked sadly at Martin Arbesh who saw the album. Arbesh said, "Oh, okay. I get it. Go ahead. Get the autograph. He's easy. Here, I'll introduce you."

"No thanks! No!" said Mark thinking, *inappropriate response, cool it, just cool it.*

"Hey," said, Martin, "what's the attitude? You're the one wants an autograph. I just thought I would help."

"Yeah, sorry. I'd appreciate the help. Sorry."

"Okay then. Who are you? What's the accent?"

"Mark David Chapman. I came from Hawaii to get an autograph. That's all I want. An autograph."

"Okay… all the way from Hawaii with his Southern drawl. Why not. Hey, Seaman!" Martin called to a thin man in pin stripes, Frederick Seaman, personal secretary to the Lennon/Onos. "Hey, Seaman, this guy here's been waiting a week for an autograph. All the way from Hawaii!" *by way of Alabama he said under his breath.* Seaman took an uneasy look at Chapman, something about the fatuous smile, the outsized dark blue raincoat that made him once again wish the Lennons would take seriously his suggestion to keep a bodyguard. "Maybe on the way out, Martin," he said. "We're in a bit of a rush!" which Seaman felt should give him time to talk with the doorman about this Hawaiian, which the doorman will say is no big deal if Martin Arbesh has him in tow. But Seaman had reasons to distrust Martin Arbesh – all those blown covers, the Lennons strolling Central Park in wide-brimmed hats and dark glasses with Arbesh snapping pictures behind trees for passersby to key on. And that time Arbesh sneaked into the Dakota as a plumber and was found wandering the Lennon's apartment. Yoko nearly put a hex on Arbesh after that one.

After speaking briefly with Seaman, Ramon the doorman figured he should take this fan's measure so made a broad smile to welcome Arbesh and friend across the street to chat. They talked about the Lennon's new album, and about the big tippers in that building. Mia Farrow especially, Woody Allen's wife, all those kids with her always, nice lady, if you can forget she's mother to Satan's spawn – "Remember that movie? Rosemary's Baby? Filmed right her at the Dakota, and she even lives here. Ain't that some kind of weird," said Ramon.

"Synchronicity," said Chapman then, "Hey, I was a security guard, did you know?"

"How would I know?"

"Yeah, a big apartment building in Honolulu and some really big concerts in Atlanta. Led Zeppelin! You heard of the Zeppelin?"

"Yeah, I heard of the Zeppelin."

"So, I mean, I know the weirdoes you see everyday in this job. I mean. I've *been* there, man. I know."

"Yeah," said Ramon beginning to accept Chapman as a regular guy, despite himself, or despite Chapman.

The three of them talked for twenty minutes about the occupants of the Dakota and about Lennon's approachability, both feet on the ground for someone so superstar, maybe to make his dick accessible to anything with a cunt or a mouth said Arbesh as a side remark that was too explosive to fade quietly. Ramon looked like he'd been struck by a hand in the face. Mark David colored to ripe peach.

"Hey," said Arbesh, "that lost weekend with Brian Epstein, a confirmed homo, and that tall blonde transvestite in Berlin. It's documented!"

"Oh, come on, Besh," said Ramon. "All the boys were fooled by that she-man. They didn't know! They were young, playing for tips in the strips bars, drunk most the time. So they got sucked by a beautiful face! Who wouldn't?"

"Yeah, I suppose, but there's lots of rumors of back alley blow jobs, anyone with a mouth, and what was that shit going down with the babysitter? They moved in together, right? Lennon and May Pang. Another Oriental babe."

"My wife is Japanese," said Chapman.

"What? Oh, sure. But hey, Besh, that was all Yoko, man! I'm telling you, she schemed it all up to keep John busy and out of her bed. The women in this place, they're spooky. They're all witchcraft and zodiac and Eastern spiritual voodoo and the guys just better watch out. You too, Martin!"

"Yeah, me too."

"Did you say homosexual? John Lennon a homosexual?" said Chapman.

"No, man," said Arbesh. "It's rock stars. They'll all, what's the word … androgynous. Bowie and Jagger in concert together. Grinding each other up there with hips and groins, cats in heat."

"No, man, not Jagger!" said Ramon.

"Yeah, bet you so!" said Arbesh as Mark David quietly slipped away down the sidewalk.

It had been a half hour since the Lennons entered the Dakota with Frederick Seaman and little Sean. It was late. They weren't coming back down. Sean had been put to bed. Lennon lit a joint. Seaman poured himself a Scotch. Yoko consulted the I Ching. Chapman pulled his collar together and walked toward the Y at 63rd street, his room there waiting for him, a concession to budgetary constraints the Minister of Finance had levied. The winter sky of New York was street lamps buzzing, tiny frozen planets in deep space; and red taillights beaming the gimlet eyes of locusts; and sidewalks swarming with the after-work rush of hollow souls, costumes and hypocrisies. Salinger was right. All these phonies!

But it could have been the weather that was affecting Mark David, that awful northern dryness of winter that Georgia never experiences nor Hawaii. Even the sinuses shrink as self-defense probably from all those dust motes, the car exhaust, particles of dead leaves, dog shit. None of this likely to seep into the earth which had already in the porous autumn months drawn vapors deep inside its now frozen, protective shell. Mother Earth had become an aged, dried twat. Nothing you eat in winter in New York City ever tastes right. Food is over spiced to compensate, wines more caustic. Women, no matter how well-heeled, smell vampy. The harmonies of perfume break down releasing the musky base note of a homeless, unwashed subway rider's pheromones. It just takes more of everything in New York in the winter to suggest a natural life. Minus the fabrications of synthetic effluvia that attack the senses, New York would be entirely without smell: a bad case of anosmia. Death! The senses are dead here, thought Mark David. And for many, that's the preferred condition. But not for Mark. He was even more prone to depression in that environment, more likely to explode in rage, more likely to escape into his world of little people, or into the pages of a work of fiction as he has here in this narrative.

Mark David walked down Central Park West along the edge of Central Park, the hackberry trees and hemlock and tupelo, the rush of after-work pedestrian pod people. Sleep walking is the best these people can hope for, thought Mark as he patted the gun in his jacket pocket, and then his wallet with those dollars borrowed of his father-in-law. For tonight, he thought, he will economize, take a room at the West Side Y, which has the smell of cleaning chemicals and urine. He thought maybe he qualified for a free room, mentioned to the fat lady with the swollen feet at the desk behind the perforated Plexiglas window, mentioned his rank as Group Supervisor at the Y in Georgia, received a ghost of a smile and a shrug of shoulders with the usual bill.

His room overlooked a brick wall and had 50s Formica-green paint on the walls, a picture of Jesus on the cross turned upside down by some previous guest: Jesus pogoing on his head. The devil making a point. Mark grunted disgust and straightened the irreverence. He landed hard on the bed with his back and felt the quoits dig with ferocious zeal the fat of his buttocks. He closed eyes, folded hands in his lap and noticed sound: the creaking of stairs outside his door and disjointed almost sinister laughter, a toilet flushing somewhere near, and a bed next door getting a very erotic workout. Someone had slipped in a girl, maybe up the fire escape. Clever. Enterprising. Mark David began to miss his wife, though he had made love to her less often than he had bought prostitutes during his Asian wanderings in Christian outreach. The bed next door began to bang against the wall upon which his headboard rested so that he could feel the thrust of a very energetic climax, which gave him a half-masted hard-on, and made him very curious to see this couple.

When the pounding abated and quiet intervened, he heard laughter, harsh, guttural and very masculine laughter. These were two men! Shit! So that's what the New York City Y had come to – the Village People! That's what! Shit! Mark pulled out the .38 snub nose from his London Fog jacket pocket, leaped out of bed, pointed the gun at the wall behind his bed, and … yes, very, very tempting. But no. Not yet. There was another homo out there that was going to feel the business end of this gun.

Chapter Eight:
Mason introduces Claudia to Jean Michel Basquiat
at the Factory

Saturday, Dec. 6th – Sunday, Dec. 7, 1980
11:00 p.m. – 12:00 a.m.
(46 hrs/45 min. before John Lennon's murder)

Mason Fisher and Claudia Fontaine – dynamic couple, don't you think? He intelligent, handsome, well connected in the art world. She well educated, cultured, fetching. This is what I was thinking as I drove the two of us from Brooklyn to Manhattan on our way to Leon's engagement party in Queens. First Claudia wanted me to introduce her to my artist, bohemian friends, someone besides me with paint under the fingernails, someone with paintings hung in a gallery, someone she had read about in the arts section of the *Times*. She wanted to feel relevant again. Sotheby's had weaned her from enthusing the art by redirecting her to a more practical application of accessorizing decor in New Jersey and matching colors in Manhattan. She couldn't take much more. She had recently, and with indigestible butterflies, sabotaged prices bidding a Rembrandt self-portrait. She had found its authenticity suspect. While staged emotion is typical of his art, a leer is not. And frankly, Rembrandt's expression was disturbing. Probably the work of an aggrieved student made to copy the master's work, she thought manning the overseas link to European bidders (her polyglot capabilities landing this post).

"*Fehlt bei der Zertifizierung der Originalität* (lacking certification of originality)," she said. "*Ja, eine neue entwicklung* (yes, a new development). May I take your bid?"

"*Das ist ungeheuerlich!*" said the wife of the Vice President of Mercedes Benz. She hung up.

"False *rappresentanza!*" said the Chairman of Acquisitions of the Uffizi, his voice fading into explosive little discharges of accusation and retribution as she gentled the phone upon its cradle.

Claudia imagined herself representing Sotheby's at a soiree for art connoisseurs at some garish Renaissance villa outside Rome. Claudia paying tribute to the withered matron of the villa ignored in her wheel chair under a shade tree. Claudia bending and leaning to address those black dead eyes, and kissing in the European way those leathery cheeks, whereupon the matron cocks a wrist and flexes a digit to unhinge an antique signet ring which deposits in Claudia's wine goblet a corrupting, tasteless poison.

Art collectors are a vengeful, incestuous and parochial people, Claudia had come to realize. They would not for long forebear the obstructions of her jejune, clerkish, academic, middle-class values, her suburban decencies. Claudia's designs on the Ph.D. in Art History had become suddenly less than nascent and more eagerly desperate. She needed to escape Sotheby's. And soon because she feared the sabotage of her body's estrogen. She wanted a baby. But before she left New York for the staid Puritanism of Boston, and the dusty shelves of dissertation research, she wanted badly to sample from the height of fame and influence the vertiginous palette of New York City art. She had studied the trends shifting back to the states from Europe. Andy Warhol had helped initiate the switch. He had helped place New York City in the center of the art world. Amazing! And she had just fucked a man who knows Warhol. She was, as it were, going to the source. Francine's party would have to wait.

I forced the usually unassertive Toyota up against a curb outside 860 Broadway incurring a whinge of rubber and a kickback of the steering wheel, which jammed my wrists, which I cursed and apologized and cursed again. I had been stressing over what awaited as greeting at the Factory. I got out of the car and looked up five stories of brick warehouse, as if the answer might reveal itself street side. I shielded my eyes from the filthy patter of rain freezing as it struck the ground. The electric hoist to the platform that disgorges the larger paintings swung in a gust of wind. The lower floors of the building were darkly asleep. But Andy Warhol's Factory in the loft was well lit. It never slept. And my memories of it were, still are, powerfully complex.

So, as I brooded over making introductions for Claudia at the Factory, I reflected briefly on my own. I was presented by the guy you never see in the film *Blow Job* who gave the actor receiving his services (as the audience sings "We Shall Never Come") an endless blow job. He is someone I had met when hanging art in a coffee house in SoHo. This most famous of un-filmed film stars told me that he really likes my work, which was nice, but then he said, No … he *really* likes my work. And that was heady stuff. Then an overture I thought a little forward. "Come meet my friends, they're painters," he said. "Well, silk screeners mostly, copiers for the master really. They need influence. And your work," he said poking with digit a facet of charcoal I had imbedded to simulate smoker's lung … "your work could amount to influence. Oh," he said, "I'll just say it. Andy Warhol. I'm talking about Andy Warhol. Are you celebrity shy? Lots of people are."

I said I grew up in Buffalo. Who the hell could intimidate me that grew up in Pittsburgh for fuck sake!

We laughed and shared a cab to the Factory where I met Warhol for the first time. Andy seemed at first attracted to me, then disinterested. He walked up to me, folded his arms, inclined his head and listened intently to my new friend describe my work. Andy wore sunglasses. The mask of his face never changed. His words fell out from the mask in monosyllable. "Well, yes … I mean, okay gee, bring him in, if you think so." Andy then skiffed stiffly away. He never did become enthusiastic about me in any way, though he tolerated my visits as he would a door-to-door salesman. Andy respects the urge to commerce, even the moribund like me. But there was nothing Goyaesque about Andy, as Dennis had led me to believe (all those disaster and death images of the 70s). He seemed more manikinesque. And now Claudia was about to meet him.

"What do I say to him?" she said. "Is he really as diffident as they say?"

"Different, yes."

"No, diffident."

"I know 'diffident.' And no, he's not diffident if you threaten his line of credit."

"I don't understand."

"He's a commercial artist is what I'm saying. His inspirations come to him from Wall Street, inside tips. He gets scrappy when money is concerned."

"That's insulting."

"No … it's not. Not if you know Andy. How do you think he came to paint Marilyn Monroe?"

"I don't know, Mason. Maybe a reverence of powerful women."

"Well, that *is* a universal homo thing, but no. It was about the suicide and how much more famous she had become, how much more interesting, and how marketable her likeness would be among collectors. Then the wild colors and the several faces and there you have it! Money on canvas! That's how he thinks. So don't get too emotional and starry-eyed at the Factory. Andy's artistic soul goes into his movies, which are shit, which tells you about his soul."

I began to feel badly about bad mouthing Warhol. I was jealous of his success. And I had always wanted to be accepted by him but never had been, and that made me resentful. I know this about myself. These are petty emotions, what the small people feel. I began to feel smaller the more I tried to impress this woman. But why should I have bothered? What was in it for me? The sex hadn't been that good. She liked my paintings but that was beginning to wear off. Why impress her, why keep her around? What if she had fucked me to chase celebrity? I really knew nothing about her. She would do well enough following her own path in New York. She would trip over celebrity often enough in her own way. There are no stars in the sky in New York. The firmament can't hold such weigh. All the stars of New York have fallen to the pavement. So many stars upon the ground it's hard to negotiate the sidewalk without stubbing toes on one.

But no, Claudia wouldn't embarrass me by slavering over Andy Warhol. She wouldn't be accepted, but what I really worried about was embarrassing myself. How would I introduce Claudia to the

Factory's silvery amphetamine operatic mole people? I was not, myself, very well liked. And Claudia was too far settled into her suburban prep-school values to do me or her any good. This was a crowd bent on judgment. *Get used to it!* is what Basquiat had said when he told me my work sucked. That was after Andy had sniffed my canvases, in the short period I was given workspace there, and asked what vitamins I was taking which made no sense until I learned Andy was piss painting and suspected the same of me. Andy's back studio stank of acetylene and burnt metal. There was no welding going on. It was the iron oxidizing from his mineral-laden, evaporating piss. Andy did say he liked the colors I was using. But that was all. He disappeared back into his piss painting and left me with Basquiat to finish the sniffing, in all manner of ways.

I resisted bringing my friends to Andy's Factory. Dennis wanted most to visit, probably yearned for the chance to commission and represent Andy's autobiography. As if there weren't already enough Andy material out there: his philosophy *A to B*, his phone conversations insinuating literature, interviews given weekly through the media, his own *Interview* magazine. Pithy Andyisms were everywhere. And then his *Popism* confirmation of self-worth in the pop art movement. Also, there was rumor Andy had been keeping a diary since back in the 60s when he was audited – his way to reconcile the outflow, a considerable portion of his vast fortune gone to parties and dinners, travel and purchases. What else did Dennis think he could get out of the guy?

I did, however, bring Leon one time – the poet/actor Ondine was there dressed in a kimono richly decorated in flaming dragons. He was poking amphetamine crystal up his nose, talking in broad gesture, reliving his explosive tête-à-tête with the melting

Nico in Andy's film *Chelsea Girls*. Ondine had an audience of the usual street people, drug addicts, artists and writers (Truman Capote was there, deep in his cups). Andy drifted in silver wigged, Brooks Brothers suited and smiling enigmatically. He nodded at me, which was like the Pope's blessing, while Ondine was quick to assert that *his* name is Pope. Then Andy disappeared into the offices of *Interview*. Leon sat in one of the pink plastic settees grinning quietly behind his beard, surrounded by walls painted silver and tin-foiled, like stepping into and behind a mirror. Silver clouds floated above, helium-filled Mylar balloons.

Truman interrupted with comical/satirical inflection: "Well, Mr. Pope, as to your movie career … schizophrenic, my dear, I must say, the split screen you know, color one side, black and white the other, but I too bite the peach, my dear, I am no saint. I bite the peach, juice down the chin, my dear, and well the soundtrack, the voices back and forth, one side silent, one side talk, too much method, far too much method, but … I too bite the peach, and you know some will say Andy simply points the camera and shoots, well my dear, I too am lazy genius, but the juice, it runs down the chin, I too am genius…." He stopped suddenly, scratched his scrotum and yawned, retreated into his Scotch and engaged a quiet spasm of hysterical giggles which everyone but Leon ignored. Shit! It *was* Truman Capote after all.

Leon told me afterward he felt he had participated in the birthing throes of improv theatre. He said, "Mimes and actors in search of a script, in search of a mythology. Inventing culture and a hierarchy. Fascinating! Seminal moments. Engendering tradition. A newborn culture gathering its best moments publicly to ingrain as communal memory. Tribal, very."

But when I brought Claudia up the wooden-railed freight elevator to the Factory loft that night, forty-six hours and forty-five minutes before the murder of John Lennon, no one was there but Jean-Michel Basquiat. He waved at us a spliff of ganja the size of a cigar. In the blue smoke of his inspiration, Jean-Michel threw down color and design upon a large canvas that lay on the floor with stacks more still wet in paint leaning upon walls. The tantalizing voice of a current love interest throbbed from a demo cassette tape in a boom box, something about virgins for the very first time. Jean-Michel had recently in a fit torn and splashed with thinner a stack of canvasses meant for a show in Italy. "Same-o! Same-o!" he had repeated as a mantra while destroying his work. Jean-Michel was told by Andy this would not do, must keep the business end of this business all business. So Jean-Michel was staying off heroin for the moment to avoid destructive histrionics. There were, however, indecipherable messages painted upon the floor which matched the graffiti of the paintings where crude almost skeletal figures twisted with pain and rage. He was a street artist, after all, oftentimes not suitable for company. This was one of those moments. I could see this instantly. But I had to make a show for Claudia.

Basquiat had his shirt off, wore only red-striped boxing shorts and flip-flops, a red bandana around his head He was lithe and athletic, his Puerto Rican, Haitian dusky skin glistening with sweat and streaked in paint, his beautiful white teeth glinting manically. "Exotic!" is what Claudia said about him. But his manners were awful. I asked how he was? Basquiat looked at me briefly, not even a smile, and went back to work. Claudia said, "Hi, I'm Claudia." Which elicited the same. Then, suddenly, he seemed to recognize me. We two had had words over the degree of genius displayed in our paintings. I had said, pointing to a large canvas of Jean's pinned to the wall, still wet in paint, "What can a skull with nonsense words all over it tell about life, Jean? This is the same stuff I can find on any subway car in New York. And, all this – bugs and coffee cans and what, cigarette butts? Now that's profound. Not like I couldn't find that shit in any alley." He never forgot my insults.

As Claudia and I watched, Jean-Michel worked silently, then bent to his painting on the floor, dipped his brush in gold paint and splashed an image, then tore the corner off. It was bright red with some black lines and his fresh, gold tri-pointed crown signature. He handed this section of the painting to me. I let it fall to the ground. Jean-Michel said, "There's the crown, Mason. Pick it up. You want the crown, Mason? Go ahead take it. Now … go the fuck away, man, and let me work."

Basquiat went back to work and ignored me. Of course I knew Claudia would recognize the similarities in our cadaver-like human figures. We both painted under the influence of *Gray's Anatomy*. There were other similarities. We were both quite ambitious. We both wanted Andy's approval. We both were bisexual (although I didn't yet know it). Perhaps we just had too much in common to like one another. Jean-Michel took up another brush, wiped fauve indigo off onto the floor, dipped into black and came at me with wrists curling tattoos if I didn't exit the loft. "Go away and let me work," he said. I shouted, "What the fuck! You're insane!" but it made no difference to Basquiat. As he advanced on me I held ground to enhance my masculine allure. Claudia pulled me into the loft elevator, closed the gate and presses the escape button. We dropped down the tunnel in a gentle sweep of rushing wind and greased cable.

It took me some time to realize Claudia was crying, a husky dry spasm but no question, she was crying. I assumed in response to the unsettling volatility of Basquiat. I said, "Claudia, sorry about Jean-Michel. He's an ass. Give me one good reason and I'll go back up there and bloody his nose!" Still crying. Okay, I thought, lift the mood, so I said, "Maybe a duel. Palettes and hog bristle rapiers. En garde!" I thrust my hips at her endearingly, but she avoided my attentions, ran out the elevator and into the street with a hand over her mouth. I knew the upset ran deeper than Basquiat's rudeness. I found her leaning on the roof of the Toyota laughing at herself, not apologizing, not really embarrassed, but amused she had gone off like that. "Like what?" I said. "I don't understand. What is it about Basquiat that upsets you? It was him, wasn't it?"

"Yes," she said. "It was. But not the way you think. I don't care that he's an asshole. I don't care that I never become an insider at the Factory, although what's left will likely be more reminiscence than avant-garde."

"More than you know. But what's so upsetting? He was insulting me not you."

"Yes, I know. He made me remember somebody."

"Oh."

"Yes. An artist I once loved."

"The cartoonist?"

"Yes, same personality as Basquiat. But also loving if immature and irresponsible and fuck him! The son of a bitch got me pregnant."

"Oh, that's rough."

"Well, my fault too, but I aborted, and that's what hurts. And I wanted that baby. And that's what hurts most."

"Must have been horrible. What was it like, the operation?"

"The 'procedure.' They call it a procedure. Like nobody gets hurt, like nothing invasive tears your guts and changes who you are."

"The abortion changed you?"

"Yes, I'm no longer the little fool I once was. I'm a bigger fool now. I pretend my life is my own, but it's not. Before the abortion, I didn't know the difference. I'm limited by my biology. I know that now. I throw this body around like it's mine to use, but it's not. It has its own agenda. Before the abortion I thought about education and career as a way to make something of myself. But that's sense-less. I may do the PhD, but that won't be who I am, because I just 'am.' I already just am. There is no 'becoming' for me as there is for you. What I am is stability, composure, self-containment, and ex-pectancy. I wait to fill a purpose. I'm dominated by the liquid realm. I engorge monthly from the oceanic tides of moon phases. Do you know that in college, in that girls' dorm, we all ovulated at the same fucking time! What's that about, Mason? Can you tell me?"

"I don't understand. You feel bad about yourself? Your self-es-teem? But you're still the boss, aren't you? I mean … you still make the decisions about who you are and what your body does? Or at least who you sleep with."

"No, I don't."

"Oh, well…"

"Sorry. Look, I have no control. I still can't stomach my favorite foods. Just the smell makes me vomit. I cry all the time, not like now, I mean *all* the time, over nothing. I keep thinking of baby names, my hair is brittle, I really can't stand to make love but I want sex. I want something *up* there."

"But when the baby was aborted, you made that decision. Right? It was your decision. See what I mean? You were in control. You still are. Do you see?"

"Oh, yes. I killed the thing that knew me best. That knew me from the inside out. I'm Greek tragedy. I've killed my own and labored in the presentation. I served it up to my parents who wanted me free of their own marital despondencies, and to the Dean of the college who suggested I wasn't ready to mother and career both, and to the Sunderbys who come to my parents' house for Saturday cocktails to brag about their children, and to the boy on the high school football team who first had me under the bleachers in the rain, and to the fucking small-town newspaper that announces graduations, weddings, deaths, but *somehow* neglects infanticide. I killed my fucking baby for everyone else! That's the worst betrayal."

"You're no murderer. You're not."

"Okay, let's be generous. Let's just say my body, Mason, is a baby factory. I fuck to make babies."

"I don't think so. I think you're lonely?"

"Mason."

"Yes."

"You're sweet. Come to momma," Claudia said stalking me as I began to retreat away from her to the other side of the car. She ran up beside me, pressed her shoe onto my shoe, rubbed cat-like, purred, licked my ear and ran her hand down my thigh. We were still on the street but then separated again as I skittered playfully away. We circled each other either side of the yellow Toyota, leaning into the car and holding hands across the hood, across the turtle top, across the trunk. Laughing noisily under street lamps, neighbors poking out their heads from sashes above to discern the ruckus, slamming windows and pulling shades. Then we were standing beside each other again, self-consciously for a moment. A woman with pink hair dragged an uncooperative miniature poodle down the sidewalk past a shattered tree it wanted to sniff and pee. Claudia sniffed my ear, said, "Tell me, Mason, that Mapplethorpe photo you have on the wall, bullwhip up the anus … what's that?"

I said, "It was a gift. He's one of Warhol's hangers-on."

"And what exactly is your response to that image, Mason?"

"Well, I don't know. I'm intrigued I guess."

"Yes, the next experiment in becoming Mason?"

"I hope not. Hadn't thought of it like that."

"Okay, consider his *Man in Polyester Suit*, large black penis poking out."

"You've seen this?"

"Yes, it came through Sotheby's, a portfolio collection: urination in the mouth, fingers up the penis, fists up the anus, a man's genitals protruding from wooden planks like waiting at the guillotine…"

"Look, I don't know what to say. I don't know why I hung his self-portrait on the wall. Curiosity? Yes, maybe. But I don't see his art as anything degrading…"

"Then you're wrong, Mason. Very wrong. Sadomasochism is about degradation."

"Okay, fine. He's a pervert."

"Not what I'm saying. Sadomasochism is his religion. His victims are martyrs, sainted, tortured and writhing half-clothed, but calm, almost serene in Mapplethorpe's work. That's the difference, Mason. He exposes with cool objectivity the wretchedness of our nature."

"I'm lost. Why is this about me? About you?"

"It's like what I was saying, Mason, about my own nature. I can't alter what I am. Mapplethorpe's photographs expose the cruelty and the aggression of our animal nature. They tie us to the pagan. Men are reduced to a status of "things," but there is metaphysical truth like tapping into a pagan religion."

"Yeah, I guess. Maybe I should paint a new series, the abortion series. Have a look at the whole process from the inside out, so to speak. Yeah, maybe. Subvert the whole manly idea of woman objectified."

"Are you nuts!"

"Why? What do you mean?"

"Do you have any idea the passions you will unleash?"

"Well, no, but that's okay. Art should stimulate emotion, don't you think? Well and I guess mine leaves some people cold. Some ready-made emotion might not hurt – right?"

"What's your stand?"

"What do you mean?"

"Pro or Against?"

"Oh, politics. See what you mean. But look, I can take an objective approach."

"You can't take an objective approach to abortion. It's too personal."

"Not to me," I said beginning to feel uncomfortably defensive. "And, well, not because I have no womb. Look … I make all my subjects objects in my work. Everything is an object if you break it down – pride is a wingtip shoe, shame the letter A, success the dollar sign, failure is bad teeth. You name it, I find the object."

"What's the object for asshole?"

"Okay, fine. Make it subjective for me. Make abortion subjective for me."

"Interesting idea. How about first I give you the objective view, the one you're most comfortable with…"

"No, I …not necessary…"

"First, injections of the cervix for numbing, then inserting dilators into the cervix. Overnight… expanding these dilators further, widening the entrance to the uterus. Next day, more shots to the cervix, then tools you would use to skin an animal inserted and the baby scraped out. Then a vacuum suction to remove anything left behind – including soul. The *procedure* lasts about 10 or 15 minutes."

"That's it?"

"Not enough?"

"That's not what I mean."

There's sexual dysfunction, Mason, and there's…"

"*Not,* may I say, a problem of concern regarding Ms. Fontaine, am I right?"

"No, you're not. No. Why do you think I fucked you with such enthusiasm, with emotion? Usually, I'm a cold, mechanical fuck. It was your paintings, Mason. I fuck a lot of guys but not like it means anything. Those paintings, they made me think you understand the emptiness of my womb. They show the damage inside. I was thinking you might be different, Mason. Oh, shit! I'm not going to cry. And how is it you will paint this *series*, Mason, this abortion series? Will it be more touchy-feely – place your hands just here on the canvas and feel … feel what? The pain, the insecurity, the damage, the God damn need to have another God damn kid!"

"Claudia, it's okay. Calm down. I was just being stupid. There will be no abortion series. You're right. It's too large a subject."

"Oh, well, then you paint only the insignificant subjects, is that right?"

"No, not that. Shit! What do want me to say?"

"I want you to say you're a God damn gay man and you don't get it yet but you could maybe someday. I'm not some projection of a hetero man's image. I'm not a swamp to be discovered, or a desert, or a fucking pet to be named. And you should God damn well know that December 8th was the delivery date of that kid that never got to be a kid and I'm God damn upset every time that date, every time that date, every time … Oh, shit! Why did you bring up the subject?"

"But I didn't bring up the subject. What do you mean I'm gay? It's just a photograph."

"No matter. Take me to Francine's party."

Chapter Nine:
A party of engagement and disengagement

Saturday, December 6 – Sunday, December 7, 1980
11 p.m. – 3 a.m.
(43 hrs /45 min. before John Lennon's murder)

"I'm truthing you, Mason. I'm truthing you." That's what my father said when doubted. He had the crabbed mind and back and the pensioned brief after life of an illiterate warehouse foreman. Boots. He trafficked in boots. Imports from Spain and South America that make their way from New York City to a warehouse in Buffalo and then on to Canada. He borrowed "truthing" from Nancy Sinatra, the walking boots song – "you keep lyin' when you oughta be truthin.'" That song. My father never had good taste in music but he bought American – wore almost exclusively Wisconsin made Thorogood work boots with steel toes, drove a Dodge Ramcharger. He was surprisingly open-minded when choosing an Italian for a mate. He died choking on a hard roll six months after retirement. He died before the Lennon murder and before my defection to Colombia with a man lover. His is an easy life to summarize. My own ... not so easy. And then, there is Mark David Chapman.

I found myself repelled by Chapman's narrow-mindedness but drawn to his single-mindedness. If that makes any sense. I was thinking this while passing a joint to Claudia in my Toyota. We were on our way to Francine's apartment for the engagement party. There were forty-five hours and forty-five minutes left until the murder of John Lennon. Both of us were lost in thought. Both were reluctant to speak because still emotionally reeling from the Basquait confrontation and from the abortion revelations. Silence had become its own language in which we indulged, a kind of burrowing under the covers so the space you occupy fills with the quieting sound of your own breathing. But when a cold hand reached under the covers, touched my cheek, when a disembodied voice said, "Stop!" I jammed the brakes as a cat slipped under the wheels. "Oh, shit!" Claudia announced as the companion to *stop.* "I can't deal," she said. "Please drive on." These were my thoughts exactly. I drove on. Clauida went back under the covers.

I began to think how easy it is to take a life. I began to wonder what it would feel like to pull the trigger on celebrity. It happened to Warhol. And that's when I envisioned the direction my art would take that has made me famous – while stoned and having run over a cat. I thought, what if I were to document the event, the murder of John Lennon, design a canvas that penetrates the shock of murder upon presumed invincibility? Maybe a series of death by murder, something like Warhol's violent death by accident in photo-redux, but in my invisible man, autopsy style. I sneaked a look at Claudia, thought I might share this idea with her, but she had gone so far down the spiral of her own breathing that I was afraid this conversation mote could throw her into brain spasm.

I wondered how a cat could stay alive for long in New York City. I wondered if maybe Chapman would run a sweep of celebrity in New York. Kill a whole bunch. Big media splash. I wondered how Andy Warhol would make money off the Lennon murder. I imagined his satirical eye interpreting Chapman's anti-heroics as book cover art for Harlequin Romance. I imagined Warhol painting Chapman as some Kiowa Plains Indian collecting scalp for the totem lodge. Blood lusty, rutting and marauding in the near nude with scalps on his belt. Kitsch for coin if Andy were willing to sell out to the pulp industry. Would Warhol sink so low? He did start out in advertising. Shoe ads. Who knows more about shoes than me?

My dad brought boxes of them home every week. There sat pudgy little Mason after school on the floor of the TV room in our suburban house of Buffalo near enough the thud of falling water over Horseshoe Falls for me to carry that sound with me even now. That pounding water had mined a room of absolute quiet into which I poured my imagination. This is where I go when I paint. This is the room where I will meet Raul Vega. That's where I went with my own crayon sketches of naked Indians scalping cowboys that my father encouraged as very American, and that my mother recognized as homoerotic. She was a grade-school art teacher then. Demur and wary of addressing signs that could alert her husband to the aberrant sexual leanings of their only son. She lost sleep over my art. She still does. Her husband dropped boxes of shoes onto the floor where I sketched. He acknowledged with pride the bloodletting taking place, suggested a massacre tableau or two, suggested a shoe style or two for me to try on – I always wore new shoes – then dropped himself into the sofa to eat his TV dinner.

Andy Warhol had long ago stepped out from his shoe ads and into the galleries. I was desperate to leave the museum job gallery. Maybe I should approach Harlequin Press with the marauding

Chapman concept. They must have someone on retainer who can write a pulp, cowboy version of the Lennon murder. Maybe after the murder, present to them sketches of a big tit farmer's wife with clothes half ripped off by a pillaging, randy Indian brave that looks hauntingly like Chapman scalping Lennon. Just enough bulge in the loin cloth to suggest virility in a man I suspected had very little. When Chapman becomes infamous, I began to think, Harlequin might consider. This could take their pulp production to a whole other level – collector's items, maybe eventually Sotheby's items. Harlequin could display books with blank pages right there at the checkout line of the grocery store and still sell out!

Yeah, well … but then I took a turn in the road that landed me and Claudia and the yellow Toyota into an unfamiliar neighborhood. Shit! Better start paying attention. I cranked the wheel to perform a 90 degree turn down an alley and clipped the side of a garbage dumpster. Claudia unfroze a moment and responded by passing the near-spent joint to me. "No thanks. Need to concentrate," I said and bounced down the trash-strewn lane and turned 90 degrees again rather than crash through the plate glass window of a Dunkin Doughnuts. Yeah, I thought, this is the coffee shop Chapman should frequent. Puffy, oversweet pastry that cloys in the throat. A little Chapman goes a long way. I began to rethink the Chapman book cover art. Despite the commercial sex appeal of a man truly homicidal, Mark David Chapman's fat ass flexed between hankies, well, Chapman was just too doughy to inspire. So I dropped the book illustration idea down the porcelain suck and flushed (too bad – imagine what that illustration would be worth now twenty years after the murder of Lennon).

I got a little heated up. I pressed the speed of the Toyota well beyond a stoner's ability to cope. I was starting to resent the commercial angle of the art business. Maybe because Andy Warhol's bank account had eclipsed Andy's art. Maybe because of the way Basquiat treated me, or because Basquiat had made it and I had not. And, well, to capitalize on someone's misfortune, that may be the American way, Andy Warhol's way, but it was surely *not* (I pounded the steering wheel with my fists) my way. And maybe I simply refused to contribute to a one-world-one-bank VISA consumption of some Harlequin Romance Rubenesque quivering tits ravaged by the obliging savage imprinted on some inconsequential book. America has become *one* (I pounded the steering wheel) mind. America has become *one* (I pounded again the steering wheel) fucking brain. Or all brains operating in synch with the bottom line. It has become a country of bottom feeders. Our only valid export is pop culture – 8 track schlock, bean bag chairs, Starsky and Hutch, the golden arches, Richard Nixon face masks. Warhol exploited this, but he rose above it, until consumerism exploited him. The masses engorge themselves on Big Macs and game show television. I will be glad to be out of America I began to think even before meeting Raul or desperate to escape the after effects of Lennon's murder. America has become a brute, ignorant nation. Maybe always has been. Single-mindedness always is. I had put myself in a really foul mood.

"Manifest Destiny is the bitch to corporate greed," I said aloud.

"What?" said Claudia.

"Oh, nothing," I said still thinking, still on automatic pilot, smoking down another joint while trying to make sense of things. Chapman's game is not a commercial one, I deduced, so can murder be an honorable pursuit? There is something ritual in what

Chapman intends to do, something artsy. I had at first thought about Mark David Chapman as another cranky tourist, disillusioned with the Big Apple and disappointed with his hero, John Lennon. He had no autograph from the great man and got hooked into the wrong subway line so let out at the 116th Street Station where he had walked serendipitously into our coffee-shop event with his sacrosanct certainties and his shadow of doom. Chapman, by turns, by his comments, seemed to take us for soapbox exhibitionists. No guts, he thought, unless someone were killed. He said I will be looking for some secret garden. Well, maybe so, but isn't everybody? And what's so profound about Chapman's horoscopic predictions that could apply to anybody? That's what I thought and nodded in agreement with myself and nudged Claudia with the joint and said, "If the kid had said I was looking for the door to gay enlightenment, it might have meant something. That's what you'd say, right, Claudia?"

"What?" said Claudia.

What I didn't know is that in a few short hours, Chapman will observe me with my hand down Raul Vega's pants at the party – not where you think – squeezing buns in the kitchen. Cheesecake! God! It will surprise me more than Raul. Maybe Chapman was right about me – no guts. At least back then, but about men, not about women. I found women easy enough back then. But with Raul at the party, my hand will go the opposite end from where my hand wanted to go. Of course Chapman will think me a Sodomite is what he will call me, defiling God's angels, he will say at the party. He will see the entire art community of New York as Sodomites. Maybe he was right. Consider what some call the "Andy Whorehole Factory." Consider Mapplethorpe.

At Francine's party, legs will lift and cocks will knock and arms will twine and tongues will tangle. Not exactly the iconoclast agenda Rowan had in mind. But boundaries will shatter. Claudia and I will arrive late, as will Chapman. Rowan will bring his Japanese girlfriend who isn't very friendly because that's her nature. And because Rowan had befriended the taxi driver, and taken unconscionably long wending Manhattan to get to Suki Miyushi who had pared her nails to spikes waiting. Then Rowan will introduce the taxi driver to the revolution. Of course "revolution" to Raul is just another body floating down a piss warm river of floating bodies. To Raul, revolution means nothing, just as taking a life by violence means nothing, but his sexual preference ... that means everything. Francine will give Suki a cold welcome, a brief emotionless "Hello." Then she will slaver over Raul's accent: "He's cute. What's his country? What's he do?"/ "Don't you mean who does he do it to?" Dennis will say. Rowan will brush past Francine's questions and Dennis' rudeness and guide Raul into the living room where Leon and Francine's friend Sharon Demy will engage in a discussion of premarital sex. Leon will say if it were up to him, no sex until marriage. Sharon will say she can see that, what Leon said, yes, definitely.

When Rowan walked into the living room with Raul, Leon and Sharon forgot their manners and gaped mid-conversation. Dennis walked into the room and began to recalculate the partnering attraction equation, but had presence of mind to amend his manners with a nod of hello. Raul's blue eyes, mestizo skin and ducktail black hair sang to them of smoky cantinas at closing time where cocaine is swept out the door like sawdust and regret and pools of blood stain benches where jealous lovers knife each other in the pitiless arc of day passing to night passing to day. Raul's white teeth trapped a Spanish greeting poised and trembling to be released on his tongue should his teeth unlock. He nodded instead but could not focus on anyone. He was nervous as hell. But the friendly intent of his botched greeting was genuine. He was immediately accepted.

Rowan sensed an animal attraction to Raul's presence, which he was not sure how to interpret, and this was not what he wanted. He had in mind an intellectual evening, a summation and an affirmation of what they all intended to do on Monday to shake the dust of complacency off established ideals. He had a plane to catch. This was *his* happening after all! For a while it didn't look like the happening was going to happen. No one wanted to wax intellectual. No one, at the moment, wanted to commit to betrayals of beloved ideals under the guise of avant-garde anything. Unless, of course, betrayals of beloved *ones*. Francine had the Scrabble board readied on the coffee table, but she couldn't take her attention off Raul. The board game became another ignored gesture. She offered a carafe of wine. We accepted. We quaffed and asked for more. We all wanted cheap thrills after Raul had entered the apartment. Yes, all. It was infectious. Even Rowan sampled Francine's cheap wine and toked Leon's cannabis in the kitchen under the oven fan.

Rowan began to assess with the remorse of a departing lover Suki's costume from a distance, her black hair dyed lightning pink, her orange eye shadow, that purple tear tattoo under one eye. He liked the face. The rest he thought was too much – a tight and torn leather jacket unzipped and festooned in safety pins and indie band patches and underneath a fish-net jersey that exposed the nipples he knew so well and that Suki wanted pinched when in her passion. And as she flirted with Dennis, Rowan began already to miss the fleshy pink blush of geisha emotion she was unable to relinquish in the genes that Dennis seemed to respond to with sincere interest. As Rowan fell away from the introductions he had made of Raul to Leon and Sharon that had become inconsequential small talk, he listened in to Suki's conversation. He recognized the same concerns he had heard from her after taking Suki to one of Teru Ishi's *pink film*, soft-porn flicks and having to shush those frat boys seated behind them. He heard, again, Suki confess what it's like to be typed Asian chick so on everyone's list as a one-time fling to experience a re-Orient-ation of erogenous zones. Caucasians, it is well known, she had said, mistake Hollywood censorship ratings for stimulation provocation. The ratings are all about body parts, she said. And chinky chicks' body parts are frequently an essential ingredient for NC-17.

Rowan knew intimately Suki's veil of self-control, knew her valves were hammering and that seams were distending with the simmering heat produced. Release was imminent. And he was counting on Suki to hold it together, to help his plan along, to help give backbone to this jellied crowd of armchair intellectuals. Francine continued to observe Raul while hanging within earshot of Suki's exposition given to Dennis revealing occidental hang-ups over sexual stimulation.

"The only chink I see," Francine couldn't resist saying to Suki, "is in your armor. I think you're afraid of who you really are."

"Yes," but aren't we all?" said Rowan stepping in because his woman had become suddenly more desirable now that another desired her. "This is, of course," Rowan said, "the sentiment behind deontology."

"Oh, Rowan!" said Francine, "drop the psycho-babble," and taking Raul by the arm, she handed him a glass of wine and led him off to a far corner of the room and behind a section of wall screen upon which an artist of the mashrabiyas has carved in teak intersecting geometrics to filter light, cast shadow and insinuate intimacies.

Francine enjoys populating a room with items and people within her means to choose. Some are frustratingly beyond her discretion. Some like Suki Miyushi, and this new one, Claudia Fontaine. But Raul Vega was a pleasant addition to the menagerie. The moment she heard Raul's voice, she knew he was meant for this most intimate of screened-off sanctuaries. The harmonies of his Spanish skin, endearing modesty and beautiful accent – all those tildes and dipthongs and upside down question marks. Just too cute. But more than that. Appropriately exotic like the Berber one would expect to hear spoken behind this teak-wood screen. Or the voice of Rimbaud who had doffed poetry to sell guns in Africa. In this case, she romanticized, a Colombian who has deserted a true love to sell drugs in America. Yes, thought Francine, this is Raul's room. She took him by the hand and gestured for him to sit beside her on the daybed behind the screen. They spoke inanities, but it didn't matter. Francine had, with Raul, endowed this room with the harmonies of an implied intimacy. And that was enough. That was more than enough. Because Francine had no place inside herself, no room inside herself, in which to nurture a relationship. Not that her womb was damaged. Just the opposite. It was, in fact, as sparkling and pure as a pearl-lined armoire. But what was missing was her ability to share any of what she is, what she had become and hopes to become with an "other." And that's why she collects, and that's why she had yet to experience orgasm. When she does, and it will happen one-and-a-half times that evening, she will not feel within herself waves of pleasure leading to the release of self. No. This demanded a trust she does not have. She feared that she would simply shatter. And she could not trust that her partner would help collect together the pieces. She will instead feel that she had added another soul to her collective self, another dependent who will be forever endeared to her. She will, of course, be wrong.

Sometime after midnight I will arrive with Claudia, who will still be surprisingly sedate but starting to shake out of her introspection as there will be others to inspect. I will struggle to follow Raul's explanation to Leon of drug running in Colombia. It wasn't the accent. I will fixate on the timber of his voice and on the imposition of his animal allure. This had never happened to me before. My rapport with men had always been, well, manly – like whose girlfriend did you lay? Or, how much money does it take to do that? Or, how drunk can you get and still drive a car? Those shared experiences that certify male virility. I feared my response to Raul would be the unmanning of me. I found myself second-guessing the receivership role of the sex act. Where can my virility have gone? I was stoned enough to find out, and Claudia, she knew and she went straight to Dennis, and well, she was *with* Dennis. Suki will brood silently in a cushy chair. Claudia will be talking ostensibly to Dennis of William Blake. The fly-on-the-wall will hear this:

"Do you pity me?" Dennis said.

"Should I?"

"If you were a Blake scholar you would."

"If I were a Blake scholar," said Claudia, "I would know better than to pity you unless I wanted to marry you."

"Then you know what happened when his wife-to-be answered *yes*?"

"He said he loved her."

"But did she pity him, Claudia? Would an artist want pity or respect?"

"From what I know of artists, Dennis, respect comes hard. But pity is bread and butter if the artist is worth anything. Don't you think so?"

"Yes, that's good," said Dennis. "That's exactly the answer Blake wanted. Pity was, for him, the grounding emotion in a relationship. Now the answer to my question, Claudia – Do you pity *me*?"

"You are no artist, Dennis. *You* are too much in control. So, no, I don't pity you. You may pretend to be an artist with your writerly dabblings, and your learned references, and your pretentious pseudo-revolutionary friends, but no, you're no writer. You're no artist. I'm not required to pity you, and I won't give you my phone number either, but I *will* fuck you, if you'd like, Dennis. If that's you're angle?"

"Nice offer, Claudia, but I was hoping for more Blake conversation beforehand."

"Blakean foreplay. How appealing. But why?"

"Well, maybe because Blake was monogamous. In a licentious time he stayed monogamous. It seems sordid to go from Blake to bed with no intellectual foreplay doesn't it?"

"Blake was a sensualist, Dennis. He loved pornography. He practiced the arcana of erotic ceremonies, elixirs, and ritual nudism. He drew women with dicks. Children fucking each other. He turned on the Swedenborgians when they pledged faith to the monarchy and away from the freedoms of infidelity. He believed in free love, Dennis. He thought wives should be shared in common."

"Yes, but he never shared his."

"Don't you think Mrs. Blake had something to say about that?"

"Well, maybe."

As Claudia regaled Dennis with Blakean anecdote she had him by the collar, pulling him into the hallway from beneath the arched living room entrance like through the portal of her uterus. It became clear to Dennis that he was being stalked by a sexual predator. It was nice to feel so wanted. The bathroom door closed decidedly behind them. The mirror still frosty with the patina of impassioned breathing from a recently vacated couple, of which Dennis was only too aware.

Guests soon disappeared in pairs into the bathroom. Claudia and Dennis, of course. Before them, Suki and Dennis. Then Raul and Francine. That took a while because Francine didn't at first like where Raul wanted to place the evidence of his attraction to her. The fact that he put it there at all indicated what he felt he owed the host of the party. Raul was being painfully polite. Then Suki and Francine. That took longer. Then me and Raul. That was the moment that remade me quite. That was after Chapman walked in on my preambular butt caressing in the kitchen which led to the denouement in the bathroom. Which led to Chapman's castigation of my new-found proclivities. But then, after all, we were are all pretty messed up on wine and cannabis, all except Chapman. All got emotions tangled and complicated, except Chapman, who was already tangled and complicated in the machinations of his committee-fried brain. Rowan said it was time for us all to get down to

the business of "I don't like Monday," which, he said, the Boomtown Rats know well enough, and which presented another icon
worth exploiting. But it was preterition of the intelligentsia time
– we all just wanted to party.

◆◆◆

When Chapman came to the apartment door, Rowan had
forgotten he had given the address to this strange man.

"Did I come to the right place?" he said to Francine. "The party?
Is this the party for icons, you know, the party for…"

"Rowan invited you didn't he?"

"From the coffee shop by Columbia University, the shop."

"That's right. Rowan Murray. Rowan!" Francine said. "Somebody here to see you."

"I'm not here to see Rowan, really, I was invited to the party. If
there's a problem … if there's a problem I can leave, but the cab, I
didn't tell him to …"

"Oh, Mr. Chapman," said Rowan smiling uncertainly, "nice of
you to come. Any trouble finding the place?"

"Yes. The World's Fair … that was no problem, but this apartment complex, the driver had no idea which …"

"Oh," said Claudia, pulling Dennis out from the bathroom,
"It's you. Still going to disappear John Lennon? Is that the plan?
Erase the phonies?"

"Yes, that's the plan. Listen, I sense I'm not welcome here."

"What is it you have there?" said Claudia. "You brought pornography to our little soiree? How nice."

"It's *Playboy*. Listen, I'll just …"

"I see that."

"It's the *Playboy* interview of John Lennon."

167

"Oh, I see. Method to the porn-ness. Well, don't let me inter-fere," said Claudia then peeled off to find Raul with the swoony accent leaving Dennis spent and dazed in the hallway.

"So, Mr. Chapman …"

"Mark."

"So, Mark," said Rowan, "shall we remove to the drawing room for introductions?" which in the doing elicited an under-stated repugnance from all but Sharon who gave Chapman se-rious consideration as conversational adornment. She moved to the sofa Leon had abandoned and leaned into Chapman's nubile voice emoting to Rowan who stood above the two of them with one ear attending Chapman and the other my explanation to Raul of "gay" in the culture of Warhol's Factory.

Chapman said, "The interview, *Playboy*, it's awful. What Len-non says about Paul, just awful, here, wait, just here – (he thumbed the glossy pages past the centerfold), okay, here, it says, '*Paul died creatively*' … after the Beatles. That's a dig! Do you see. And it says George was a nobody following him around like a little brother. Ringo had no talent. And he's saying this from a penthouse with a hundred fifty million dollars in the bank, telling us to change the world, that there's too much greed and corruption, and he's doing drugs, and even says he does acid and marijuana (Leon looked at Rowan who looked at Leon who trod into the kitchen to hide the pot), and mushrooms, and said LSD was made by the government, imagine, what crap, and he talks about screwing Brian Epstein, well…not exactly *screwing* him but close, and just him thinking 'maybe' it happened is enough! Isn't it? And about how he has no respect for other musicians, listens to muzak, can you imagine! And how Yoko had all these abortions – just awful! Says here, let's see (flipped the pages, began to sweat, his breathing become irregular and hasty), says here…says here, okay here: '*She has had too many miscarriages and when she was a young girl, there were no pills, so there were lots of abortions and miscarriages; her stomach must be like Kew Gardens in London.*' Awful! Isn't that awful?"

Claudia said, "Change the subject!" and walked away.

Sharon Demey said, "Yes, awful. Please change the subject."

"Okay then, says about religion, says religion is …" turned pages furiously, turned back again, "says he put down Hare Krishna in his walrus song, I mean, well, maybe he's not so wrong about the Hare Krishna, when, well… but and then he says … okay, here, he says about Dylan being one of us, I mean a Christian, a born-again, he says, '*The messenger is worshiped, instead of the message. So there would be Christianity, Mohammedanism, Buddhism, Confucianism, Marxism, Maoism – everything – it is always about a person and never about what he says.*' So, you see, it's all about him – it's about the messenger. He's the messenger, our savior, right? This is bullshit. He's got to go down!"

"But, Mr. Chapman, I don't think that's what he means. I think …"

"Rowan."

"Yes."

"Let it go," said Dennis.

"Let it be," I said. "May I see that magazine, Mark?"

"Yeah sure, here."

I thumbed through, saw the reference to Charles Manson. "Ah," I said, "Here is more reason to villainize the man. Remember the helter-skelter Manson killers? Of course you do, rhetorical on purpose. It seems John Lennon talked directly to Manson. The devil speaks! Spooky! Yes? And now, it seems, he talks directly to Mark

David Chapman. He says, put a bullet in me. Is that right, Mark? Lennon is speaking to you right now. This *Playboy* interview is, what did you say … synchronicity. Am I right?"

"Are you insulting me? Is that what you're doing? I was invited here."

Sharon Demy moved to the far side of the sofa. Chapman reached deep inside the pocket of his London Fog raincoat where Dennis saw an oblong and vaguely threatening shape. Dennis said, "Look, don't go emotional on us? We're all just a little fucked up."

"What do you mean emotional? What do you mean fucked up?' said Chapman.

Claudia said having returned from the kitchen with a beer, "So, Mark. You're here for the Rowan Murray project … is that right."

"Well," said Mark, "I was invited …"

"Yes, I know but … you're here for the iconoclast thing, the happening, right?"

"Yes, that's right."

"And, Rowan, what was that question you asked of us as a way to identify icons of personal relevance? What was the question?"

"Oh, yes, I said, identify the thing you most love. Identify that and agree to destroy it."

"Yes, that's right. Now, Mr. Chapman, unless I'm wrong, you don't seem to love Mr. Lennon very much."

"No, I hate the man … I hate his phony..."

"Yes, so it seems. Then if you don't mind, I'd like to suggest you may have come to the wrong party."

"What's that? Well … the hell with you then! And," he said, looking at all the surprised faces, "the hell with all of you. Especially John Lennon, which I intend to do something about." After which he told me I am a homo, said he saw my hand on that man's ass (pointing to Raul) in the kitchen, and he can smell the marijuana and should really report us all to the building superintendent, and this is when he mentioned that we were all a bunch of wimps anyway, all talk and no action.

Chapman stormed out leaving behind *Playboy* on the coffee table. Claudia said, "Good riddance!" but couldn't resist examining the Lennon interview with a curatorial zeal. She found the reference to Yoko and read further and found herself wanting to defend Yoko as an impressively acute businesswoman married to a difficult man, but was conflicted in assessing her art. She said, "Okay, enough about John Lennon. Let's get some perspective on Yoko."

Rowan said, "Yes, why not. What's to say of the good lady?

Claudia continued, "For one thing, she is recognized a shark in the waters of finance. We should grant her that. And, Rowan," she said abstracting away from the pages and tapping into memory, "here's a Yoko 'happening' to compare your own – *Cut Pieces* if I remember right. It's Yoko expressing the female as a victim of societal violence by sitting on a stage and giving the audience permission to snip away at her clothes until she sits there with nothing but a bra strap in her hand. I don't know … maybe that's not so bad."

"That *chica*," said Raul, "she is *gran parte de otro mundo.*"

"She's what?" I said.

"Of another world," said Dennis. "Why is that, Raul?"

"I give Yoko Ono a ride in cab."

"Oh, yes?" said Claudia

"Yes and very odd in behaving. *Si.* She is with a man that is art collector and they talk of Persian mummy she buy and have in house that is much like her face and she say to man she want Egyptian room in house with mummy and she say mummy is herself of three-thousand year time ago …”

“Oh, yes,” said Claudia, “Yoko believes in reincarnation. Many do.”

“Too bad she doesn’t believe in hari kari,” I said.

“Not possible. Is jigia for woman,” said Suki. “She also believes in the I-Ching, astrology, tea leaves, tarot, and gurus,” said Claudia. “Many do.”

“Yes,” I said, “but Andy Warhol doesn’t like her at all. He thinks she’s pushy. She practically blackmailed him to come to her gallery opening. What was it called? *This Is Somewhere*?” If you want to know, it was nowhere. I went. All the way upstate New York for running toilets and rotting apples. Ridiculous!”

“Yes, but she keeps a home for John Lennon, and that can’t be easy,” said Claudia.

“Oh sure, Claudia. Very loving,” I said. “Do you want to know what her decorator has to say? Let’s assume you do. He dines with Andy regularly. What I heard at the Factory is Yoko manipulated her man to ten days of silence in order to climb back into her bed?”

“Interesting idea,” said Francine.

“There’s more. And rowing the East River an hour a day by his lonesome, TV viewing allowed but no sound, and finding a tree in Central Park to communicate with intimately. What the hell! What kind of crazy is this girl? Talking to a tree!” I said. “Maybe Chapman *should* put Lennon out of his misery.”

Suki had meantime reclined in a stuffed chair in a corner of the living room with a gooseneck floor lamp melting heavy eye makeup. Rowan was tempted to say he could sing a melody off the orange notes upon her cheek, but he knew she would not take this well. She said, "Mason, please consider, Yoko make significant contribution to music."

"Oh, yes, the screaming. Screaming come cries – very influential. Yes, prominent role in punk scene. You not know sat? B52's most especially."

Yoko Ono make primal sound. She make primal therapy on record. Very prominent in vocal technique of emotion. Very prominent."

"Yes, yes," said Leon. "Women have the inside track to God's twisted plan. Certainly, without a doubt. They will be the ones to tell his secret."

"There will be proof of this?" said Dennis.

"Yes, certainly, there is proof."

"Very good, Leon, we are waiting," said Rowan.

"Yes, proof, well," said Leon, "take the Virgin Mary. Wouldn't she know God's intentions? He knocked her up, made a mockery of her marriage – I mean, God makes Joseph a cuckold. Nice work! – and then he tortures her son to death."

"Leon, you're a Jew. You don't believe in Christ or the immaculate birth – right?" said Francine.

"Yes, well, no. I'm not sure. Well then, take the Delphic Oracle. We can discuss that."

"Discuss away, "said Rowan.

"All right. There is the case of the pythia impregnated by the goat God of the oracle."

"Well, of course, there is that," I said.

Leon continued unfazed: "Lagerkvist wrote about her. He should know. Nobel Prize writer. Very learned. Profound. He said, gods are mean, vengeful, hateful, but without them ... we are nothing. And they don't seem to know. He said the Gods envy our humanity. We fear and pray for their love and protection. They don't love. They just *do*. Do what they want when they want. Willful children. She has a child of God, this pythia …"

"Excuse me, excuse me," implored Sharon Demy, "… not to be an obstruction, but can you please explain pythia. It's all new to me. I wasn't told we would be discussing the Delphic Oracle. Wish I had known to brush up on the Delphic Oracle. You know…."

"Yes, no problem – the pythia of the oracle descends a cave, the rock has a fissure, there are gasses and poisoned snakes writhing on the floor for effect, she breathes, goes into trance and wails and says all manner of wacky things priests interpret as oracle. Yes?"

"Yes, we see. Hooked on drugs. She has visions," said Claudia.

"No, more like hooked on God, breathes his stench and complains," said Dennis.

"Oh, I don't blame her. Do you?" said Sharon.

"I blame no one," said Dennis, "but Leon, what's the point?"

"Oh, well, point is, as I was saying … what was I saying?"

"You were saying about the child the pythia has of God," said Rowan thumbing through the *Playboy* interview of John Lennon he had taken from Claudia.

"Oh, him, the child, yes, an idiot, certainly. Can't speak, nor hear, nor anything. But beautiful hands and feet, beautiful enigmatic smile like the ancients paint on idols, a face that never ages."

"Sounds like we're getting set up here – the idiot savant? Am I right?" I said.

"Yes, no, somewhat… he does ascend to Heaven, much like Jesus, mountain top rescue and all that."

"But what," said Rowan, "does this have to do with the superiority of women and how that should make a difference in our iconoclast gesture?"

"That they are closer to the Godhead. Do you see? They speak for him, bear his children. Ultimately, any gesture that hopes to shake the status quo of the God/man relationship must come of woman, not of man. See?"

"Then, Leon, what you are saying is you feel inadequate to the job of comparing the powers of Freud and Moses. Is this right? You are looking for a way out. This is disturbing, Leon, rather much so," said Rowan. "Well, all right then. To break the ice, may I suggest a kind of parlor game."

"Oh, yes. Please," said Francine.

"Yes, well, what if we all say a list of those things we categorically would *NOT* desecrate were we moved to iconoclast?" said Rowan.

"You mean," I said, "the things we hate?"

"Yes, just so."

"Just so we can relate to Chapman," said Claudia.

"No, no. To decide whether or not this exercise in deontology is worthy of pursuit," said Rowan.

"Good. You first," I said.

Rowan said, "No, I think rather not. I think better to go last, as this undertaking is my idea. I would like the summary position."

"All right then. I'll go first," I said. "Those things which most bother me in art are assumptions of perfection, *not* the kind of perfection I feel Warhol accomplishes with his Marilyns. No. His perfection is recognizing the imperfections. I mean the kind of perfection that announces itself perfect. A Vermeer might be a good example."

"Oh, sour grapes in a vase! Vermeer *is* perfection," said Claudia.

"Yes," I said, "of a kind – those delicate touches he produces so minutely. They confuse the spectrum. Do you see? They flirt with white light and mesmerize the retina. Manipulation – but done so quietly. Do you see?"

"Where did that come from?" said Dennis.

"I've studied Vermeer. Are you surprised? That's why you can't take your eyes off his work. It teases and patronizes and flimflams perception."

Claudia was amazed. She took a serious, re-evaluative look at me. Dennis was pining to ask questions. Francine felt the fun had just begun and said, "Well, that was interesting. Who's next? Dennis, what about you?"

Dennis was, despite himself, a little intimidated. He still couldn't understand where I had found the rhetorical acumen for that response, and he was not sure just what he wanted to say. He, like Sharon Demy, had not prepared ahead. He said, "Okay, give me a minute to collect thoughts." He pulled imaginary lint off his legs, rubbed the back fur of his neck with a hirsute hand, said, "There is a kind of book I dislike with a kind of character I *really* dislike, and there is a kind of author I don't warm up to…"

"Come on Dennis, out with it!" said Francine.

"Okay, fine. What I really don't like in a writer is a confessional, self-aggrandizing wallowing in self-pity. Like torturous navel gazing, like warts in a magnifying glass, that kind of thing."

"Well, that's saying it," said Claudia.

"Sorry, the words imply vehemence, but I really have no one special in mind."

"Oh, bullshit!" said Claudia. "What about Bukowski?"

"Poet. He doesn't count," said Dennis.

"Okay, Henry Miller," I said.

"Yes, maybe," said Dennis.

"Knut Hamsun?" said Leon.

"Who?" I said. "How about Salinger?"

"Salinger, yes, maybe *Catcher in the Rye*. If we can fairly assign the author's sensibilities to it's whiney narrator. A preachy, depressing, poor-little-rich boy psychosis. Nice choice," said Dennis.

"And there's what we know about the writer himself," said Claudia.

"Well, yes. He's paranoid, antisocial, megalomaniacal. All the good things. He qualifies. I would *not* desecrate a work of JD Salinger's if it would, by so doing, enhance the writer's status in the annals of world literature. How's that?"

"You won't have to. It's being done by someone else," I said.

"What do you mean?" said Dennis.

"Chapman is going to kill Lennon as Holden Caulfield, remember?" I said.

"Yes, I wonder?" said Rowan.

"That's right," Dennis said with implied foreboding. "That will put *Catcher* back on the best seller's list." *Nice to get a piece of that action* is what he was thinking.

"Good! Well done," said Francine. "Let's see. Let's hear from Suki! What about you, Suki? This is fun!"

Suki looked venomously at Francine, tossed a lit cigarette in her wine glass, which Francine took accurately as statement, and began to pace the room theatrically drawing with her finger letters in the air, smiling in a mask of feminine cute.

"Oh, charades! Excellent. How many syllables?"

"Oh, fug you!" said Suki.

"What? What did she say? Leon, what did she say?"

"Let her explain, Francine," said Leon.

"A fug is a warm atmosphere in a room. It's a compliment, Francine," said Dennis.

"*Kawaii*," said Suki. "Kawaii *katakana*." And she drew these words in the air with her finger, placing little hearts above each of the two i's and tracing the ears and eyes and nose and whiskers of kitties where the a's should go. "*Koneko ji,*" she said after each kitty. "Kawaii mean cute in Japan."

"Oh, yes, I see," said Leon. "Cute writing. I've heard of this. School teachers go crazy over this, students insist, horizontal, left to right, rebellion against Japanese traditional writing of the verti-cal, and English words too, stars, hearts and silly faces. Inventing a whole other language. Fascinating, truly fascinating."

"Yes, sat is correct. Sat I hate." The smile faded. She threw her-self into a chair and lit a cigarette with disdain.

Rowan said, "All right then. My turn. I have been observing a fe-male sparrow of late outside my basement apartment window. She is song filled. There are different pitches and messages as I interpret them. I find that in myself I must *interpret* these songs. There is full song when a mother sparrow repeats phrasing which I have come to recognize from among other bird species –- the signature of sparrowhood. But then she is alone. She has a nest under the eave of a utility shed in the alley. That shed is used as storage for the building super and is rarely visited. So – good place for a nest. But why the song? To whom? For what purpose? A busy chatter attends bug catching, as she must feed, and there is a warning rat-a-tat she voices as I become too nosey. But why the continual beautiful song, its complex cadences and spirited delivery? She cannot now be courting a mate as none of her kind ever responds. Is it to fill the air with her presence? It is as mysterious to me as to John Lennon wherein this *Playboy* interview ... (Rowan pointed to the page and tossed said magazine upon the coffee table where I picked it up and began to read), this interview suggests Lennon's debt to the 'Aeolian cadences.' Aeolian, as it happens, refers to a sighing, moaning sound as of wind whispering or a storm announcing its secrets, or what we academics call the natural diatonic scale."

"Oh, shit. Here comes the lecture," I said.

"Yes, sorry. Residual effects of the erstwhile professor. But, this is the point. Do you see? A beautiful song might be taken as no more than what it is, a beautiful song. Why should this bird mean anything else? But then the academics take over and voilà, there you have it – meaning in nomenclature."

"But, Rowan," said Dennis, "you're the professor here. It's you that worships Cage and Glass and convinced Joseph Papp to produce that extravaganza of operatic avant-garde you wrote."

"Yes, and it was shite! All of it. Dreadful shite! I have absolutely loved the life, the intellectual life defining aesthetics, but it is a sham, and it has to go."

"Your career? Your art? You're saying it's worthless?" Francine moaned.

"Yes, he say sat. He say sat clear enough even you can hear," said Suki.

"Oh, fug you," said Francine.

Ambient party music, the B-52's *Love Shack* filled the gap. Suki lit another cigarette.

"Music is organized sound," said Rowan. "What follows when melody and harmony cue off jackhammers and trains or women crying and wolves howling? Still music if organized – collage and emotion. It's all there. That's what we say, we moderns. Yes? Well, bollocks!"

"Whose balls?" said Francine.

"Well, perhaps my own finally. I am soon trading my academic credentials for druidical apprenticeship at Findhorn."

"Where?" said Francine.

"So you *are* leaving us," said Dennis. "What Suki says is true. You're off to some commune in Scotland, contingent upon the success of your iconoclast happening I suppose."

"Yes, that's right. After my final concert at university, one for which I have primed critics to expect disharmonies of the twentieth century, but for which I intend to reinstate a taste for bird song. And then …"

"Birds? said Francine.

"Yes, bird song. And then a bird in flight," said Rowan.

Which was pretty much the intellectual apex of the party. Rowan took one of Suki's cigarettes and lit it there in the living room in Francine's despite. There were further inquiries into Rowan's intentions. Was he really leaving the States and all he had worked for? Was he leaving Suki? Suki, it appeared, had already left him. She got out of her chair, took Dennis by the hand and disappeared with him into the bathroom, again. And what of the iconoclast gesture? Rowan said, "Yes, still on. But do as you please. I shall."

The engagement party had become a going away party. And as if to cut the ties that bind, as if to cast away all ties of friendship and fidelity, the sinsual undercurrents of friends wondering how it would be to be with a friend's girlfriend/boyfriend, wondering what if I did this/that, wondering if it would make a difference in our tomorrow. It was all suddenly available. Wherein Francine came within a capillary's breadth of achieving the big bang with Suki working her tongue in places unfit for description. Whereupon Suki will return later the next day to get her there. Whereas Dennis came nowhere near to filling the emptiness that haunted Claudia. Whereof Dennis clawed and stroked per Suki's request all the little unattended places she had never wanted to share with Rowan. Whereupon Rowan attempted Sharon Demy but couldn't get beyond petting, couldn't find the wherewithal to assert his urges. Whereto Leon got no action whatsoever. Whereby Sharon Demy had no clue that Rowan wanted to be the submissive. Whereat Raul took Francine to a place she had never been and from where she may never return. It hurt to get there, but she got there. Whereafter Raul took me to that same place, after which I have been trying to find my way back ever since.

Chapter Ten:
Chapman from the Y to the Sheraton
to John Lennon's tree in Central Park

Sunday – Monday, December 7- 8, 1980
12:05 a.m. -10:50 p.m.
(36 hrs/40 min. before the murder of John Lennon
to 5 minutes after)

When Chapman left the party, he wasn't thinking seriously of turning us in for drugs or for breaking the rules of hospitality. It wasn't a good time to call attention to himself. He found a pay phone and hired another cab. During the ride to Manhattan, he consulted again the committee in his head. They thought, on-the-whole, it was good he had left the party as he was not afforded the respect that is his due, especially given the seriousness of his project compared to damaging a painting or discrediting Freud.

And Chapman was glad he hadn't threatened violence with the weapon concealed in his jacket pocket. This would have been beneath him. He had been tempted to open the doors onto our small minds and small lives. But he was sure we, the iconoclast brotherhood, would pay more attention when he put down John Lennon for the dog he is, when he stepped into Chapter 27 of *Catcher* and inhabited the role of Holden Caulfield, which we would read in the amended text. Then he remembered – shit! He had left the *Play-boy* behind. Well, no matter. He could still hear Lennon's voice, his self-righteous, phony, celeb-enhanced voice. And he could still see the centerfold, the golden skin and the soft brown hair languid and inviting male assertion. Well, he *was* just then feeling very asser-tive. Maybe when back at the Y he should blow away with hollow points those homos sexing it up in the next room.

Mark asked the cabbie to drop him off two blocks from the Y so he could walk and clear his head. The cabbie didn't expect much of a tip, which is what he got. Mark shuffled along beside the shabby storefronts with his head down thinking. He knew he had few hours remaining to satisfy the flesh before he killed Lennon and metamorphosed into the sacred "word" of Chapter 27. So … before that, he decided on the Sheraton and he decided on a hook-er. Why not? Holden Caulfield had brought a prostitute into his hotel room on a Sunday. So he tossed in his sheets one last night at the Y, which was gracefully unpolluted with aberrant sex, and then he checked out and into a room on the 27th floor of the Sher-aton late Sunday afternoon. He called an escort service that of-fered extras for tips. He showered and lathered cologne then dined extravagantly in the Sheraton's fireside brasserie. The prostitute arrived early evening at the Sheraton, an oriental (good, excellent, like Yoko, like his wife), nervous though courteous and slender in a tight green dress (even better – same color as Sunny's dress, Holden's girl's dress). Chapman put the girl to ease – "Don't worry," he said, "no sex, just, you know … companionship." Same as Hold-en. And, like Holden, he had no sex – except with himself, unlike Holden. In fact, Chapman won't want this to get out, but in his first twenty-five years he had intercourse less often than Rocky Balboa has had sequels. And most often with someone other than his wife.

The prostitute slipped out the door Monday morning $190 richer having waited for Chapman to fall asleep. He had talked to her soothingly of the offenses of John Lennon while massaging her. She had pretended to fall asleep. Then he had massaged himself. Only he, not she, had responded sexually. When Chapman awoke, the room was empty, cold and uninspiring in that hotel way of impersonal, over-used accommodation. He reached over and touched the lamp stand, behind him the headboard. He shivered. Reminded him of the medical wares showroom he had passed by Saturday night on his way to the Y with its windows dressed in motorized chairs and motorized beds and artificial limbs. Even fresh sheets and fresh soap can't take the impersonal out of a hotel room. But then Mark realized. *He* will bring to this room an historical significance.

Not that the Gettysburg Address will be written here, but something like that room in a castle in Germany where Martin Luther tossed an inkpot at the devil and the stain remains there still on the wall. One room forever transformed by Luther's gesture.

And now, *this* room among millions here in New York where Mark David Chapman has committed irrevocably to remove a false prophet, and has prepared to step into the pages of *Catcher*, which (and he became briefly mirthful with this tiny brainstorm) ... which will replace the *Gospel According to John ... Lennon*. Mark pulled the hotel copy of Gideon's New Testament out from the lamp table drawer and flipped the pages past Mathew, Mark and Luke and wrote after the name John the name LENNON in bold letters. He tossed the book onto the bed and projected its discovery there by some incurious maid who will toss it back into the drawer, and then he knew: this room needs to be properly staged. His deeds will ensure a police investigation of time spent in New York prior to Lennon's execution, maybe even inspire a cottage industry of fans researching and writing of Mark's achievement. This room needs to make a statement.   There may soon be a plaque outside the door in commemoration.

Mark consulted the committee in his head before installing objects his public will want to study. This took all day. He considered reserving the room for another night, knowing he will be gone and that only his things will be there, but dismissed the idea and settled in for a long session of difficult meetings.

The Minister of Morality thought it a nice touch to leave behind upon the bureau a letter of recommendation from Chapman's supervisor at the Fort Chaffee, Arkansas, YMCA, although he questioned leaving photos of Chapman and orphaned Vietnamese children because, as he said, Mark will soon make Sean Lennon an orphan.

Collateral damage said the Minister of Defense. Move on! he said.

A small poster of the movie *Wizard of Oz* found a place there too because, and Chapman had to argue this point with the Minister of Defense who thought the gesture showed weakness, because as Chapman said the movie is about good vs. evil, and because he is himself some part of all these characters missing some part of themselves – Dorothy a home worth returning to, Scarecrow a brain making its own decisions, Tin Man a heart that holds onto relationships, and Lion the courage to withstand his own roar.

Then there was the eight-track cassette tape of Rundgren's music lampooning the Beatles which the Minister of Public Relations thought crass but no on listened to him, and as a final gesture, which the Minister of Morality thought especially piquant, Mark placed the hotel Bible on top of the TV opened to *The Gospel According to John LENNON* with a hollow point bullet as bookmark. All had to be sanctioned by the Chairman, but he was easily swayed by the gathering momentum. The meetings were over.

Mark having no stomach for lunch took a nap, slept fitfully, a warrior on the eve of a decisive battle. It was then past 3 p.m. on Monday. Maids were dinning to get in to clean. In their Polish accents they enquired in growing agitation: Was Mark staying another night? Or does he have a late check out? Because it is not on the room card – Rm. 910 (the one after 909) *overnight guest*, it said, *light clean*, they explained. Chapman said, no, not yet. He said this twice and twice closed the door on them. The front desk phoned (Chapman didn't answer); then hotel security knocked, two brawny x-cops impossible to resist. So he packed, except for what he left behind that the maids will eventually find and the investigating police and the media after them. It was dark, almost 8 p.m. He left his bags at the front desk with the implication he would return shortly to retrieve once resettled. The clerk was too polite, or too tired of dealing with him at that point, to challenge.

Chapman went out onto the street. It was a dry, black night, the odors of New York vaguely stale, like the breath of someone leaning over to read your newspaper on the subway. He started to feel edgy, a loss of personal volition, locked into something much larger than himself. He knew he needed simply to surrender to and trust those forces propelling him. There was a policeman jangling in a belt of hardware down the sidewalk. Mark forced a smile and gathered his disarming southern accent, but the cop ignored him, stopped to issue a ticket for double parking. Chapman was on his way up Central Park toward the Dakota. He badly wanted to leave an impression of normalcy so decided to address the policeman who was tearing at the perforation, a snap of the wrist, a thick wrist like the one his father owns that sent Thanksgiving dinner across the table and onto the dining room wall. Chapman stopped.

The policeman looked up, said, "Yes?"

Chapman said, "The ducks."

"Oh, shit," said the policeman.

"Where do they … in winter, where do they … oh, never mind," he said, "I'm not that stupid. There will be corrections made in Chapter 27."

The policeman will remember this kid in the dark blue London Fog with the silly Russian fur hat asking a question he has heard from every preppy on school holiday that has come to this town since that son-of-a-bitch Salinger went into hiding. Disgraced most likely for creating a social nuisance.

Chapman arrived at the Dakota at 9 p.m., just in time for a white limo braking at its front gates. The doorman who gestured for its attention disappeared a moment, then ushered Yoko, Sean and John Lennon out the front lobby toward the waiting car. Chapman shouted, "Wait! John!" and the Lennon family instinctively back peddled. John crouched as if aware of a threat then realized: just another autograph seeker. Sean who was five years old held onto his mother's thighs and peered around her legs at the awkward trot of Mark David Chapman crossing the street, his smile full on, his two arms pushing the air ahead with *Double Fantasy* as baffler. Yoko shielded her son, any mother would, but in this case the mother felt Sean could be the next messiah, so protection was a matter of universal import: born of rock star parents thereby superbly positioned to manage the media, and as Yoko had manipulated the birth to fall upon October 9th, John's birthday (some say November), surely Sean had inherited his father's soul. A martyrdom of John the father would be perfect for Sean. (Makes you wonder if this were a commissioned job.)

Then Yoko got it too, Chapman was only after an autograph. But she had no patience for another interruption and another reminder that she came second after John, always. Since the studio sessions had ended, divorce plans were again in motion. John didn't know. John had recently come off a sailing trip to Bermuda revitalized, and yes, he had poured his long-dormant creative energies into the album, but she did *not* see this as collaboration. There are two sides to the album after all, hers and his. And maybe she was a little strung out on all that "devil's dandruff" that helped them through the long nights of studio work. And there was no question, after the album's release, John intended another spell of "watching the wheels," another free-fall into drugs and chocolate bars and fucking any girl named after a calendar month, and more crying to be forgiven by mamma Yoko. Well, no more! *"Oh, Yo-ko, Oh Yo-ko,"* he sang pathetically, *"my love will turn you on."* No! Not anymore. And yes, John makes melody and Yoko screams. And as he sings he believes "Starting Over" – but it will never happen. More like, "I'm Losing You." And, no, she had never, ever stolen another song and made it her own. Only George does that. And there are some that say her music has textured the punk rock scene. Well, yes, why not! And there are some that say she can sing pretty when she wants to. And, yes she can. But, what's the point in that? Let John wink at the world. For her the world is a serious place! If not for her, John would have got nothing from Apple. If without her readers of tarot and numerology and astrology. If without her advisors and her weighty negotiations. That Klein son-of-a-bitch! Four years work and only 5 million! Who does John think earned the other 50 million? Yoko, that's who! And what of this agoraphobic, live in a cave thing, one Thai stick after another, scared of the plumber, shy of the piano tuner, the antique restorer, yelling at the cook (well, she *is* Korean, and she does have an awful temper) but of tempers John is the worst – throwing furniture, cursing, making Sean so afraid he has nightmares. She has become so depressed she sleeps until noon. #72 has become an asylum for psychoses. Her "readers" tell her, leave this building. Something bad will come. Well, she thinks it has already. When John tore a piece of embalming cloth from an opened mummy sarcophagus in Egypt, in that dank crypt they had sneaked into, he had engaged the mummy's curse. They are all, John & Sean & Yoko, living under that curse today. She has tried to make a marriage of a business arrangement. She has tried but she cannot. Her "readers" tell her this. But she has tried. She has composed public love letters to John: *Sean is beautiful. The plants are growing. The cats are purring. The town is shining, sun, rain, or snow. We live in a beautiful universe.* Lies! All lies! And she will *not* have a Beatles reunion! What purpose will it serve? And John is not ready. He never will be. And for this she is villainized. So, let them call her dragon. She will breathe upon them the fire of truth. She will purify them in the flame of truth. And yes, she has placed many witless little cunts in the path of her husband to keep him out of her bed. She wants him away from *her* cunt. He wants to curl up in there and go amnesiac. He will need to find another womb to disappear into. His thoughts are always of hard dick and release. Let him release somewhere else! But she has also, and this is quite humorous, convinced him of the benefits to his libido of tantric yoga. Let him sit there in the twat of another and abstain from climax. He thinks his sperm will build and lift to his brain and enlighten his thinking in some primordial ooze—hah! Good one! And yes, all right, she made the phone call to her relative in Japanese customs and put that son-of-a-bitch McCartney in jail. He was taking illegal drugs into her country. She had to do something. She has a social conscience, a well-developed social conscience. And John must not know. But he is so ignorant. He filled her house with gardenias on her 47th birthday, 1,000 gardenias, the flower of death in her country. John is so ignorant.

John rose from his crouch, pretended to have dropped and picked up something, then waved Chapman on and reached for the BIC pen offered like a flower. He wrote: "John Lennon 1980." He had signed his own death certificate, then handed back the pen and bent into the car. The windows went up automatically, black glass in which Chapman could see reflected back his fading smile. And John was off with his family for a good, solid meal. He was experiencing another brief moment of elation. Everything in his life was beautiful! The album was finished. He had done some of his most melodic, sincere work, and he knew it. And Yoko knew it. And it was for her. She knew how much his family meant to him. And soon, as she had promised, they will buy a house in the Bahamas, and he will sail every day. And compose music. Maybe the critics are right: maybe there are Aeolian cadences in his work after all. Maybe it was his recent sailing trip with Sean that re-connected him to his music. It was maybe because they had been on a small boat, a sailboat. The crew were practiced but when the storm came, even they were noticeably insecure. Everyone had to help. No free ride. No assurances. They heaved rope and strained muscle, the boat shivered and shook and wanted to shed its masts, gusts at 70/80 miles an hour, the language become salty, and a fatalism took hold that God confers when disciplining his children. And then a stubborn obstinacy to resist powers greater than themselves. John had learned to steer by compass, and could steer "full-and-by" and "close-and-by" and could box the compass, all 32 points and back again. But that was nothing like riding a storm. Wood, iron, rope, canvas, and polymers, all somehow compelled to ride the swell and stay in one piece. You learn to be wise in weather lore, or you swallow water with the fishes. But, they had survived. And this was *not* a miracle, no, nor anything ordained, nothing to do with Yoko's magic spells nor interventions – this was by the strength of their collective wills and muscle and … and then you understand why a boat is like a woman, why a storm is like a marriage, you understand that even in a storm you must gentle your woman, you must tack her without deadening her in the water. These are things you learn in a storm in a small boat. And these are lessons John will apply to Yoko, to his stormy life in the Dakota, to his music, his family. He is blessed, truly. And without Pat Robertson and Club 700. Praise God that he had survived God! And if he had to, he could spit in God's face and throw down another challenge. He had become that salty.

Chapman paced and sweated, his eyes darting everywhere, his arms slapping each other for warmth as the committee in his head began to stir. There was an argument, a heated one in which the Finance Minister emoted in his three-piece suit, very upset over recent expenditures – I mean, well, 190 dollars and not even a blowjob! The girl gets a massage and you get screwed! Or don't get screwed as the case may be, but my God! That and this hotel bill. How can you justify … please explain!

The Minister of Defense stepped into the fray, his medals and balding head gleaming, and said there was precedence for steep spending in times of war.

What war? This is a pop singer we are pursuing for crying out loud, said the Minister of Public Relations. How can this end any way other than in disgrace? If we don't shoot John Lennon we're a failure of unrealized potential. If we do, we murder an icon, a beloved pop icon. How exactly is he harmful if allowed to go about his business of song singing? I just don't understand.

Of course you don't said the Minister of Morality. You don't know this man at all. You take his songs at face value. You don't see the drugs and the deviant sex, the hypocrisy and the devil's influence. It will take an exorcism to rid him of these influences but no Christian can get near enough with that oriental by his side with her Egyptian magic, her tarot and I-Ching, or whatever!

Yes, I suppose, and did you know Yoko Ono has gone to Cartagena, Colombia, to pay a bruja there $60,000 to do a little dance and cast a spell and pronounce her business investments sound? That is just crass, said the Minister of Public Relations. Good thing for the Lennons that little story never got to the press. If I were handling that business …

Yes, yes all right, but let's be serious, said the Minister of Morality. If we keep on with this project, if we keep on with this "murder," and make no mistake, no matter what we decide in terms of righteous jihad or cultural modification or exposing phonies that justifies taking down Lennon, many will attribute this to the work of the devil.

This deed will put the UR back in mURder.

Yes, very bad press, said the Minister of Public Relations.

And so, said the Minister of Morality, if the church gets involved, we should expect Mark himself will undergo exorcism … it's unavoidable.

That's ridiculous, said the Minister of Finance. There's hardly room enough for *us* in here. Where do they think we hide the devil? Our bookkeeping is exact and open to the public. We have no secrets. There is just us. No devils on the payroll.

Yes, but in cases like this, it is de rigueur, said the Minister of Morality, or if not this, we will be subjected to public incrimination by some attention-seeking psychologist in a very public court case.

Just then Chapman saw Mia Farrow walk through the wrought iron gates of the Dakota with several of her adopted children in tow. He stopped to assess. The voices in his head quieted as Farrow and her brood worked on his sentience like optical brighteners. She wore sunglasses even at night and hair wrapped in a scarf, but he knew it was her – that fair skin and willowy, little-girl figure and tentative ego that needs Woody Allen to help her know who she is, these adopted kids to help her feel worthy, and Mark remembered *Rosemary's Baby* was filmed at the Dakota, and the devil fucked Mia Farrow, and the director Roman Polanski shortly after lost his wife to Manson's disciples and Sharon Tate's blood and her baby's blood helter-skeltered on the walls in the words of a John Lennon song. Who in their right mind could possibly doubt the synchronicity of this moment! There was a murmur of consent from the voices in his head. Chapman had won. The shoot was on.

He flapped the tails of his overcoat with hands in pockets to cool the dampened, gnocchi body whose thought engine had over-revved in a tide of blood now thinning to viscous impurities and draining out the glands under his arms, between his legs, beneath his eyes. His face was flushed with his body's discharges, and he lost focus rubbing eyes with fists. His mouth was tacky dry. There was a ringing in the ears like bees swarming. He moved slowly into the park where street lamps failed to penetrate, flapping his coat still, and found a bench beneath a centuries old beech tree that had spread its roots and consumed its fill of nutrients in a plot of earth so rare in this city of concrete and steel that its feeding must be considered a usurpation of territory by all other breathing, growing entities, including Chapman. But this tree had steadfastly maintained its proprietary rights in the face of opposition of many kinds.

When it was just a seed, it had struggled to push aside gravel and sod to get its fair chance of growing an inch where shoes trod the earth unaware of urges green and buoyant beneath their step. And so the beech had arisen two inches above ground, then was pressed by a booted fur trader counting guilders in the patois of the Dutch. The infant beech was crooked now and bowed as before a mighty weight but determined to regain the light of sun. Twisting and thrusting in movements too small to measure, the beech began to right itself. And so, despite urban horticulturalists realigning and reapportioning green spaces in later times, despite drought and the heavy rains that exposed roots and swept away top soil, despite the stealthy chopped away parts of depression-era denizens eager to warm a barren fireplace, despite the dalliances of citizens like Chapman who sat beneath its branches and carved its trunk with hearts and initials, the old beech dominates this little corner of New York. And it holds all others in contempt. Chapman

especially. His runny nose and rheumy eyes and emotional debil-
ities, his silly dreams of potency and his intrinsic impotency, his
feminine softness, his guilt and anger and self-hatred, which the
beech could intuit as well as any living creature within the proxim-
ity of Chapman's shivering mass of exposed nerves and perverse
intentions.

Even John Lennon had made small impression. He once court-
ed the sentiments of this ancient tree, sitting beneath its branches.
With ceremonies prescribed by Yoko he introduced then seated
himself cross-legged upon the bench. He stated his intentions,
breathed deeply with contrived awareness then attuned himself to
the telepathic relay of feelings and visual images the tree would
send to him. He received nothing. This was a new experience for
John, who was most used to receiving without having to give anything of himself. Chapman knew he was unwelcome here too. He
looked up at the big tree and had not the authority to gainsay its
assessment of his condition. Forlorn again he moved away from
the bench and back to the street. The Dakota waited for him like
a nightmare he had to finish in order to awaken from this dream.
The beech considered sending telepathic warnings to John Lennon, but gave in to its indifference and decided instead to attend
another century in profound silence.

Chapman jagged back across the street. He had no wish to hear
the machinations of the committee or of himself in negotiation. He
saw the photographer he had met earlier who waved but Chapman
went straight for the gates of the Dakota. As he crossed into traffic
listing and bending, he imagined himself struggling in a current
of colorful bright fish snapping at him with big, chrome teeth. He
felt the suck of wavelets swirling in a vortex from a whopper fish

parting the tide and gliding close by his legs and into the gates of the Dakota.

A concerned citizen saw Chapman nearly knocked down by a white limo with beautiful fins and shining aluminum cutting across traffic and bouncing into the gated entrance beneath an arched ceiling of sandstone and Egyptian columns. The driver's window was down, his head and torso twisted rearward, his black moustache chatting personably, irresponsibly with his passengers while imposing unbridled the slick gleam of General Motors tonnage upon the unwary, and so the citizen emoted with dB's rising: "Hey, you, driver … *Careless! … Careless!*"

Which Chapman ciphered as proceed "without a care" and pulled the .38 with hollow points out from his coat as the driver braked and dismounted to open the doors of his passengers, and Yoko stepped out first and gave a hand to Sean who was yawning because it was almost 11 p.m., and Yoko pulled him along up the sidewalk in past the glass doors toward the elevators, and John was collecting a stack of cassette tapes off the seat of the limo and stepping out the door and turning when he saw Chapman quick stepping down the sidewalk just outside the gates and with nothing to sign in his hands, and so John thought nothing of concern/interest and so walked toward the glass doors Yoko and Sean had already gone through, and humming something from *Double Fantasy* and anticipating maybe popcorn and chocolate almond bars and fucking Yoko with porn on the telly as Chapman turned in at the gates and aimed his gun at John's back, and as the Minister of Morality was saying, "No, Mark, not like this!" another voice, one Mark couldn't make out that he felt must be the Minister of Defense saying, "Do it! Do it! Just do it!" Mark cocked the gun and

John still whistling with that portion of his lung that will soon be eviscerated, and Mark heard the Minister of Morality once more cautioning, and he saw the face of the Minister of Defense, his medals gleaming, his features ugly with resolve and anticipation shouting, "Do it!" And Mark pulled the trigger once. The hollow point left the gun at 975 miles per second and traveled less than twenty feet where it met John Lennon's back and ripped out a one-inch hole where it entered and expanded through his flesh taking three inches of lung and chest out the other side, and Mark saw the face of the Minister of Defense morph into something even more ugly, and he looked up at the gargoyles that sentineled the stone wall and realized *that* was the face, and the face shouted again, "Do it! Do it! Do it!" and Mark fired four more times, and one bullet ripped away Lennon's kidney and another exploded a length of intestine and the fourth removed his stomach and somehow, even as the light began to dim in his eyes, Lennon's feet were still moving, and he crashed through the glass door and started up a set of stairs, and the heart over rich in adrenaline pumped more fiercely the blood that leapt through arteries and vessels into the void of torn and dismembered flesh and found its unnatural course through the push of gravity down that set of steps to pool at the bottom where a rope mat reads DAKOTA.

Mark awaited transformation. He had dropped the gun. Taken off his coat and hat. He held *Catcher* in his hands. He stretched out his arms and awaited transformation. But he did not become the next chapter in Salinger's book, and he felt he should have fucked that whore, and he realized love is not sex, and he wanted his wife Gloria but she was in Hawaii, and he wondered why he did this, and he could taste car exhaust, and he asked the voices in his head but they wouldn't answer, and he put down his arms and dropped the book and realized there was a crowd circling him and men pointing at him and shouting and a woman screaming and the crowd was getting hostile, so he put his arms over his face like bars to protect himself and slid his fingers deep into his hair and cried.

Chapter Eleven:
Rowan's gesture

Sunday - Monday, December 7 - 8, 1980
2:30 a.m. - 11:05 p.m.
(20 minutes after the murder of John Lennon)

After the party, Rowan asked Raul to taxi him back upper west side of Manhattan to his apartment. Suki had stayed behind to inhale drugs and to court Francine. Her second-ever orgasm will arrive the next day via Suki's attentions scripting their relationship as one of those corny romances where eventual lovers first work through mutual loathing. It was not as easy for Rowan to leave Suki behind as you might think. They had been simpatico in grievances imagined and real since Rowan's failed opera. They had shared his depressions and they had worried together over his finding spiritual solace at Findhorn. Rowan's escape to Scotland seemed a desperate act to Suki, a surrender to forces that had kept him down. She thought Rowan should stay in New York and bask in the afterglow of his iconoclast gesture, even if he had to do so from a jail cell.

Suki's pilgrimage was of another sort from Rowan's. She is, thought Rowan, more the cultural warrior than he. He admired her for this. Suki's aspirations to feel good about anything, as she had told Rowan, had been leached away by a Freudian who had finished off what a Buddhist monk had started. Now she simply wanted to bring it all down, collapse the foundations, humiliate the puppet masters, jam the gears of industry with its own waste product. And she will not hesitate leaping off the ivory tower to do so. Wherever she lands will be fine with her, so long as she's irritating someone. Her father will be first. He will soon discontinue subsidizing her stay at NYU film school. The day is fast approaching where Suki will plant both feet on a stage below which bewildered fans will mosh to the punk-rock wave of her discontent: she was making connections with New Wave bands looking for chicks with attitude who could carry a tune. She possesses one of these attributes.

Rowan was quietly sitting in the cab listening to all this Suki speculation loop through his mind. Raul mistook Rowan's silence for an attentive study of Raul's concerns as he had presented them in Spanglish to his new friend: "And so, Rowan, I must say to you, *¿cómo puedo decir,* this one of your amigos, this Mason, he must have the new life of man love, *Sí, sin duda,* he must suffer of his soul if cannot, *perdón, pero debo decir la verdad,* if cannot make this new life. *¿No es así?* And, *señor …*"

Rowan was not listening. He had already declassed his friendship with Raul, as Rowan could no longer make room in his own life for more than his own needs. There had been too many disappointments of late, and he was desperately worried his recent gesture to initiate an iconoclast brotherhood would add another. It was more about whether his ideas would be accepted and given the weight that was their due. It was more about the right kind of attention from the critics to be frank, not that he should, as Suki had suggested, take his gesture to jail to prove his worth. Although that creep Chapman might follow through, and Mason might, and well, if he were really serious about… and but, oh dear, and he looked guiltily at Raul who sat animatedly in the cab beside him, his left hand on the wheel, his right gesturing as he spoke. Rowan had at times ducked that hand to save his left eye. Rowan reached out and snagged the emphatic hand and placed it back on the wheel, but it broke loose again. Rowan couldn't adequately address his own thoughts while fencing with Raul's conversational aggressions.

"Raul!" he said, "Please attend the road."

"But, señor, my friend, por favor, your amigo Mason. What must we …"

"I cannot say. Truly! We all have revelations become disappointments, Raul. Leave it at that!"

The words had come with a strength of delivery beyond their intent, which left a very loud moment of silence inside that rattling cab. But as a musician and a composer, Rowan knows how to play the silences. He used the ambient sound to further distance himself from Raul, the bend of glass and metal and polymer adhesive as the road jounced their vehicle, the wind outside the window he had cranked to evacuate the sweat and the confessions of previous riders, the late-night occasional lonely laying on of a car horn echoing off empty streets and sleeping buildings. These were assurances to Rowan that the impersonal had realigned Raul's expectations of this moment he presumed they were sharing.

Then, after this timpani of cacophonous interruptions to the main theme's introduction, Rowan began again: "Raul," he said almost tenderly, "you must understand. We all run from our disappointments. We are lemmings gone off the cliff. Our migrations are instinctual. They send us away from disappointment. Our disappointments do this. This is routine. If," he said with escalating significance, "as I think you imply, Mason has moved within your circle of affections..." and now within the octave a digression, "and of course one must guess where that leaves miss Fontaine who has partnered with the brotherhood entire, well ... all but me it would seem, but placing her aside for the moment," back to the main theme, "consider that Mason will now be in the free-fall state of disappointment. Mason may not want to cozy with the man who has sent him there. You may, of course, spread your arms and break his fall, but he is desperate with disappointment and running from such. And he may run from you too. Don't you see?"

No, he did not. Or he chose not to. In any case, he was very, very disappointed in Rowan. He pressed the brake outside the address Rowan had given him and disgorged a passenger whom he had mistaken for a friend.

Rowan simply walked away. His mind was still in a whirl. It was, he thought, exhaustion that had turned the corner into wired; it was the in-your-face observation of old friendships falling apart; it was the stress of the big evening he had planned for his own iconoclast event that would forever exile him from university. Things were speeding up and breaking apart, like matter itself, which Rowan had always viewed as an unnatural condition of atoms resisting being pushed apart. Breaking apart is the natural way of things. It was 4 a.m. Monday, the day Rowan would surprise a select body of musicologists with his experiment in iconoclast deontology. He had invited only academics and critics whom he thought would have a predisposition to detest television as a pedestrian media, so he could overwhelm their senses in 50s American TV jingles masquerading as avant-garde opera. There were others that intended to sneak in, including Rowan's students, past and present, and some members of faculty, musicians too, but none of the brothers iconoclast. They seemed to have no interest. And this was hurtful.

Rowan considered the gathering at Francine's to be his going away party. It was Mason and Francine's engagement party too, of course, but they were not going away, unless from each other. And while the brothers seemed to understand he was leaving town, no one but Leon seemed concerned. This too was a bit unsettling. Rowan had thought the brotherhood would be going through a kind of postpartum blues. Who now would give them direction? But, no petit nor grand mal sadnesses had erupted. Typically American – no sense of history, no reason to miss anything because it is all replaceable. As far as the iconoclast gesture goes, Rowan had not really expected any more from the brothers iconoclast than he had got from the brothers Che, or before that the brothers abstinence, or the brothers libertine. Rowan's first experiments in intellectual activism had appealed too much to the visceral. There needs to be a balance. He realized this now. Although debriefing Mason's struggle to resist touching the flesh of New Orleans was a hoot, the counterbalance to this, the brothers libertine, went too far in reacting to Dennis's attraction, discomfort, and guilt over Bowery alley liaisons as low-rent prostitutes became the stuff of experiment and intellectual query.

Rowan's most successful gambit had been the brothers Che. If for no other reason than what they had discovered culturally. He had immersed the brotherhood in Little Havana, west downtown Miami, a long weekend of rum and festival to honor the Bay of Pigs sacrifice, a way for the brotherhood to absorb Latino culture. But these were not the Latinos Rowan had expected. Despite having taken small steps to learn English and wholesale treason in failing to obtain social security identification, these were seasoned Junior Achiever Spanish/Americans, entrepreneurs playing the system to pay rent and then send what was left to relatives in Cuba. There was no heat for counter-revolution, for overthrowing the dictator. There was more fear of becoming that which they would replace. "Un dictador es un dictador, no importa lo que brazalete lleva," had been the refrain: *A dictator is a dictator, whatever armband he wears.* Rowan had cut the visit short and had convinced the brotherhood to help organize a campus-wide protest of migrant worker abuse. Chanting outside the Chancellor's office at Columbia University to protest the university's complicity. This had been his best effort to direct and harness the intellectual/recreational energies of the brotherhood. And being hauled off to a brief stay in jail had given them a sense of closure. Well, all except Dennis who had skipped away unnoticed and avoided jail.

This time, Rowan just wanted some movement in the direction of evaluative iconoclasting – assessing those "things" that take personal, symbolic relevance and then some consideration of the consequence of a life void of said particulars. What do you really love and why? This is a worthy question, thought Rowan. And further, is this a sincere love, a deep love, or a conditioned response? Destroy it and find out. He did not really think anyone would seriously consider damaging any one of these *particulars* if it meant breaking the law, hurting the self, or another, as Chapman had asserted, and then the party got out of hand, so he was unable to test the resolve of the potential law breakers, and then ... well, the party hadn't ended well. The boundaries of common decency had blurred, and not the way Rowan had in mind.

All this deontological theorizing Rowan had initiated was very self-serving, of course, and only Dennis really understood this, but then he was one of the brightest and certainly one of the most selfish of the brotherhood. It takes a solipsist to know one. Rowan had not held up well under the criticism he had received in his debut avant-garde opera, *Tillich and the Burning Church*. Joseph Papp had supported his effort, indeed had laid out tremendous dollar value in scenery and in fitting two theatres for tandem, concurrent performances. And the university was pleased to have one of its own so prominent a figure of debate among the franchised critics that publish in the *Times*, the *New Yorker*, and the credible street mags. But Rowan tended recently to agree with the lay public and with the most churlish of critics that purely intellectual stimulation, as his opera had seemed to be, despite the gorgeous stage settings, just isn't enough. Certainly Suki had been vocal in condemning Rowan's cerebral purge: *Dry bones clacking*, she had said, or something like that. Which made Rowan think of the koan, *one hand clapping*. Which was pretty much the response he got from his audience.

Suki took Rowan to see in concert the Sex Pistols, his competition at the time, and yes, he had to admit ... that was a show that pulled at the guts and at the intellect. The Sex Pistols were working the same end of the spectrum as Rowan, but working it ferociously. Theirs was the true deontological experiment. Their rage had annihilated the bloated pomp of pop music. Their song

"God Save the Queen," written for her majesty's Silver Jubilee, very clearly wanted her, supreme icon, dead, and it rose to the top of the charts despite the BBC's reluctance to air it and the BBC being 9/10ths the available air time in Britain. Johnny Rotten and Sid Vicious: "All we're trying to do is destroy everything," said Rotten. Glenn Matlock, base player, was ejected from the group because he liked the Beatles. He was replaced by Vicious who couldn't play guitar but had the look, and was clearly bent on self-destruction: *All we're trying to do is destroy everything.* When Rowan saw them in concert in New York, their album *Nevermind the Bollocks* had recently been released. And such an inspired phrase! Because bollocks means several things: in old English it means "priest," in the parlance of polite it means "nonsense," and as anatomical reference it means "testes." During the concert, Vicious had addressed his audience as faggots, had encouraged a feverish fan who had leaped upon stage to simulate upon him a blow job, had carved into his chest the bleeding words "gimme a fix," and later that night had been beaten up by his own bodyguards. This kind of nihilism was, to Suki, endearing, and to Rowan oddly compelling.

In contrast to the demands of Rowan's university job, the tenure committee ever watchful, the department chair positively intrusive, Vicious and his band had no wish to please anybody, which is why it pleased the many who are similarly disposed, including Rowan. This performance, which Suki had to seduce him to attend – she had promised transformative drugs and public sex performed upon him in the balcony – Rowan had attended shortly after the short run of *Tillich and the Burning Church.* The Sex Pistol's performance was both inspiring and chastening. Shortly after the concert, and as

a tribute to the Sex Pistols, and as a ploy to establish his own wor-
thiness among the avant-garde, Rowan had staged the theatrics of
mock suicide with student participation which nearly got him fired.
Rowan needed to do something more vicious with his approach to
music. He knew that now. Destroy the thing you love. That's what
he had to do.

So he explored all the ways music creates and continues to
stimulate in its auditors an abiding craving for more, like a heroin
addiction romancing the pleasure receptors in the brain. Music, he
considered, is an emotional signal sent to the cortex. It has been
exploited since the first stick beat the first taut animal hide, exploited to sell an emotion, to enhance communication, to send a
message: love is here, or fuck me now, or I'm at war so be afraid, or
I'm imperial so be impressed, or buy this product.

Every 50,000 years mankind evolves through adaptation,
which means we are still manipulating and reinterpreting music
the same way our ancestors did when they lived in caves. Maybe
that's why Ringo Starr performed so effectively a grunting cave-
man in that filmic documentary of a day in the life: "October 9th,
One Zillion B.C.," or something like that. And of course Ringo
was very happy to have met Barbara Bach who had invited him to
her bed in present time shortly after filming and has yet to boot
him out. A testimony to the testosterone delivered from behind
the groin's valance of a modest set of animal hides perhaps? The
point is that in the year 51,980 we will have evolved again in our
pedestrian need to manipulate music, and we will have by then
merged with its harmonies in metabolic/psychic/emotive/ and
intellectual ways.

Consider then: "Harmony of the Spheres." The Pythagorean

concept of three fixed notes imposed upon the chaos of possible sounds of untied notes. Chaos meant for the Greeks evil. Limitation meant good. The entire universe is, in fact, a musical scale: it is organized numerically and musically. Kubric's movie *2001* uses Strauss as the glue that coheres his space waltz. NASA has released the music Saturn makes, its magnetosphere of waves, played through a synthesizer – a slow, intoxicating melody. Which makes sense as all things oscillate: celestial bodies, nature, humans, molecules, atoms! They all sing! Together these sounds make a Uni-Verse. Yes? Yes.

If we should subvert or destroy certain innate harmonies, release the chaos that is also among us (consider when the butterfly wing flutters and alters forever what was imminent or not to be: the tornado that does not happen or that does as a result, "the butterfly effect" of random imposition), then we simply realign the harmonies. The world will, again, settle back into an harmonious pattern, but with a different set of priorities. This is the job of the iconoclast musician then, to disrupt the current harmonies in search of a more meaningful order, an order more in keeping with the zeitgeist. Rowan decided that his opera had got it all wrong. He will now, instead, reintroduce the audience to its century's most compelling harmonics (the commercial jingle) and then he will *No Wave* the proceedings by showering upon his audience filthy language, violence and pornography – the jarring non sequiturs of unpleasantness foisted upon us in the midst of our musical, harmonious reveries. This will destroy the thing most loved, the memory muscle of harmonics as capitalized upon by the capitalists, and Rowan was betting the hole left to fill will not be filled by the dissonances and intellectual atonalities of Glass and Cage and

Murray. Rowan intended to shock academics back to placating the harmonies where the universal truths lie, where the next great discoveries will lead.

All this Rowan contemplated anew while sitting in the oblong glow of the last desk lamp left in his denuded apartment, and upon the remaining spring-sprung and cigarette-scarred sofa intended soon for roadside trash. He sipped a nice red Chilean wine and brooded. He sipped and then suddenly he had finished the bottle. The sun had meantime rolled up over the buildings beside him, the sparrow had sounded its chant outside his alley window, the soot and grime of his grated windows had filtered the light to sepia as if submerged beneath the Hudson River, and Rowan found himself suddenly plotzed. He thought, why not just go with it. It was just past noon. Nine more hours to the performance. He opened another bottle of wine and a box of Ritz crackers. He decided to phone his department chair. She did not know Rowan was planning to depart New York City once the concert had ended. She did not know she will need to find a replacement teacher before second semester.

The phone jangled other end of the line for a long time before Doctor Janice Giuliano answered, her hoarse voice vibrating the diaphragm of the receiver Rowan held an arm's length away – "Yellow! Doctor Giuliano here. Who is it may I ask?"

"It is 'I'" – Rowan responded in kind – "Doctor Giuliano. It is Doctor Rowan Murray."

"Oh, *yes,* Doctor Murray? Are you *not* in class as we speak? Do you *not* have a class in session as we speak?"

Rowan envisioned the purple miniskirt and the black stockings that hugged her strong legs and the large white teeth of her wide jaws and the way she twirled her eyeglasses by the stem in one hand while talking on the phone. She drove a purple Pontiac Trans Am, a convertible muscle car, her long black hair streaming out behind. Her voice in conversation peaks and dips for emphasis.

"Yes, Doctor Giuliano, as we speak I do in fact have scheduled a class in Symphonic Dynamics."

"And, *so*, if indeed, may I ask how it is you will be phoning *me* as you will be engaged in teaching as we speak?"

"Yes, excellent question, Doctor Giuliano. You see, as it happens, I have been drinking myself into a bit of an existential crisis."

"I see. You are going through another moment of self-revision *as it were?*"

"Indeed, yes."

"And may I ask if this will be conducted with or without a *gun* in your hand?"

"Oh, well, indeed you may ask. In fact, within your purview to ask I should think … very much within your purview."

"Yes, I *am* glad we agree. But the answer to my question…"

"Not so easily answered."

"Yes, I *see*. This will be a portion of the matter under consideration as it were?"

"Exactly. If I understand you rightly. Yes, exactly."

"Then shall I phone security and have you ushered out the building if not indeed restrained and committed to Bellevue?"

"Ah, yes, difficult to achieve I am afraid."

"How *so*, Doctor Murray?

"Well, Janice, and please excuse my addressing you in the familiar, but I do feel we have become quite close over the years, and I should say my behavior may eventually be amenable to correction but I must report that it is currently connected to my legs which are loath to move off this sofa."

"You are *not* at work in other words?"

"Nor shall be ever again."

"*I see.*"

"Yes."

"Hmmm."

"Yes."

"*I see.*"

"Yes, indeed, but I do have such fond feelings for…"

The complaint of the dial tone resulting from Doctor Janice Giuliano's disconnect was deafening, but also liberating despite the fact that he felt the sting of another missed opportunity – he so enjoys strong women. Of course the hangover that will accompany Rowan to his swan song performance will be more debilitating than liberating, but a necessary component to the process of separation, as Rowan came to understand it.

As a prelim warm up, Rowan brought with him the wine bottle and took a seat before his old friend the piano who had of late suffered neglect and resided in dejected anticipation of abandonment by his owner. Rowan played the keys at random, then went where the piano wanted him to go until the voice he knew well rose plaintively.

I have 88 keys, Doctor Murray, and they all think you are wrong.

"Yes, I know."

My lowest key vibrates at 27.5 hertz per second, which if you don't know is the rate at which still pictures presented as slides make the illusion of motion. I can suggest a movie if you no longer have the ear for music. Is popular culture your next evolution? Music is passé. Is that not so?

"Yes, no, but look … I'm here at the keys aren't I? Just give me my chastisement in the mode of our bond. It will make the matter more piquant, don't you think?"

I'm sure.

"You were saying?"

I am saying that as you turn away from music you turn it off.

"If a tree falls in the woods …"

Yes. I will likely be reduced to ornament in my next ownership. Isn't that right? He is a medical doctor, yes? Is that not so?

"Yes, that's right."

Wonderful! Sunday afternoon lessons for the kids, banging the high range like shrieking "I won't go to bed! I won't!" Glorious! Tunings seldom and less-than thorough. I have the greatest range of any instrument, but to what end? Maybe someone at a Christmas party knows Broadway tunes, but even should Rachmaninoff attend and stimulate my vibrators with his genius, he will not be heard. You know this. Like the tree in the forest, if no one hears, no one with the ear to know, there will be no music. Yes, the tree in the forest. You know this. And Rowan, who will tickle the membrane of your inner ear? Use it or lose it. Is that not right? The hair cells that vibrate sound will ossify and place you among the geriatric impaired. What am I saying right now? (261 hertz rings out)

"Middle C."

That's right. And soon Middle C will be high range for your receptors, Rowan. Are you prepared to surrender your gift of gifted hearing?

"Yes, said Rowan. "I think I am."

And with that, he prepared for the evening performance. The rented tux came out of its plastic cocoon. He stepped into black pants with a military stripe of gray on the vertical, hooked black-capped buttons through silky gashes in a spotless white shirt, pulled up suspenders and snapped them once with his thumbs for good luck, placed the satin-tailed black jacket at the ready back of a chair, and rolled a ribbon of blood-red fabric into a passable town-tie knot. Rowan pulled his long red hair tight, threw on a ponytail clip. He looked pin-up spiffy.

When he arrived at the chamber hall of the music college at university, security had detained his street act. His little coterie of hookers, heroine addicts, indigents, and chart-topper crazies were some pissed. Their language was so disgusting, their body odor so offensive, their presence among spiffy sophisticates arriving for the concert so disconcerting that Rowan had great difficulty convincing authorities that these were "his" people. So he resorted to a lie – "The concert, gentleman," he said, "is a charity for the homeless. These are the recipients of our efforts and of our good will." Oddly as Rowan handed out scripts to his people, as he explained and prayed there was a modicum of understanding, he found the light of purpose begin to shine in their otherwise purposeless and blood-shot eyes.

Rowan took a seat at the piano. Despite being hung over, sleep deprived, and nervous as hell, he jumped to the main theme with abandon, as he knew he must. No introductions, no justifications. Just this: jingles. His audience were at first disinclined to make sympathetic connections to these particular television commercial harmonies, but they were nonetheless captured in its cadences – a sixty minute jazz improv beginning with an operatic *No Wave* punk diva screaming the Meow Mix lyrics: "meow meow meow meow/ meow meow meow meow/ meow meow meow meow meow meow meow meow" then interpolating "I want tuna, I want liver …." which would be inane and maybe even insulting but for the scientific certainty that consonance in a simple jingle fires neurons in the auditory cortex in intoxicating ways even with the juxtaposition of Ginsberg's "Howl" stitched into the performance in random readings by these street indigents Rowan had hired for a meal, a fix, a room for a night – whatever it took. The piano established rhythm through meter intrinsic in these jingles. Despite Rowan's inspired tickles of meta-jazzy misdirection, the jingles pulled the memory reflex toward a comforting center of cute and catchy and toward the universal with "I'd like to buy the world a Coke" (images of bucolic hillsides, crowds of smiling people holding hands, holding lighted candles and singing) then "Snap! Crackle! Pop! – Rice Krispies" and wailed by the diva in various languages. She being the one professional in the arts beside himself he had included in the spectacle. In German she sang "Knisper! Knasper! Knusper!" And there were choruses of "Hey, Culligan man!" Concurrently, the street dwellers: one man of indefinable age with a scar on his cheek and walleyed and with the sour aroma of the un-bathed and the diseased, he toured up and down rows of cologned and fresh-shaved cheeks and perfumed throats and coiffed hair reading from his script, "yacketayakking screaming vomiting whispering facts and memories and anecdotes (mispronounced *anti-dots*) and eyeball kicks and shocks of hospitals and jails and wars …," and another who was too skinny seemingly to be ambulatory, a young black girl with mucus eyes and shiny skin, curled in one corner of the room reading, "What sphinx of cement and aluminum bashed open their skulls and ate up their brains and imagination? Moloch! Solitude! Filth! Ugliness! Ash cans and obtainable dollars!" She read in a quiet, disembodied voice with a haunting British accent like she had attended acting school and thought this might be her big break, or maybe she had emigrated from Jamaica and found acculturation more comfortable on smack. Others wandered the isles in various states of decay with voices cracking, pleading, some adlibbing while panhandling. All a calculated distraction to enhance the longing for harmony.

After the performance, the reception, and while arguing and flirting with Doctor Giuliano, Department Chair, explaining the significance of Findhorn in his future and in a world at a loss for spiritual direction, a world that destroys but knows little about what most needs destruction and what works best as replacement, and Mark David Chapman had shot John Lennon as they sipped wine & chatted & intellectualized, and so a graduate student who had snuck in late in the performance shouted the news of Lennon's murder over the din of clinking glasses and chattering tongues.

When Rowan heard, he was appalled. The audience was amazed. Pop icon brutally slain worked perfectly with Rowan's program. Some even wondered if this weren't a ruse, the Lennon slaying, but no, the university was awash in the news – kids outside the chamber music arts building milled and shouted the disaster up through windows and sang old Lennon songs. The audience seemed now to better understand Rowan's statement. There was a buzz then silence then a single baritone lifted his glass and said, "Maestro!" The room erupted in warm applause. Rowan blanched, froze, and his heart, that single most vulnerable organ of demonstrable chaos in rhythm, began to fibrillate so that an ocean of blood washed past his ears and drowned out the congratulations of his audience. He fell into a chair to catch his breath. This was *not* in response to the audience's response.

Chapter Twelve:
Leon's gesture

Sunday - Monday, December 7 - 8, 1980
2:30 a.m. - 11:05 p.m.
(20 minutes after the murder of John Lennon)

Leon Rozen was utterly shaken by the conclusion to his (dis)en-
gagement party. Francine had broken his heart. As had most of his
friends. Leon had such low expectations of me that my moment of
revelatory sex with Raul failed to move him one way or the other.
Only Sharon Demey had remained unsullied in his thinking, despite her making out with Rowan and encouraging a grope or two.
Leon wanted out of there. He left without ceremony and without
speaking to Francine. He offered Sharon a ride home in City Garbage, which she failed to understand which gave Leon something
to talk about besides the tumult of emotions that were spilling
around in his guts as he steered the clumsy Buick into Manhattan's
Bowery district where Sharon and a roommate of questionable
morality and only one working dress shared a room. It was 3:00
Sunday morning.

Leon felt he had descended to hell. Everything there in the
Bowery moved slowly and in a disorientating oscillation – neon
signs cut out and reignited, street lights did the same, car head-

lights like urban fireflies blinked in and out of cobbled lanes limning the white and black legs of hookers swimming in a mash of car exhaust and vomit and street slang. He throttled the car to idle and slid along in synch. His wreck of a car was perfect, Charon's ferry floating in a river of debris. It thrust its nose contentedly into this collage of steam and yellow light, graffiti and boarded windows, bad teeth and short tempers. Leon saw skanks in an alley shooting gallery staring timelessly from hollow eyes. He had seen those eyes a hundred times at the psych clinic in Brooklyn where he interned. He understood the attraction to drug addiction. It was their answer to the weight of time advancing humorlessly on its cogs – tick and graduation, tock and occupation; tick and choose a mate, tock and separate; tick and retire, tock and expire. Leon had come very close to marrying Francine. Yet again the ties of matrimony had eluded him. Or he had eluded them. Either way he was free to fuck Sharon Demey, and that's exactly what he intended. There were, all around him that night, encouraging markers of amorality and heedless self-indulgence.

As Sharon sat demurely in the cracked and stained and scabrous synthetics of City Garbage, she could feel Leon's eyes rounding her curves while enquiring of her life in the Bowery. This was the price of her passage. She knew it was too late at night to safely journey home by subway from Queens. And taxis don't deliver to the Bowery no matter what the hour. She had not wanted her workmate Francine to know where she lived or how. Francine had always assumed Upper West Side or Yonkers, which would have been a considerable upgrade. And she was too flipped out by the behavior of Francine's guests, and by Francine herself, to ask for a ride home or to ask to stay the night, but she saw how vulnerable

Leon was, and knew he wanted to get away as badly as she, and let's be honest, maybe this was her chance to land a doctor. Isn't this what Francine would advise? So Leon will see her circumstance and wonder, how can anyone so charming thrive in such an environment, and then she found herself telling the debt that has leached her salary, paying down her mother's rehab, her mother's debt, and telling why these ghosts of flesh and blood that inhabit the Bowery are a comfort because having grow up with a hippie mother who never could be responsible, who was only half there in the flesh because always high on something. Sharon too has had to silence the ticking of the clock. And after Leon had learned all this, what was it she had overheard Dennis say – to pity is to love.

A black girl with scissors legs encased tightly in a pink dress with tits like rockets fell off a curb, pink wig askew, heel of a red shoe cracked, pocket book spilling a clatter of contents, and bleeding mouth streaming obscenities that Mason couldn't hear until Sharon rolled down the window, told Mason, "Stop the car!" and called, "Rose, Rose, what's wrong?"

"What the fuck, motherfucker? Why you have to mollywap me, fucker!"

"Rose, over here, Rose. What's wrong?"

Rose was over the top. She didn't hear Sharon, didn't notice City Garbage grinding rusted brakes and rasping spent shocks. She took the broken heel of the shoe and charged a black man in a fur coat like slicing with a dagger. He stepped back lightly for a big man and smiled beneath a do-wrap, burning a bleezie in his left hand, his face scarred from corn squabble, but his grill a perfect specimen of ivory and gold, his right hand resting on a deuce-deuce shining in his belt.

Rose said, "Fuck this shit, Tyrone, fuck this shit. Who gonna clean this up, now – who? Who gonna tap this damage? Bargain hunters is who. That's who the fuck is. You want I give discounts today? This be what you want, motherfucker?"

"Why you gotta act all hifee, girl?" said Tyrone. "You wants a glass dick to suck to sweeten you mouth. I gives you one. And you still one bitter hoe, girl. Get along gone. Don't make me mollywap you no more."

Sharon said, "Rose, over here!"

Rose slipped off the unbroken shoe. She did it sexy, falling into pattern, straightened her pink wig and smiled as best she could at City Garbage, but she was not spliced into the scene properly, still high and still somewhere acidly steeped in anger because Tyrone had reduced her earnings to the bump-and-grind tips of an a.m. stripper. That was why the purse had gone over the curb and Rose to follow. Tyrone had taken his cut and tossed the rest.

Her skin was dark but not so dark as Tyrone's and light enough so Leon noticed the bruised eye blossoming beneath the halogen gasses of a street lamp. He was beginning to feel nervous, said, "Sharon, what are we doing here?"

Rose slanted over to City Garbage on bare feet, wouldn't look at the occupants even as Sharon touched her arm, said, "I don't do tag team, but what you got in mind, sugar?"

"Rose, Rose, it's me, Sharon."

"Oh," she said, "Sharon? What you doing here? This ain't your scene, sweetheart. Get you on home. Make no more stops neither. Just get you on home."

"Rose, get in the car. We'll take you home. Just get in."

City Garbage slipped back into the stream of tidal flotsam with

Rose laid out in the back seat like old cork bobbing, insensate, rancid with come stain.

The tenement apartment that Rose and Sharon shared made a dim impression on Leon. Exhaustion from the day's events at this point bordered on hallucinatory as he helped carry Rose up a flight of stairs to the door with five locks and five keys, as if what lay behind were something anyone in their right mind would want to pillage. As it happened, Sharon had a touch of the domestic, a small touch – doilies and art posters and cute ashtrays belied the poverty and the perversion of scrap furniture and drug paraphernalia and filth. There were two rooms, one with two beds, a television and sofa with end tables, the other a kitchen where food rotted and dishes tipped in a pile in the sink. The bathroom was a shared room down the hall. It was the cleanest room they inhabited. Sharon and Leon placed Rose in bed with her clothes on, such as they were, and covered her with an afghan. Sharon then had the wherewithal to appear embarrassed. She did so charmingly. Leon was, of course, smitten. No, make that lusty and invited to be so. As Rose snored and Bowery trash cans tipped over outside the windows, as bottles broke in alleys, and the sun began ruthlessly to rise, Leon schtupped Sharon. Not as a gentleman would, but as a man angry with the world and eager to make his dick show what it was made of, tired of being the victim, tired of having to react rather than initiate. Sharon, in her intuitive wisdom, played the chalice to his questing need.

But when it is over, Leon felt like a shit. He found his clothes as Sharon dragged a towel with her down to the bathroom to clean up. Leon dressed in a rush and jogged out the door. City Garbage, as it happens, was gone. Leon had no wheels. He went back to the apartment, banged at the five locks and said, "I have no car. I have no fucking car!"

Rose came to the door. She was docile, her wig gone and her natty hair sprung alive and fetchingly childlike. She smiled lopsided with a cut lip, one eye swollen shut. She stepped out the door and asked what was wrong and said Sharon was not in. And "I know you?" Then said, "Jest a minute," disappeared and returned with her wig, her pink dress flashing beneath a man's dress coat overused, vermiculated and shoddy but warmly draped against her slender and bruised body. She said, "Now these be my streets. If you be a friend ah Sharon won't no wrong be done you. Your car not so far away gone if I know my people."

Leon was about as awake as he could be. He was, of course, on adrenalin assist. He knew without a car he would not get far outside that neighborhood, knew he would not find a cab, and he was fascinated by the edgy imperfections of Rose. She was suddenly more human, and he had never met anyone so honest. She told about her drug habit and about her pimp Tyrone who kept her locked in a bathroom for three days to break her in as a whore for his stable. She told about the day she had met Sharon at rehab where Sharon's mother was making small progress and herself none at all. She told about the cancer that had taken her breasts which is why Tyrone is so hard on her as she is deformed but with a pretty face. And she is so lucky to have a pimp that keeps her knowing these falsies (which she had left home, which explained the trim fit of the man's overcoat) makes it impossible for her to render more than a mouth or hand job although she tries, God knows she tries to push her cunt into the world if it will have it. Usually it won't.

Leon asked, "Listen, this is unusual, and I'm sorry to lay a burden on, but, as it happens …"

"God damn, mister. Spit that thing out!" She shivered in the cold and pulled the coat more tightly around her.

"What I mean … I'm making a decision that will change my life. I don't know how. Maybe I just don't have the guts… but maybe you can help… you seem so certain…"

"Everybody knows nothin', mister. I'm certain about that."

"Yes, maybe. What I need to do is decide whether to follow Freud, finish my internship and heal minds, or follow Moses and … I don't know, maybe join a kibbutz in Israel."

"Moses?"

"Yes, Moses. You know of him."

"Mister, I been about Mosessed to death when I was a chile. I be a Baptist, a good little southern pickaninny. Ain't no more Moses you will ever find than that. I been half drowned in the waters ah righteousness. I been told the promised land so much I must own a address there."

"Okay, let's talk about Moses."

"Your dime, mister."

"I'm paying for this?"

"Every god damn minute!"

"Fine, fine. We getting anywhere near my car?" Leon looked around him and could see only cars stripped for parts, bars on darkened windows, those eternally flickering street lights.

"Don't know yet. Jest keep walkin' this away till I get a notion who will be snapped and tweaked enough to make a heist ah your wheels this god awful time ah the day. There won't be many, not down here, not this time ah day. Most is in they squat by now and which is where I should be but for you will pay me."

"What happened to friend of Sharon?"

"That be gone soon as we talk money."

"Okay, fine, so I was saying. There's Moses and there's Freud. Put them both on the couch and psychoanalyze. Which is the least fucked up? Make one a God and debunk the other as idolatry."

"What the fuck you talkin'?"

"Let's get started. Okay. About Freud, he was a mommy's boy – 'my golden Sigi' is what his mother, Amalia, called him. She was beautiful, twenty years younger than Freud's father, who was a nobody. Maybe that's why Freud pissed all over his father's side of the bed."

"I startin' to like this boy!"

"Yes, I suppose, but, irksome, in some ways, I mean that whole Oedipus thing … kill his father, fuck his mother…"

"Not so unusual, mister. Happens in my neighborhood every day."

"This neighborhood?"

"You think it be the promised land? Shit. I'm getting the shakes. You got money for a rock of coke?"

"A what?"

"Oh, shit, mister. Speed ball. A dime bag. A blunt. Any damn thing! I need a bump! Just a minute. No … okay, yes come here. In here."

Rose took Leon by the sleeve down an alley where a curtain of wool blanket overhung a doorway, smoke blowing out the seams. She pulled Leon to cross inside but he refused. She said, "Look, I be getting the shakes. I need to shoot up. You got a 5 for a C or a 10 for a D? Let's do a D together. What you say?"

"No, no drugs."

"Shit, man. Okay, a short dog then. You must got enough for that."

"A what?"

"Thunderbird is all."

"Rose, what are you doing? Look, the drugs, they are a dependence, a conditioned need. Break that dependency. Just learn why you do it and break it."

"This be Moses talk?"

"No, Freud talk. Look, your nervous system craves the drugs, the "id," the pleasure principle, it wants! Could be anything… sex, money, power…"

"It be the rush, yes, but also it be the forgetfulness is what I craves."

"Yes, because the "superego," the conscience knows this is wrong … you feel the guilt … you want to forget the guilt so forgetfulness through drugs…"

"How this make me feel better?"

"The *Nirvana principle.* The death wish. We all have it, admit it or not, we all have somewhere in us the desire to just end, to empty out, to just end."

"That do sound good."

"Yes, so you know what I mean."

"Every day I know. But what the fuck I care. Listen, mister, this Freud shit, it don't help me whatall. I need a fix is all. And you owe me …"

"I think it's moral anxiety, Rose. Guilt. What is it that's bothering you, Rose? What do you dream about at night? What do you keep in your thoughts you can't run from?"

"My thoughts?"

"Yes, what do you think about *all t*he time?"

"Well, I think about my children."

"Ah, I didn't know. Where are they?"

"Ask the state. They be taken away at my last rehab. I don't know where. But I don't care whatall! What good they do me. What good I do them? Better they be gone. Why I must think about them? Does no good whatever."

"That's what it is, Rose, that's why you're so harmful to yourself. It's because you can't find anyone or anything else to punish. You punish yourself. Your drugs are a magical gesture to undo the harm. They are your ritual and so your dependence. Don't you see? Now let's talk about your pimp. What is his name?"

"Tyrone."

"Okay, Tyrone."

"He be some upset to have us talk ah him."

"No, I'm still talking about you. Why do you put up with him? You say he's the only one that will see you as useful after your mastectomies, is that right?"

"Something like, maybe."

"Was your father a factor in your life?"

"He be dead now, God bless him in hell."

"Ah, an interesting projection, yes, but when alive…was he *there* for you? Was he your protection?"

"Well, yes, until I be knocked up and leave school and then leave home."

"But until then, he was a strong presence."

"Oh, he be strong all right. He be placing outside the door anything not right in his home. He be the wrath of God is what he be when something not right in his home."

"Well, don't you see the parallels?"

"What you mean?"

"Tyrone, his fists, your father, his rejection. This is no coincidence. This is regression. Do you see? When you feel pressured, unable to deal with difficulties, you seek a firm hand, so to speak, a male who will put things right in your world, like your father, a man who will smash everything into place, even you. Do you see?"

"You say Tyrone be my father?"

"Yes, in a way."

"Sick motherfucker. Just give me the juice and get out my way. You owe me. Get me the juice, motherfucker! You and Freud ain't no good to me. A blunt be good right now. You know? You got a blunt on you? Everybody got fucking weed. But not you, motherfucker. Shit!"

"No, look, I'm tired. There's no sign of my car. Let's get something to eat."

There was an early morning breakfast place across the street. *Eggs with Legs* said the menu written in black marker on cardboard nailed to the door and listing a dizzying variety of eggy carry-out specialties. Leon looked inside. There were tables. Leon bought Rose a coffee, she liked it black, and himself egg and cheese on toast. They took a seat. She saw money paid elsewhere but drugs and became huffy and silent. Leon wolfed the breakfast. It was approaching late Sunday morning. He would ordinarily be cooking brunch with Francine. Crepes or quiche Lorraine, mimosa cocktails, reading and a nap after. He looked around the place. There was no Francine. Rose was fading, as roses are wont to do. She had rested her nappy head on the Formica tabletop, flies buzzing in a urine scent that rose off the man's coat she wore, maybe a gift from a street sleeper Rose had known or ripped off in his stupor and her need. The 99 cent special of home fries and egg anyway you like had a ubiquitous presence among these castaways and ne'er-do-wells and substance abusers and escapees and homeless that occupied the other tables. Rose called these her people. Awful thought. Maybe she would want to take them to the promised land. Looked to Leon like they were already there – outpatients at the clinic, most likely, getting their meth for free and their breakfast from coins in a cup. Can life get any simpler? What is it we think we need to do to earn our place on this planet? Isn't the will to take another breath enough?

Nothing made much sense anymore. How the hell was he going to get out of this place? Rose had not been much help delivering City Garbage. He pushed her head, shook her shoulders to awaken and inspire Rose to exit the door. She did not respond gracefully: "What the fuck, motherfucker! What you want from me? You owe me!" she said, her head raising slightly off the table top.

"Hey," said a woman of indeterminable late years with so much dirt on her face she could be a geological land formation, and with fingers sticking out her gloves, one of these raised in the air for effect. "Leave her the fuck alone, mister." She was up off her seat and coming fast toward Leon with attitude, which ignited interest from the other denizens of this greasy spoon. Leon shook Rose more vigorously. "Rose, we have to leave!" he said with urgency but with less volume, which still had more effect on the other patrons than on Rose. A man seated directly in front of Leon who seemed almost comatose except that he was mumbling to himself, had a nose like WC Fields which he was constantly picking, lifted his bloodshot eyes off his untouched plate of food, said, "You don't belong here, mister. Leave our Rose alone!"

"How do you know I don't," said Leon, beginning to feel some pique himself.

The woman who charged him was leaning over Rose and asking, "Is this man bothering you, sweetheart? "

"Hell no," said Leon. "I'm Rose's boyfriend."

"The hell you are," said the nose picker. "Look at those shoes. You ain't no Bowery citizen. Get the fuck out of my town!"

Leon remembered he was still wearing party togs, which included wool socks in Birkenstock sandals. They may have a point. This was clearly not Bowery wear. Two men in a corner turned in their chairs to face Leon. One a black man bedecked in gold chains and a purple overcoat and diamonds in his ears, regal; the other an Hispanic wearing an orange construction worker's tee shirt like it was summer time and smiling so hard that a long purple scar from the corner of his mouth to an ear made another smiling face. Leon couldn't help staring at that scar.

The black man said, "Hey, ain't that Tyrone's bitch?"

The other said, "Bring her mouth over here I'll tell you so or not."

Leon said, "What the hell is the matter with you people?"

Which compelled the black man to push back his chair and the Hispanic to pull a knife threatening, "You like my face, motherfucker? I make a smile on your face just like mine!" and charged Leon who grabbed his fork and shoved it into the man's neck who went down instantly leaking blood and guttural Spanish and clutching the fork that was buried in his larynx, and everything seemed to stop, like a glitch in time, finally the eternal clock taking a break, but what a moment. Leon looked around and everyone seemed to be shouting something. Only he couldn't hear a thing. It was like he was deaf and stuck in this time warp while others were moving forward in slow motion. Their faces were ugly with hate. Even Rose had pulled her head off the table and moved her lips violently like a stuck record repeating, "What the fuck? What the fuck? You owe me!"

But Leon didn't answer. He was listening to the voice in his head saying, leave, just leave, like the man with the nose who said, *you don't belong here.* So Leon was out the door and running down the sidewalk. He was the only one moving with pace as others had remained slowed in time. The traffic lights blinked yellow, but there was no traffic, stray cats atop trash bins calcified as fast-food wrappers wafted in a small wind, a policeman in profile in his patrol car at first seemed a cardboard cut-out. His windows were down and his voice at first sounded like an echo from inside a well. He was calling in the plates on City Garbage which had been left running, one wheel over the curb, smashed into a fire hydrant leaking water. Then everything moved double-quick. Leon jumped into the car, waved to the officer, who said, "Hey, you Leon Rozen?" / "Yes, but, I can't, please just right now, I can't …" and punched the accelerator, which inspired the cop to chase until he heard then saw the mob from *Eggs with Legs* charging down the sidewalk toward him, shouting obscenities, and figured another riot against the police, it's happened before, so called in a code 10-103 and pulled his gun but thought better of this because no witnesses on his side so jumped back into the cruiser and motored away, thinking he had made the right decision. He had defused a potentially bad situation, bad for him.

Leon had no idea where he was – lost in the wilderness, he said to himself. Masada hopeless, he said to himself. And no traffic to follow. He turned the wheel and turned and turned and got nowhere. This was not the Jew he wanted to be. He had been the good Freudian up until he had killed a man and left town. Now he was a Moses Jew. If the kill were righteous, then this could be a significant start to his new Jewishness. And, yes, Leon thought he may have made the right decision. After the shock, after the blood on his hands, literally, wiped clean on a rag he pulled out from under the car seat, after slamming his hands on the steering wheel shouting, *What the fuck kind of Jew are you! What the fuck kind!* The fork, he had begun to feel, went where the fork was meant to go. If he became a known murderer, the state would put him to death for this, as the Pharaoh would have Moses for killing an Egyptian to protect a Jew. Of course in Leon's case the Jew he was protecting was himself.

Leon needed to regroup, rethink, begin again. He couldn't go home to the apartment he shared in Sheepshead Bay with Mason. Couldn't go back to Francine's. The brotherhood had disbanded. The marriage was canceled. He must, finally, go back to his father's house, back to Brooklyn where mother will blintz him and worry him with bills and speak weepily of her departed husband Merrill and what he would have to say to every direction in life Leonard had chosen while away from home (yes, Leon is short for Leonard), and what father would say to every feint and dodge and shift and conceit that Leonard has used to distance himself as his home life had become too heavily larded with protection for him to *feel* the world as he had wanted.

Leon's father, Merrill Rozen, was a dominant presence in that home. And he was a man of prominence in the neighborhood. He was proprietor of a house wares and novelty store on Flatbush Avenue, an easy subway ride from home, a depository of goods Merrill had gathered into three rambling stories of brick building, a collection of quality home goods, from kitchen sink to brass bed, all remarkably inexpensive. If anyone were to ask how come so cheap ("affordable" Merrill liked to say), Merrill would identify a ding ("fallen off the truck") or an imperfection ("factory worker fallen asleep") but really, there was something in Merrill's dealings with warehouse foremen, truck drivers, even factories that was a little suspicious if not criminal that no one, including the police, would question. Because, well, there were appropriate discounts to be had even by the police. As a result, Merrill had furnished most all the new households in Brooklyn Heights. Newlyweds especially would go straight to Rozen's for furnishings but for something more – good counsel. Merrill Rozen had become a macher (big shot) but a haymish besides (someone you feel comfortable with) and a mensch (a man of worth) that youth would consult with the naïve expectation of supplicants to a secular rabbi. And that was the man that Leon (Leonard) needed badly to separate from.

As a boy, Leonard could make no decisions of his own that weren't weighed and examined by his father, even if only assessed by a raised eyebrow or an accepting nod. Everything Leonard did and said in that household of Brooklyn Heights, nestled in the humm of traffic crossing the Brooklyn Bridge, seemed destined to pass through the filter of his sage father. Leon understood Freud's need as a child to piss on his father's side of the bed. Leonard could easily have done the same. There was a kind of emasculation going on in that house, a kind of evisceration that gutted his youthful surge and whim, his urge to leap and land where he may. Not only had the ground been prepared upon which he would land, but the projection of his leap, the velocity, the purpose, all had been pre-programmed by the very caring secular god that was his father.

When Merrill Rozen died, Leonard did not consider this one

of those deaths that took him by surprise or that placed lead in his soul, not the death of innocence that had early in his life defined the compass of his world as a series of catastrophic gestures by God. Leonard had welcomed the death of his father as a kind of release. His sister and his mother were his only concern. They keened and brattled, surrendered emotional and neurological control, flopped and fainted. Leon was concerned. They worried beyond reason that Merrill would not be accepted in the spirit world of ancient Jewry because he did not want cremation in the plain cedar box with wood pegs. Merril must have the ornate brass and silver casket he had bought before his death somewhere at a very reasonable price. And, yes, Merrill's best suit which he had carefully folded and placed inside the silky folds of the silver casket as if to predestine his remains, that suit was summarily gifted to Goodwill and replaced with a sewn white shroud. And, yes, the cremation had gone ahead despite Merrill's wishes. But the family were told by Rabbi Soloveitchik not to worry. Merrill might at first complain as one betrayed – the keening of mother and daughter had then become truly obstreperous – but the rewards in the next life would be so considerable he will mollify. Not to worry. He will mollify.

Merrill had died a slow and uncomfortable death from liver disease. He had kept his symptoms secret – the back pain, the rectal bleeding, the abdominal distension – as if he could counsel them to perform quietly and in moderation as a gesture of respect for one of his stature reduced to this deteriorating condition. Only when he was found one morning curled into himself in bed like a mollusk in a shell did Dara know to be alarmed. He and Dara, Leon's mother, used separate beds and separate bedrooms, so it was late morning before Merrill was found. Only Osheroff's Bagel and Lox knew something was amiss, as Merrill had started his day there seven days a week by 6 a.m. with poppy seed and salmon and cream cheese and black coffee before going to his storeroom office at Merrill's Variety to file receipts and review stock. So, they just knew. Merrill will no longer want of the kosher sustenance yeast and dough provides.

As Leon waited the five minutes it took Dara to realize someone was knocking on her townhouse door, Leon's boyhood home, as the traffic sang to him over his shoulder from the harp strings of the bridge that had destroyed the Roebling family (crushed legs, lungs, and lives), Leon began to imagine he would see his father again. Because this house was still more Merrill than anyone – his furnishings, his voice, his smell, his rules. Dara peeked out the mullioned glass of the side panels to the front door, blinked and removed her glasses, rubbed them upon an apron, blinked again and said, "Who is it? Is someone there? Meshugas, who is there?"

Leon had a moment where he nearly back-stepped quietly away, but Dara sensed someone was there, and she was getting agitated, "*Gay avek!*" she said, "Go from my door!"

"But mother, it's me, Leonard."

"Leonard?" Dara's blinking increased. The eyeglasses came off and went on and off and on and received a thorough buffing upon her stained apron. "Luftmensh, my son, you are returned to me for what reason? What naches do you bring?" The door opened a crack, as if gifts alone would bring admittance. She said, "How are things, my son?"

Leon said, "Mother, open the door, please. I seek refuge. This is not a casual visit. Please. I'm in trouble."

"Ah, *gai kakhen afenyam*! Your father should know. He should know, no *naches* do you bring. Your suffering mother. Your suffering father. No *naches* do you bring to us that suffer."

"My father's suffering is over, mother. Mine, however, is about to commence. Will you bring me through the door, please? Do not have me beg at my own door."

"This is no longer your door, Leonard. You have left this house. Oh I am *verklempt.*" Off went the glasses, the apron came to her eyes. "You have left this door to potchka about. If your father should know. If your father …"

"My father is *dead*, mother. And I am *no* nebbish. I have a degree. I fix people's heads. People *meshugge* in the head."

"*Meshugge?*"

"Yes, *no*! Not me. I am a doctor now. You know this, mother. Please let me in."

"A doctor?"

"Yes, a doctor."

Ah, you bring naches indeed. Your father should know."

"Yes, let's tell father. Let me in, please."

Leon had to admit, the house smelled less of his father now but more of spoiled food. His sister, Sara, had been looking in on Dara, or so Leon thought (it must have been a year since his last visit), but the place was oppressively hot – oven heat – and food was piled everywhere uneaten. There was bakka, borscht, gefilte fish, blintz, latkes, schnitzel, and of course lox.

Dara said, "Leonard, sit. Eat. But no. Wait for your father. It is not like him to be so late … he will join you … it may be just, well… he …"

And so this will be Leon's life, many years more. Leon will settle into the basement of his father's house, his mother cooking for his father so refusing to eat until he arrives, refusing to feed Leon until he arrives. And, of course, he will never arrive. She will, however, cook a breakfast for herself and for Leon, as Merrill always takes his breakfast out, but lunch and dinner will be tenderly prepared and left uneaten.

Leon will make a home for himself in the Platonic shadows of the foundation of the home his father still dominates. The food he smells, the breakfast he eats, this will be his only connection to the corporeal world, as his life with Francine is over, his career abandoned. He will have begun a life of hiding from the police who aren't looking for him (the man with the fork in his neck survived and was so criminal himself he thought better of bringing criminal charges upon another).

Down in that septic basement Leon has appropriated the heavy, oak desk brought there from his father's office in Rozen's Variety, and has begun to plan the Moses/Freud psychoanalysis. He will present his session notes to the American Board of Psychotherapists and to its publications bullhorn *Psychology Today*, where it will make a considerable stir – naches, his gift to his father.

Let us imagine Leon placing his lips to a fissure of stone wall foundation from which gasses and dreams issue. Let us picture Leon summoning the inchoate then assembled essences of Sigmund Freud and Moses. Leon entreats them to attend group therapy, an event intended to probe the significance of their contributions to a modern world. What he doesn't say is that he wants the two together to tease out and expose hidden identities. Moses is intrigued. Freud demurs. Maybe doubtful of Leon's qualifications to apply the tools of a science Freud had originated. But Freud eventually agrees having decided Leon is neither a frosty physician nor a clammy priest. Leon convinces the great doctor that he is the appropriate evolution of psychoanalysis, a "secular minister of the soul."

Doctor Sigmund Freud drops noisily into the faded paisley, damply soggy stuffed chair imprinted with Leon's fretful sleep. This is the Freud who has come to America after escaping the Nazis, a man with few years to live because betrayed by the tobacco he so loves, the great man who has introduced a new field of science to fathom the human psyche, no less dramatic than the first sputnik sending signals back to Earth from the depths of space.

The prophet Moses enters Leon's basement hermitage with a smile of amusement, the desert sand having worn and the sun having baked his wizened face and etched deep lines, but eyes steady if averted and reddish brown as agate. His beard is white, long and wispily thin, unlike the Michelangelo statue whose beard could nest a piteousness of doves. He seats himself before Leon upon the slats of a wood bench, quietly smoothes the burnoose over his knees, nods gracefully to Freud. The cloak is pastel blue and white with purple and scarlet trim, the color of the Tabernacle.

Leon feels remarkably calm, grounded in purpose. He has been planning this a long time, and he is in his element (that being the shadows of his hallucinatory mind). He looks first to Freud, whom he knows he must draw out, as the great man leans guardedly away from Moses and his eyes track over the top of Leon's head where mice run through the joists. Freud is repulsed, those libidinous busy rodents tunneling into his unconscious, and is having too a moment of totem aversion, finding it difficult to acknowledge the imposing presence of Moses, the ultimate father figure.

"So, Herr Doctor and Moshe Rabbenu" says Leon, "to hear your voices in this modest home, well, I am blessed. First, may I ask Herr Freud, your system of associative dream interpretation, it is more intuitive than intellectual is it not? And, therefore, very like the Kabbalah?"

Freud looks warily upon Leon's uncharitable Kabbalah provocation. He is puzzled to be so betrayed by a Jew, buts finds it historically resonant. He rubs with tobacco stained fingers the thinning hair of his skull; his brow porches over his eyes showing concern; his watch chain sparkles defiantly from a wool vest. Freud sinks more deeply, disquietly, into the worn, stuffed chair facing Leon behind his father's desk and boldly states: "There will be nothing derivative in my system, my friend."

"Ah," says Moses, "you must know dreams come from God."

"Not your turn," says Freud, his unlit cigar tremulous in his hand.

"You must know," returns Moses, blithely smiling and staring into space, "even the mystics derive Kabbalistic ciphers from God."

"Yes, well," says Leon distracted by Moses, examining his eyes gazing deeply out onto desert horizon and thus deeply inside himself. "So," Leon says refastening on Freud, "was your father not an Hassid? Can you really be an atheist?"

"I do not accept precepts and laws handed down by a primal father who watches over me. I believe in fate's cruelty. Yes, I am an atheist."

"But, Herr Doctor ..." Leon begins.

"Oh, God," says Freud."

"Ah! You summon the deity!" says Moses.

"Convention,' says Freud, "as you would know were you attuned to our modern sensibilities."

"But, Herr Freud, is not modernity a relative consideration? Please, one more question: what do you say of the convention of murder? Where does it come from … this very human quality, I mean, should a man commit murder, even unintentionally, say from self-defense…."

"Mr. Rozen," says Freud, "take my word. There is no unintentional murder. It goes back to the original son's murder of the king father. Even Moses was murdered by the Israelites he tried to free."

"Yes, I see."

"No," says Moses, "Neither of you truly sees."

"Moshe Rabbenu," says Leon, "blessings on you. May I trouble you with my questions so that the world can better know your story and its meaning in our lives today?"

"I have come for this purpose. You may ask your questions."

"Thank you, Moshe Rabbenu. First, is it true that you have taken lives?"

"Ah, yes, but in the cause of justice. An Egyptian trader beating to death a hapless Hebrew. Could I watch indifferently?"

"Freud will say, Moshe Rabbenu, that you have ritually killed your own father in this action. Does this make sense to you?"

"Hmmm," says Freud. "My words from your mouth, somehow … castration of the father comes to mind. But please, allow me to address Herr Moses."

Leon nods his consent.

"To be frank, Herr Moses, your idea of circumcision as a male child's introduction to his God, when the first touch of God terrorizes the libido... well, I appreciate the work you send me, but such trauma! Your God is so threatening. The best way to begin a life do you think?"

"A light touch of the knife. No more," says Moses. "An agreed upon symbol of a chosen people."

"So you say," says Freud, "but what of Herr Rozen's question of murder? Have you not also murdered Jews whose foreskin you have first removed?"

"Yes, I have murdered Hebrews as God commanded. I have killed many engaged in idolatry," Moses says then hesitates, thinking through his answer then adds, "I hear their cries even now."

"You are bothered by your conscience," says Leon.

"Oh, no. This was exigent."

"But of course you feel no guilt," says Freud. "Your acts were avenged. You were killed by your own people."

"Not at all. I died an old man humbled by his trials, one hundred twenty years of age, upon Mount Pisgah looking out to the promised land of Israel. Glad in my heart."

"Glad?" says Freud, "For killing women and boys? You have killed the innocent!"

"This I did in the name of God."

"Your belief in God is childlike," says Freud. "You yearn for the parent you never had. You fixate on pleasing the father and have taken the lives of innocents because of this."

"No one is innocent in the eyes of God. We all deserve to be punished. It is his will when and how so."

"To be sure, such wisdom overwhelms," says Leon. "May I ask just one more question? (Moses nods his consent.) Is it true that esoteric meaning is placed in the Torah, in the laws of God given to you and placed in Hebrew scripture?"

"Ah yes, it is true. God has yet to present to us the Nasi of the Great Sanhedrin who shall reveal through his understanding of

Kabbalah God's teaching. Your man Freud has tried and failed. (Freud groans discernibly.) He will not want to admit his failure. But another will succeed. This will be man's supreme understanding and the beginning of the end of days, when Herr Freud shall meet his God. Oh, and you should know. Your friend John Lennon has been shot dead. A good singer, but not a profound one. He also is not the Nasi of the Sanhedrin. Not to be mourned an innocent."

"Yes, I understand. No one is innocent. No one escapes punishment."

"No one."

Chapter Thirteen:
Dennis' gesture

Sunday - Monday, December 7 - 8, 1980
8:00 a.m. - 11:05 p.m.
(20 minutes after the murder of John Lennon)

Dennis Zamora thought maybe Rowan was right. The waiting needed to end. Something needed to happen and Monday was as good a day as any. Waiting to quit his job. Waiting to know if the murder of John Lennon will happen. Waiting for the right woman. And it was one of those winter skies that hangs leaden, heavy and gray, like screened off from God's intervention, if he were still up there. Leon might think so. Dennis thought he had gone to some Greek island in his retirement. Looked like rain, maybe snow, but it wasn't doing anything yet. Waiting to decide. And there's nothing you can do about it. It will do what it wants. Or, it will do nothing at all in your despite. And Dennis had waited long enough. First, high school in nowheresville New Jersey with the towers of New York City looming in adjacency, and there was Dennis pretending he wasn't getting A's in his classes. And he certainly was *not* enjoying those books in English he was made to read (Henry James and the Brontes and Hawthorne). And Brenda Sampson, the luggage family princess whose parents own a mansion on a hill and were polite to Dennis but suspected he took their daughter to the old quarry to fuck.And when Dennis and she went to different colleges, he promised to wait as did she, but neither did. Then college and thankfully out of his father's house (not the kind of father Leon had who controlled with his superior reasoning, but the kind of father that controlled with his liquored temper and the back of his hand). Then in college the surprising numbers of kids who wanted nothing but to get high and get laid, and so Dennis again masking his academic ambitions in order to fit in. Then grad school at Columbia Teachers College which turned out to be a fool's game (selflessness promoted to the point of self-annihilation). Then writing stories that no one would publish. Then his job at the literary agency promoting other writers so less talented than Dennis but working within a recognizable niche so sellable. How long will the wait to be Dennis go on!

He read again portions of the Wyatt Earp novel. It was still just too good. Dennis Zamora was tired running errands for his two Type-A bosses Holmes and Stout and tired of making follow-up phone calls to his friends' girlfriends (perhaps not as tired as they) and tired of having no clout in the world of letters.

Dennis found the writer's bio and phone number. It was Sunday morning. The writer was recovering from a week delivering mail on the back roads of rural Oregon, but mostly recovering from a Saturday night with the boys at a roadhouse bar where rockabilly had never died – Billy Lee Riley's "Red Hot" still playing in his head. The phone rang. The writer figured one of his buddies calling to remind him Laura Jane Seward, the councilman's daughter and his fiancé, will be on her way presently to take him to church and so that tall redhead with the runaway freckles and the simpering giggles should be out of his bed right about now. The writer answered the phone said, "Shit! I know. She's leaving. I'm working on it. I am," to which said redhead responded, "Take my tits out of your mouth, cowboy, if you're sending me home." / "Not yet, darling," he said, "God can wait. Lets us conspire a bit more in this our redeemable sin."

To which Dennis replied, "Mr. Writer (name withheld upon request), I am a literary agent in New York City, not without sin myself" (he paused for effect, heard only quick breathing and rustling sheets) said further, "I am interested in your novel."

"Oh, shit. Beg your pardon all to hell … darling, get your tits out of my mouth. I need to talk to this man. Yes, go ahead, please. No, not you, darling…."

"Your book has made quite an impression on me. Apart from the flaws one would expect from a first novel, and my fee will be 20%, the extra cost of editing and promoting new talent, you understand. But yes, your book… I would like to represent it in a new agency here in New York City."

"Well, shit and hallelujah! Why the hell not. Honey, get your hand away. What's your name again?" and so on until the writer and Dennis had agreed that a contract would affirm the following – that nothing written by the writer beyond December 8th, 1980 will go out to any publisher or editor or agent but Dennis per contract stipulation of binding exclusivity with termination subject to … and etc, etc, etc, all which the writer heard along with the redhead's escalating passion throes, as her hips straddled the prone cowboy, arms and breasts flapping, riding the bull as it were, and then Billy Lee Riley in his head again: *my gal is red hot; your gal is doodly squat,* and the writer was starting to think maybe Mary

Jane needed to go to church by herself, and maybe the redhead was a keeper, and this in conjunction with alcohol dehydration constricting the flow of blood to his brain, which is when he does his best thinking, and this throbbing more pervasive than the love knot distending his dick. He thought, if I die this moment, my life is complete.

Dennis, however, was experiencing ambition anxiety. He was considering how best to leave the service of Holmes and Stout so as to avoid the usual contractual machinations that attend dissolved partnerships, and the restrictive assignations of intellectual properties that he intended to impose upon his own future employees as the cowboy writer's books become movie scripts, video games, television series. Dennis justified his betrayal with the rationale that this writer was, after all, his to find in the slush pile reading that had burdened his evenings at home – raking through all those homeless and homely words that will never find representation because unschooled and undisciplined and sadly unaware. Dennis had suffered through mounds of this wasteland detritus. Now – the rewards!

Dennis decided he should maybe phone Francine Carlton. He should. Yes. She would need solace as her marriage plans had ended per Leon's Rozen's unmistakable revulsion as Francine had last night begun to fuck anything with legs, like the dam had burst, and really it had. Francine had finally orgasmed, as she confessed to Dennis in their last moments together in the bathroom, and it wasn't Dennis, but that was okay, and it was like, well, very much like that limitless credit card Mason had posited as enticement, but with no interest for ninety days, and with debt forgiveness built into the plan should she get herself into trouble. Francine had just let herself go wild. Call it capital gains. Francine now realized she had been looking all this time for another room to decorate. Now that she has found it in the silky walls of her uterus, she intended to experiment with color and with the wildest variety in furnishings. Only Francine wasn't quite sure what to do with this feeling once she realized she no longer had a partner. Dennis decided he really should not phone Francine.

Since Dennis will be, like Leon, dissolving a partnership, albeit a business affiliation with Holmes and Stout Literary, he was eager to form another relationship, as he was never really any good at being alone, and right now, with his career about to accelerate, he will need a woman to validate his vision of ascendancy. He will not want a Charlotte Corday to stab him in the bath nor a Tadzio to dazzle him with the aesthetic wonders of partnering. He will need someone like Monsieur Curie, the Madame's selfless partner, someone who will do the groundwork for his high-rise career and live quietly in the shadow of his expanding ego.

Shit, Dennis was getting ahead of himself. He decided to slow down the speculation. He walked over to the frig, cranked the top off a Molson – call it a brunch extravagance that will calm his brain with its foamy, yeasty, malty enzymes and whose latent fatness quotient he would counteract soon with a battery of sit-ups. Dennis looked up through the window with the East River view. The rarely-seen gondola slid past to Roosevelt Island. Synchronicity! Exactly. Where did he get this word? Didn't matter. This was Dennis's moment. The timing was right. Which meant that bastard Chapman, that son of a bitch, Chapman, he was going to do it! He was going to kill John Lennon. Just as Leon thought he would. It was Chapman's word, synchronicity, wasn't it? Now

Dennis remembered. That kid was going to shoot John Lennon and Dennis knew all about it. Should he phone the police? No. They would think Dennis a crackpot or an accomplice. Sorry, John, but the thing to do is wait and see if it happens, and if it does, sell this story to the media for the seed money Dennis needs for his start-up literary agency.

He phoned Francine. But why? He hadn't meant to. But the in-decision was killing him. She picked up but there was no love in her voice. She, like the cowboy writer, was nursing a hang over. Dennis should have phoned Claudia. Francine's number was just in his head. Well, go with your mistake he told himself. At the party, while Francine had acted the libertine, and had certainly had too much to drink, there was something very controlling go-ing on. She knew what she was doing. The alcohol was a cover for something she had planned all along – maybe a last fling at multiple partners before settling in as doctor's wife, a last orgasmic titillation before eternally relegating her over-revved clitoris to the bland attentions of husband doctor. Whatever it was, Dennis saw a woman who knew what she wanted, kept her own counsel, imple-mented the plan in disguise, and was willing to push beyond the boundaries of decency (also willing to deny as much if the need arose). A mate worthy of a Machiavelli. A mate worthy of Dennis.

"Dennis, why are you calling?"

"Francine, how are you?"

"You know how I am, Dennis. I am without a man."

"But you were very much *with* men last night, and woman."

"This is not a laughing matter, Dennis. Leon has left me. He has taken Sharon Demy home. That's what he said, but really, it was his excuse to leave me. He has been gone all night. I haven't slept.

A phone call, maybe, you would think, at least he should call, and apologize, or well, maybe I should apologize, and you should too. I mean, you and I, last night. You're his fucking friend…"

"Nice adjectival attribution, Francine, but we were all drunk, stoned, the boundaries fell away. We were not in our right minds. But, Francine, what I saw of you, you were glowing, not like I've seen you before. Something happened last night that goes beyond Leon, beyond the orgasm. Am I right? You're not the same Francine."

"I'm flattered you noticed, Dennis. But I had hoped the man I marry would make me glow. Guess it takes a whole room of randy men, a dike and a homo to get me off. This is not a convenience, Dennis, if you know what I mean. This is not at all a convenience."

"No, I guess not. But let me ask you a question."

"Keep it polite."

"What is your assessment of Chapman? Will he do it, do you think? Will he shoot Lennon?"

"Leon thinks so. He says Chapman is … oh, well, I'm not sure why, but yes, he thinks Chapman will kill somebody."

"Francine, tell me … what are you going to do without Leon?"

"Well, pretty much what I did *before* Leon, I suppose."

"What's that?"

"Television for one, lots of good shows I have ignored to sit and chat with Leon while he reads, so he should make himself intellectual to be a good doctor. But that just spreads my rear end, sitting and chatting does. And, well, I should catch up on my shopping. This Arab décor has to go! I did it for Leon, you know, make a place where his mind spirals in. That's what *Architectural Digest* said, make a place for a man to get all introspective and stay-at-home comfy – that's a word, right – (Dennis asks, "What comfy?"

/"No, introspective." / Dennis grunts, "Uh, huh."). Right, so a place where a man with a good brain can burrow in and tap the riches of an intellectual life at home, that's a direct quote, I think, pretty direct. Only, he's not here to burrow into anything anymore, me included. Maybe I need a new apartment. Some place with lots of windows so there's no more burrowing in. Maybe that's what I did wrong. Maybe men don't want to burrow so much anymore."

"I have an idea about that, Francine. Tell me what you think?"

But he couldn't get to the point. Couldn't say the words, "marry me," so he talked around the idea, as obscurely as one of his favorite metaphysical poets. He talked about bursting hearts and caressing hands and the fondness eruptions of dreams he had experienced lately when he thought about her (yes, sexy stuff and meant to be so), and he said there can be no static relationship now between himself and Francine, since they had both broken with Leon, and Dennis just couldn't let this be the end. There are so many lonely people out there, because so few are right for each other. And those few so seldom find each other. But surely this was not the case with himself and Francine.

"Dennis," Francine said, "what are you saying?"

"Think of it as a marriage of convenience," said Dennis.

So Dennis had at the time of this phone call essayed three business arrangements – one with his former agency (although this will transpire sometime Monday), one with the cowboy writer, and now with Francine, to whom he had indirectly proposed marriage and to which she responded ambivalently.

Francine became unusually quiet. Said she needed time to think. Said call her back Monday, no Tuesday because Monday is never a good day and, well, there was too this Rowan Murray "happening" to sort out. Sharon Demey might want her to go to Rowan's concert. But she didn't see the point if Rowan were off to some commune in Scotland. She needed time to think.

When Dennis hung up the phone, he was pretty sure he had a wife on standby. So, that was decided. The next step was to feel out the media. Whom did he know at *Rolling Stone*? They would get behind this Lennon murder scoop. Dennis consulted the Rolodex – so many names. He flipped through eagerly then urgently, as nothing seemed to turn up. Then he thought he should just cold call. They will know Rowan from his opera. He could use Rowan Murray as an introduction. Rowan had stormed down there and made a scene. They will remember. He had gone on about the Sex Pistols getting all the press and where's their cultural soul, or something like that, or that's what Rowan said he had said. So Dennis consulted the phone book then dialed the number, got an intern on the phone. That's right, he thought, it's Sunday; the salaried people are sleeping.

Dennis said, "Listen, this is not a hoax. I'm a friend of the maestro Rowan Murray. You know Rowan."

"Who?"

"Look, I have a big story but it won't develop for another day or so, if it does, but it most likely will, in which case your paper will want this scoop. Is that the right word, *scoop*?"

"Oh, sure," said the girl at the phones, "scoop works just fine for retro-detective work. Where do we drop the money?" This girl has a lot of attitude for an intern Dennis thought.

"No, look, it's not like that. I have credentials. I'm not on the con. That's the right word, *con*?" (Dennis had not taken the time to work through potential scenarios before making this call, so his language was woefully un-hip. Why hadn't he read some Hunter Thompson before placing the call?)

"Look, either hang up the phone or tell me what this is about."

"Okay, but who are you? Why should I tell *you*?"

"Because I'm the girl holding the phone that says either you're a lunatic and go away or I connect you to the city editor, who happens to be here today. Which is it?"

"Okay, but I can't say much. The thing is there's a very famous musician, a pop star, living in New York whose life is in the balance. He may soon be killed, an assassination, a hit, a psycho may soon put him down."

"Do you own a gun?"

"No, look, this is not a game. This is real. Just patch me through to your editor and I'll explain in more detail. I'm for real. This is for real. I know the killer. Or, well, the would-be, soon-to-be, potential killer."

The phone went dead. Dennis said, "Shit!" Then the line became alive again with a crackling recording of the current issue's top stories ("… three American nuns killed in El Salvador; was the U.S. Army involved? Subscribe today or pick up a copy at your…"), then a young man's voice: "Yes, hello. This is the city editor. What's this about pop star assassination?"

Upon which Dennis waxed eulogistic in extolling the as yet alive pop star's virtuosity with a protest song (the editor said, "Dylan?"), no but think notable import from beyond the big pond (the editor said, "Clapton – my God, and so soon after alky rehab."), no, but think sexual perversion ("Oh," said the editor, "You mean Polanski, but he's a movie director, right?"), yes, I mean no, not him, think married to the dragon lady? ("Oh, shit, you mean …")

"Yes, the walrus himself."

After which Dennis explained in extravagant detail the Mark David Chapman weirdness at the coffee shop that none of the brotherhood ... /"What brotherhood?" said the editor./ "No, no, not the mob," said Dennis, "a brotherhood of intellectuals, like Samuel Johnson's *Literary Club*, ours is *The Shop*, Rowan's idea for a café klatch that well, never mind, but this Chapman..."

During which Dennis explained that "Chapman had not been taken too seriously by the brotherhood until he had had the balls to attend Francine's engagement party, which turned out to be her disengagement party, as well as Rowan Murray's going away party ..." /"How do I know that name?" said the editor./ "Avant-garde opera," said Dennis, "if you remember, a Joseph Papp mistake that you guys at *Rolling Stone* panned." /"Oh, yes," said the editor, "I remember a visit from the maestro."/ "Exactly."

In consideration of which Dennis then steered the conversation back to Mark David Chapman, "Who exhibited very strange behavior at the party. He spoke openly about wanting to put down, is that the right term, *put down*, well ... assassinate the pop star in question, *and* he had a gun in his rain coat pocket which flipped everybody out."

The conversation with *Rolling Stone* went better than Dennis had thought it would, his having been so unprepared. Now came the waiting. The awful waiting. Waiting to know for sure if Francine will marry him. Waiting to quit his job. Waiting to know if the murder of Lennon will happen. How very unlike Dennis to drink to excess, but he did, all the Molsons he had left in the frig, then a half bottle of Chablis, then to bed with clothes on, and when the phone rang it was Monday and the cute secretary from Philly who meets and greets at Holmes and Stout Literary asked was he all right? When was he coming to work? And blah, and blah, and blah, until he blew up. Again, very unlike Dennis who said he would call back when he knew exactly what he was doing. And don't bother him again! Which may not seem like a very big blow up, but for Dennis, a very big blow up. It was 11 a.m. No wonder they wondered where he was.

Dennis pushed himself out of bed. It took effort. He shuffled to the bathroom, stripped off clothes and ran a shower. There was so much hair on his back he could benefit from a full-body coiffing, but the hair was blonde so less than simian and more… more what? Nordic is what Dennis likes to think, Bergmanesque. But when he came out of the shower, as the vent fan pulled away moisture from the mirror, Dennis saw a nearly bald, paunchy, hairy guy with fat hands and an overlarge head for short legs. This was time advancing. This was his father's visage and torso and hirsute extravagance. How unfair! This was Dennis at age 27 looking 47.

Dennis ran back to the bedroom, his schlong dripping water, the hair on his head matted like a cheap wig, his back hair glisten-ing, and grabbed the phone and rang, again, Francine at home. No answer. Oh, yes, work. Rang again and Francine answered in a funk which Dennis wanted not to attribute to himself so ignored his insecurities and asked what she thought about his idea for a "partnership," and then said, "Well, you know, if you hesitate be-cause, well, because our sex together is not exactly what you want, if like you say, it takes a room full to get you excited, I just want to say I'm not opposed to multiple partners even in marriage. If that's what it takes to get you *on board.* Shit, can't believe I said that. I just want you to know, I'm not looking for exclusivity that way. What do you think?"

She said, "Dennis, I'm at work. And it's Monday. What is the matter with you? Do you really expect a bright, chummy little conversation from me at work about sex and marriage on a *Monday*? And with Leon still missing, probably doing something stupid and criminal for Rowan's stupid iconoclast thing."

"Yes, but, what's wrong with Monday?"

"Shit, Dennis. What's the matter with you? Think about it." She hung up.

So, Dennis had to think about it. He couldn't imagine why Monday should be any different from any other day of the week. It's the start of the week, but so what? The week had to start somewhere. If it started Wednesday, would that be a Monday? He draped a towel around his gut and padded wet still into his living room to consult his shelf of reference books. He saw Blake miss-shelved, made the correction and thought a moment of Claudia. Dripping on varnished hardwoods, he selected volume M-P of *Encyclopedia Britannica,* last revised 1968. Under "Monday," from the Old English Monandaeg, he read, means MOON's day, which makes sense as everyone seems so damn moody, loony, under the moon's influence on Mondays. But Monday's child is fair of face, so why all the bother? Wednesday is the bad day of the week. Wednesday's child is full of woe. If Monday were a woman, she would spec out on the zodiac as Cancer, intelligence informed by emotion. Maybe too emotional: most suicides fall on Monday. Maybe because it's painful to be back to work after a Sunday rest. In New York City, for generations, Monday was "wash day," clothes rubbed by hand against metal-ribbed wash boards then strung with line between telephone poles and tenement windows fluttering, the scent of lye and tallow. But why would Rowan choose a Monday for his iconoclast event? Well, why not. The government creates holidays on Monday to get the max out of a weekend, like Christopher Columbus chose a Monday to discover America which got its name from the wrong Italian. Did Columbus take the weekend off? All that really happens is the mail gets backed up and we get a day to recover from drinking while watching the game on TV. Ask my Dad about that, the original Monday morning quarterback. Or let's be a good Christian and repent on Sunday what we did on Saturday and are going to do again on Monday. Like kill someone. Jesus. Is this really going to happen? Well, yeah, it did a year ago in Cleveland – who was it? Brenda someone, somewhere in Cleveland, Ohio, just a teenager, sat in her apartment with her father's gun and shot elementary kids outside their school, did it for TV coverage, did it because she hates Monday, like the Boomtown Rats say. Maybe this Chapman is the same kind of Monday hater. Synchronicity.

Dennis laughed then looked around to be sure no one had noticed. Dennis never feels alone. He always carries with him a company of evaluative companions. Not, thankfully, socio-pathological companions like Chapman's little people, but bad enough. Dennis always wants to please. It was beat into him by his father. Dennis has never trusted authority because he has never felt he can appease authority. And what Dennis was doing, blowing off work, blowing up at Rashana Whitfield on the phone, that cute little black girl from Philly who flirts with him, that is very unlike Dennis, the blowing up part. And here he was naked and dripping water all over his living room, the book on his lap sopping up water, his father's chair in which he sat absorbing water from the wet towel wrapped around his waist. Very unlike Dennis.

He decided maybe the thing to do to mitigate the waiting was to get some of his own writing done, get a character going and put him through this kind of shit and see how he makes out. So Dennis pulled himself off the chair, wiped the encyclopedia with a corner of towel, wiped off his father's chair. Didn't know why he bothered as beer stains are indelible. He flapped over to his writing desk in front of a window facing apartments whose people he nightly observes and pities and shamelessly borrows for his fiction, his as yet unpublished short stories. But when he looked through the window, he forgot it was daytime, and there was probably no one home there, and if there were, he couldn't see in anyway even if their lights were on. What he saw again, instead, was himself looking out, or a ghostly image of himself twenty years from now with thin hair wetted down to bald and sunken eyes and pale white flesh. A memento mori like what artists of the Renaissance placed in portraits as a reminder of the vanity of this life and of the fate that awaits all flesh.

Goddamn, this was depressing. Which was very unlike Dennis. There was no time to fuck around. Dennis decided he really wanted a woman, no more party life, nothing more to prove in bed. He had as yet no commitment from Francine. He thought again of William Blake: "Do you pity me," Blake had said to his wife to be. Why wouldn't she? The guy was a mess. Dennis was a mess. He decided to phone Claudia Fontaine and get a definitive answer from a decisive woman for once.

She was not at work. The receptionist at Southeby's said Claudia had taken a sick day and gone home to her parents in Westport.

"But," said Dennis, "she told me to call her today. I'm on the line from Brussels – in Belgium …"

"Oh, is that somewhere East of New York City? Mister, I know where Brussels is *at*. I grew up in Jersey, maybe you guessed, but my degree is PoliSci, NYU. Now, you want that phone number in Westport or do you not?"

Dennis wondered why it was every secretary in town had it in for him. When Claudia's mother answered the phone, Dennis was, for the moment, at a loss. He had expected to hear Claudia's voice and had prepared his remarks, but this go-between needed finessing. Dennis imaged an overweight dowager still leaning on her late husband's status and living off his largess, a woman who died her hair with Spanish Chestnut to appear as youthful as her daughter and who had the little moustache above her mouth waxed biweekly.

He said, "Oh, pardon me. I thought this was a direct line to Claudia Fontaine, the Sotheby's Art Assessor. I'm calling from Brussels … Belgium."

"Yes, I know where to find Brussels."

"Oh, my mistake. But would Ms. Fontaine be available. I have been told to contact her for specialized service in an arcane point of identification concerning a mannerist painting by Pontormo … (Nice! thought, Dennis. Where did he get that name?) Or," he said, "presumed to be so. But then Ms. Fontaine will know. May I speak to her, please?"

"Well, I'm not her secretary, but I can tell you she takes this day off for very good reason. She takes every December 8th off, as she should. It's a personal day. Some don't believe in personal days. I'm a great believer in personal days."

"Yes, I see that. May I confess to you that the nature of my call is really more personal than business. I'm a good friend of Claudia's."

"A friend from Brussels? Well, let me see what I can do."

Moments later – "Hello, this is Claudia Fontaine. I'm afraid I am unable to…"

There exists only one greeting that will be effective after Saturday night. Dennis applied it shamelessly: "Claudia, do you pity me?"

"Oh, shit, Dennis, from Brussels. Yes, I guess I do. After that party, after what happened between you and me, between you and your so-called friends, yes I guess I do pity you. You all smell like dead fish."

"Nice olfactory image. What does this mean exactly? It's not the kind of poetry I would expect from a Blakean scholar."

"Dead fish. You know the smell of dead fish. And I don't refer to the piscine smell of after-sex, so don't get me wrong, Dennis. I am, for once, being exact with my inference. Dead fish in a dried out creek bed is what I imply."

"Okay, fine, please explain."

"When I was a kid, there was this creek in a small wood near my house in Connecticut, where I am now as we speak, and well … where the creek *used* to be before developers bulldozed the hell out of the woods … anyway, I'm just maybe 5 or 6 years old, and one summer day, it's real hot, I smell something awful, like the trash bin when sitting in the garage a week in the heat while your family is gone on summer vacation, like that…"

"I get it. Go on."

"So, I walk into the woods and follow the smell and it's coming from the creek, only there is no creek, only just rocks and moist dirt and a whole lot of dead fish lying there. It smells awful."

"I see, but what does that have to do with me?"

"Not just you – you *and* your friends, last night, and me too, all dead fish, that's why when I left New York last night, I'm not coming back. I'm not going to be dead fish."

"Well, Claudia, and I don't mean to step all over your childhood memories, and pardon me all to hell for this, but what does any of this have to do with me and my friends?"

"It's a memory I have never shaken, one I have puzzled over the years. It's this, Dennis – those fish, they must have known the water was getting shallow. All they had to do was swim out to the river the creek empties into. Easy."

"Yes, I see. Why not?"

"Because they're fish, Dennis. It's in their nature to ignore their fate, the walls closing in around them. All they care about is sizing up the other fish next to them – if bigger, it eats you; if small, you eat it. They're fish. That's what they do."

"You're saying my friends and I are cannibals?

"In a manner of speaking, yes. You swim around each other in the same pond, all very incestuous, you fuck each other in every way conceivable, you depend on each other too, and you do *not* see the walls closing in around you. Last night, well. I smelled the dead fish. I saw the walls closing in. I'm not coming back to New York City, Dennis. Even John Lennon doesn't know enough to swim away. Chapman is going to kill him. I think he will. It's shooting fish in a barrel. I don't mean to diminish the potential for tragedy. But Lennon is just a big fish in a pond that's drying up and he won't leave. New York City is drying up – intellectually, morally, aesthetically. I don't know. I guess I'm cynical, but I want out."

"Where are you going?"

"I'm following Rowan Murray to Findhorn."

"Don't they have fish in Scotland?"

The phone's strident buzz signaled a profound disconnect. Dennis chose to ignore the implications. She'll be back, he told himself. She is not a searcher in the way of Rowan, he thought, not inclined to go Druid and talk to plants. She's a true academic. She will want security in the ivory towers of elevated thought, which will be a different elevator ride from the one Dennis will apply to attain his desires. But she'll be back. My phone will ring one day and it will be Claudia. She'll want to know if I still know my Blake. And then he thought, shit, he's going too much the opposite direction from Claudia. Once he begins his rogue career as literary agent, once he negotiates with the media for a slice of market share when Lennon is killed, he will have forever tainted his moral profile.

Which left Francine. Unless … unless Suki Miyushi? She has potential that one. Of course it doesn't hurt that her father is an ambassador. And Dennis was quite sure there will be a substantial trust fund, as no one can live so defiantly while attending an ivy league graduate school like a temporary imposition to a life so clearly directed toward the avant-garde. There is *no* money in bleeding-edge art, in challenging successful formulas and popular trends. Dennis knew this from his knee-deep slog through the slush piles of querying authors at Holmes and Stout, all those young writers who feel they are doing something "unique," who invoke the names of William Gaddis and Thomas Pynchon, sainted writers of post-modernism whom nobody reads but pretends to which is why their books sell, as pretense will always find shelf space.

But about Suki, she took quite well Rowan's co-opting her inspiration for his gesture, what Rowan preferred to call, what was it? Deontology? More like Demonology. Suki tries very hard to mask and distort her refined, innate sense of propriety and proportion. But it's there. She's a woman of refinement and breeding looking for legitimacy, once daddy's power and money are no longer an obstacle to her self-worth. Dennis could help her with that, he thought. Where's that number? (Dennis thumbed through the Rolodex, leaned back in his desk chair, avoided his reflection in window glass and dialed with the self-assurance of a confidant).

But this was misperception. Suki had no intention of sharing anything meaningful with Dennis – neither her thoughts nor Saturday night's orgy, neither her feelings towards Rowan nor her understanding of Chapman's potential to murder. And certainly not her hidden desire to accept daddy's wealth and connections gracefully and maybe even Dennis' offer to partner. She did, however, intimate that something significant had happened between her and Francine which she might want to explore, then hung up.

This left Dennis holding the dead phone between his legs like an impotent appendage of male vanity. This can not be. He must not allow his ego to wither. His anomie must bloom even as the women in his life take flight. He went back to his short story writing, which is a world where he has all the control, and summoned his collection of characters observed from apartments across the street upon whom he inflicted damage as the afternoon passed unseasonably warm into a late December evening. Dennis had entered the "zone," a world where writers manipulate from behind the looking glass of shattered images characters who imprudently gaze upon the face of God. Dennis extracted himself from this place only when the burn from his own radiance had become too great to endure. He had written ten pages of what he believed to be transcendent prose. This was huge volume for a bleeder. He was both emptied and refreshed. A glass of chilled white wine, Concord grapes, cheese and an apple refreshed him further. Then the phone rang.

The city editor of *Rolling Stone* said, "Shit, you were right. He did it."

"He did?"

"Chief Detective James Sullivan said Chapman did it. 10:43 p.m., three shots with hollow point. A fucking blood bath."

"Incredible. I was right."

"Come to my office."

"Now?"

"I have a contract for you to sign. And an advance on your story."

Finally, someone wanted a Dennis Zamora story! The rest for Dennis will be all contractual: a prenuptial agreement with Francine Carlton, signing the cowboy writer (name withheld upon request), breaking contract with Holmes and Stout Literary, the deal with *Rolling Stone* to give an exclusive account of the Chapman/café brotherhood weekend that had launched the shooting of John Lennon, and the loan for a town house in Jackson Heights at the foot of whose stairs Dennis and Francine and his lawyer (provided by *Rolling Stone*) will meet the questing TV and newspaper press so Dennis can answer just enough questions to accelerate the fever of a media frenzy.

Chapter Fourteen:
Mason's gesture and long after
Monday, December 8, 1980
7:00 p.m. - 11:05 p.m.
(3 hrs/45 min. before to 20 minutes after the murder of
John Lennon)
and
Bogota, Colombia, December 2000
(twenty years after the murder of John Lennon)

You will now understand why I placed Dennis Zamora in the Judas chair of my cover illustration for *Time* magazine. I made up my mind about Dennis twenty years ago when crossing over into Mexico with Raul. I wasn't always so clear in my thinking back then. I was all hyped on making a life change after making a statement the world would recognize, proving something to Rowan and to myself. I was just stupid. That Monday night twenty years ago, I had signed on to guard a fashion gala of the Costume Institute at the Metropolitan Museum of Art. It was my moment to come through on a promise to Rowan Murray to iconoclast.

I was there early for my shift walking the halls quietly and deeply into Modern European and American painting, my usual post. These would be dead halls during the Costume Institute's celebrity dinner and ceremonies in the Great Hall below. No one would be in these upstairs halls but the guard currently at his post. And yes, there sat Levi Gurney at the end of his shift leaning against a wall in his folding chair napping, his wrist watch draped around an ear, the alarm set to chime. A good Quaker communing quietly with his God, agreeably naïve, his thinning hair cut page boy, his nautical beard somehow youthful though gray.

I sneaked past Levi, made a left at Degas, a right at Diebenkorn, then down the hall past Pollock's shouting canvas of suicidal red splashes to Warhol's *Four Marilyns*. I took out my penknife and slashed three times – up, across, and down – tried not to think what I was doing. I had already spent hours sleepless in the arms of Raul Vega worrying myself over this gesture. My life was about to change entirely. I was ready for this. As was Raul. He didn't understand what I had to do at the museum – I spared him the details – but he did grasp the resentment I felt for the worship of mostly dead artists while the live ones scrape by on stale toast, and the hope of a gallery show should the zeitgeist of home decoration swing their way. We planned an escape to Colombia once I had completed my part in Rowan's Monday gesture.

The funny thing is, it was more difficult for me to work through the nerve it takes to destroy a piece of art than to disassemble years of hetero-conditioning in favor of sex with men, or I should say, with this particular man. And maybe that was the difference. Raul has been my only male lover. And maybe it's because I didn't feel I was disappointing anybody (parents dead, thankfully, and no marriage to dissolve or kids to humiliate). While as an artist, I had betrayed the unwritten code generated since my first days copy-sketching stuff in museums. Then of course guarding the same stuff. And in between rubbing my ego up against fellow artists navigating the dimly-lit paths after art school and before that expectant break-through gallery opening which for me never came, at least not in New York. Everyone looking for new angles in representation, fresh perspective, tasteful bohemian digs for network parties, the best interest on their trust fund (well, all but me it seemed). And some going commercial and some holding out for conventional taste to break their way. And some gone so far down the rabbit hole they need to ingest uppers to welcome back the sun. I did not, somehow, feel as though I had betrayed Andy Warhol in my decision to iconoclast. But I did feel this gesture will take me so far off the grid of accepted behavior for an artist with formal training that a new category beyond iconoclastic will need to be invented to explain my actions and my art. No one that I knew in the world of art would any longer associate with me. No more alumni bulletin mailings from The Manhattan Institute of Art. No more invites to loft parties. No more galleries to consider my work (or maybe I should say coffee houses, as that was the only display space I had found lately). And no more association with the Factory, or with Andy's Pop Art groupies and hangers on where, contrary to experience, I still I felt I had a chance to get a helping hand. Well, maybe not with Basquiat in my way. And now I will be considered another betrayer of Andy, maybe as bad as Valerie Solanas, the scum that shot Andy. But maybe it was better this way, a clean break with New York City.

I sneaked down the hall to the men's bathroom in European painting. Wiped fingerprints then dropped the knife into the water tank of the toilet, which I had seen in movies, although that was a gun, but that's okay. All art is derivative. I then descended an echoing set of stairs to where employees punch time cards and the

Shift Officer occupies a desk behind perforated glass. When the piston shot through my card, I took this little demonstration of time's violence with me down the hall to the locker room to wrap myself in the latest design in security wear when Levi Gurney ran past me shouting, "Breach! Breach! Security breach!" his page boy flopping, arms raised as if someone were holding a gun on him. These were decibels of angst well beyond Levi's comfort to perform, so his voice cracked and his eyes darted unsure where to fix themselves. The Shift Officer had meantime jumped off his chair and beckoned with both hands for Levi to focus on him and calm the hell down.

Levi stood before the Shift Officer other side of the glass and shook and said a painting had been desecrated, said he was taking a final tour when he noticed a painting had been desecrated. Exactly how much desecrated? asked the Shift Officer, to which Levi replied with three dramatic eviscerating slashes the length and breadth of the Shift Officer's torso. The Shift Officer, now very concerned, looked to me, said, "Fisher! Get up there quick! Find the painting in question and secure the area!" A military operation, it seemed. Very appropriate. These Heads of Security are all x-city police who anticipate the worst in behavior of their fellow man. They have learned patterns of response to deal with such, like "securing an area," and like assuming the malefactor will likely be the security guard who reported the damage. Which, as it happens, is not far off, as the guards I worked with were either frustrated artists like me, or obscure writers, or criminal. Ninety percent of all theft can be traced to employees. Just recently a rare Roman coin had been lifted from a display case and found in a security guard's locker. Say both criminal and stupid.

Two burly Heads of Security had meantime approached Levi then pinned his arms behind him to use as a ruder to steer him down the hall to interrogations. They hoped to have the truth sweated out of him before their shift was over, as OT for city employees had recently been curtailed by Mayor Ed Koch despite his administration's having the worst crime rate in the city's history. Much of this crime related to drug abuse. Maybe if they could trace this wanton damage to the side effects of drug addiction OT would be approved, is what they thought. But not likely to happen as this Levi was known to be clean of drugs and prompt and courteous, one of their best employees. Which is why they trusted Levi with the *dead shift* (those hours the museum is closed), as others will likely sleep or steal through those hours. So, what to do with Levi? And then, in interrogation, it came out – as they assessed Levi's opinion of the painting by Warhol, they discovered his Quaker prejudices against displaying icons in "meeting" as Levi calls it, which they discovered means communal worship, and not so big a stretch to see these herds of citizens venerating the art as a "meeting," and those three slashes – Father, Son and Holy shit! Of course! They tell it all. Levi is their man.

But this was their thinking before taking into account the possibility that as Levi slept, which he did confess to, and quite readily, as they began to believe he was telling the truth about napping, there were many, many possible perpetrators among the guests of Diana Vreeland's costume show, including Warhol himself, who they believed was not above staging this kind of thing for publicity. There were punk rockers prone to violent acts, jealous artists whose star status had been eclipsed by the Warhol brand, mavens of haute couture Andy might have pissed off, maybe the oddball caterer who dislikes modern art. Or maybe someone sick enough to feel he was doing Marilyn Monroe a violence through her portrait. Or her four portraits. So maybe this was a kind of multiple rape? Why couldn't this have been some Renaissance art that doesn't matter?

I had a lot of time to revisit my own worries as I paced the hall in front of my Marilyn desecration. I had already justified my actions to myself, so why so prickly with guilt and apprehension as I awaited arrival of the museum curator? Maybe it was the idea of interrogation, as in what just happened to Levi. Or maybe second thoughts about tossing my future into the untested affections of this strange and wonderful man from Colombia? Maybe it was the worry that I will fall just as hard the next day for a woman? Or that Raul will. God knows Raul was active and effective with every gender during Leon's party. Poor me. I will never be the same is what I thought. And poor Leon, his wife-to-be serviced to perfection, fine-tuned and vibrating still when Raul got done with her, then again after Suki. There could simply no longer be any question that Leon has been replaced. And the brotherhood was over. Or maybe for me it had morphed to another kind of brotherhood. Now that I was one of "them," one of Raul. And I was trying very hard to figure out what that could mean.

My voice had not changed. I had no desire to wear women's clothes. I still have no interest in S&M or in gay bars and I didn't, still don't, give a shit about single sex marriage. Nothing had changed. Except that I found myself under the influence of this man Raul, who can do whatever he pleases to me in any way conceivable and I will gladly submit. Does this mean I'm no longer a man? I didn't know. I'm not a sheep. And how significant is it that I had desecrated an icon of female seduction? Maybe all that intellectual justification, all that assertion of master art, Warhol's masterpiece, the work I loved, maybe even this is really all about identity – a gay man paints Marilyn, another gay man destroys her. Each telling his identity in his own way. All I really knew was that I had to follow this man Raul Vega to Bogota.

Soon there was a swell of noise and a stampede of Vreeland dinner guests, hundreds of them charging down the hall to view the Warhol damage, including Andy Warhol himself. I really didn't know what to do. I first stood center of the hall entrance and waved arms like I remembered from cowboy movies when the rustler falls off his horse in a rampaging herd of longhorns and just stands there and waves his arms and stands there still when the dust settles. But I didn't have the nerves. I jumped aside then squeezed into the flow of the gathering wave hoping to wash up somewhere beside the damaged painting to assume my post of authority, minor though that may have been among this throng of dignitaries and the titled and the entitled.

What I heard and saw among the throng was Warren Beatty with hair that Andy Warhol thought too Californian, "Topiary," he said to a paparazzo clicking shots beside him, and "carved like a bush." Which focused the photographer on sullen Beatty, and maybe, Andy thought, sent this insult into the crowd like a virus because Warren had snubbed him on the elevator. And there was Mick Jagger with Jerry Hall and both were already plotzed before dinner was served, Jerry having just appeared on the cover of Italian *Vogue* which impressed Andy, but not so much as the risqué cabaret she had performed in Paris with Grace Jones, which Andy thought were her salad days, and there have been maybe 50 appearances on fashion magazine covers, so ... Italy now too, that's nice, and really, he thought, what do you say to Mick who was dumped by Bianca?

And then along came Basquiat all coked out, hair like snakes, wearing jean overalls that smelled of turpentine and sweat. But he was thankfully in one of his shy moods, one arm gathering the waist of an even more distracted young material girl wearing fishnet stockings and a large crucifix necklace and leaning into Jean-Michel like he was a sofa. And the newly wed dancer Ron Reagan Jr. in alligator golfing shirt that showcased his muscle and talking to Andy about Jimmy Carter's dismal performance in the Iran hostage episode and his father, President elect Reagan, really wants Andy to come to the inauguration, which explains why he hasn't had time to see Ron Junior at the Joffrey Ballet, and maybe also because he married without Nancy's consent, and didn't Steve McQueen die a horrible death? And did Andy know that John and Yoko hire someone to buy their clothes but that that someone can't write a book about them because he was made to sign a contract of intent? and "Oh, my God! This is horrible," Ron Jr. said, the crowd having parted so Andy and his retinue strode elegiacally to the fore to view the damaged canvas.

Andy looked startled, a little embarrassed, said nothing in that Andy way of his for what seemed hours, then, "That must have hurt." Which set everyone tittering except me. I had made my way to the display and in the presence of Andy nearly broke down, said, "I am so sorry." To which Andy said, "Oh, that's okay. I'll just make them another one."

Andy didn't recognize me as anyone who had trod the outer edges of his Factory coterie, although Basquiat dragging Madonna along walked up to me to have a good look. But couldn't get his mind around this costume, this blue/gray military suit that would never have made muster as Factory wear. Clever pantomime? But no, he thought, never would this guy receive an invitation to this exclusive opening. No, this can't be Mason Fisher. I averted my eyes like I was the Queen's guard in London, although the tears might have said otherwise. I turned aside to present a profile that Basquiat was sure he had never seen before, as he usually came at me head-on, and that paunchy tummy, well, nothing Jean-Michel had encountered at the Factory except maybe Truman, but no chance *he* would wear this silly outfit, not even for a laugh. Basquiat dragged his date away from the Warhol painting so he might uncork a small vial and inhale another bump of stimulation with a hundred dollar bill.

Then a ripple of solemnity, all now unearthly quiet, except for my choked-off emotion, and in waded Diana Vreeland. She was sharp as a knife in a long, lean black suit by Coco Chanel whose work was the focus of the evening, until the slashing of Andy's painting, which she resented as upstaging. But as it happened even Andy pined to return to the opening because, of course, Andy must attend and be seen, as it is said he would attend the opening of a drawer. And as Diana confronted the damaged painting, layers of pearl necklace spilling into shimmering ovoids, she said, "Andy," her very large lips smacking, her large ears and sculpted jet hair projecting an Incan ceremonial mask, "Andy, this is tragedy." Upon which Andy replied, "Yes, the girl who wore only Chanel #5 to bed. She dies again."

A besotted Truman Capote stumbled in leaning upon the arm of lover Jack Dunphy and asked, "What did I miss?" Said, "Oh, I see. Well, if you think that's a crime, Random will pay a million for *Prayers* three times unanswered. Huh! What do you think? (silence) Do I have any friends here?"

Andy stood silently beside Truman ignoring the question, gazing curiously at his painting, his lips slightly parted, his platinum wig gleaming in the shock of flash bulbs as the press captured him, hands locked at his pelvis where he palmed a miniature tape recorder which he had engaged. He seemed distant emotionally but was secretly reveling in the words spoken around him because preserved for posterity by those tiny busy magnetic heads vibrating in his hands.

The curator arrived at the painting. Short and violent in motion, his tiny arms splaying all over as if his brains were at the tips of his fingers and signing intentions. Lips were pouty and round head oversized, hair unruly and flame red. He said, "These halls are closed! To the public! Closed! The Press especially. *You* must *all* leave, immediately!"

To which Truman responded, "Surely, *we* are not the public!"

Andy whispered, "Depressing to think so."

Diana Vreeland, hardly fazed, said, "In fine, we should claim our seats at the banquet downstairs. Let us not forget why we are here. And besides, the offender has been seized. Another religious zealot I am told. This way, please."

After which all 650 best friends of Diana Vreeland descended the fan-like granite steps to the Grand Hall to confront a quandary which ensued from name tags replaced, hidden, discarded, upon which guests had imposed their own seating arrangements indicating favors earned in some cases and vengeance in others. The meal, the pheasants, there were many, still in their costume finery were brought to table under glass surrounded by thin reservoirs of liquor set ablaze that drew applause and temporary distraction from the politics of assigned seating. As guests pulled apart their birds and pacified their faces with the succulent white flesh, the retrospective of Coco Chanel's line arrived displayed upon bulimic models streaming by one after another.

The tables were assembled in a sinuous link of conjoined half circles through which models glided then to glissade en arrière, then faded away as Diana, microphone in hand, explained each creation lovingly: "… a cream silk linen woven butterfly jacket … a black silk hand beaded jacket featuring the most intricate beaded dragons and phoenix … a yellow bouclé jacket and skirt suit fully lined in silk, jacket trimmed with signature Chanel gold chain …"

The press were careful to photograph specified attendee targets as they emoted over costume, or what have you. And as the event was going swimmingly, as the evening began to feel appropriately choreographed, Diana skipped one costume, then another, a model stopped in her shoes, then another and they began to stack up like planes at LaGuardia. Then some words that were best not heard coming from Diana. And then finally, this announcement:

"My friends," said Diana. "I am shocked. I don't know what to say. I had expected Yoko Ono would have joined us, but well, of course, and if she had, but that cannot be … well, her husband, John, John Lennon has been shot. Just now. Our chef has told me. He has a radio, in the kitchen, and he has called the *Post*. And it is all quite true. John Lennon is dead! It was the gesture, say the *Post*, of an overzealous fan."

I had been sitting top of the stairs above the Grand Hall numbed from fatigue, floating in the white noise of Vreeland's costume chatter. I was hardly missed in the gallery. There were so many police and curators chasing clues, examining other paintings. But now *this!* That son of a bitch, Chapman. He did it. He killed Lennon! I hated that kid from the start – his little boy act. There really is something wrong with that kid. Didn't he have a gun in his coat pocket when he came to Francine's party? Have the brotherhood barely escaped John Lennon's fate? And the way he left. So paranoid. Shit! Rowan should have known better. What good will this collective iconoclast gesture do to change ideas should one of its participants prove to be a psychopath?

The room downstairs exploded in pandemonium. People were out of their chairs, hugging neighbors, crying, some running to the cloakrooms and to the phones to call their car services, and I thought out loud, *Well fuck them! Now one of their own is dead. How vulnerable they feel. No amount of money and fame can insulate them entirely. They must feel that now. Yes, and how criminal they are. Really. Think about it. Maybe no better than Chapman. Their hypocrisies and petty dislikes, the people they wish dead, the ignorance that passes for sophistication, the flatteries that poison, the influence that corrupts.*

But this invective didn't help me feel any better. I knew that at that moment I was myself entirely criminal. I took my uniform off and hung it in my locker. I had abandoned my post, didn't bother punching out at the time clock. Why should I? I was now a fugitive and a man without a country. Raul Vega will smuggle me across the border and use his drug connections to lead me along clandestine routes to Bogota. We have already spoken of this. When we arrive, Raul will drive a taxi, I will paint, and we will live on a cobbled back street in the small house that Raul's father built. We will love each other. We will be the only family each other needs. I was then, more than ever, convinced I had done the right thing in destroying Andy's painting. If only to send a message.

I know it's a silk screen, one of a series by hired hands, and that Andy meant himself to be far removed from the production end of the process. But this idea of Andy's, it seemed so pure because so risky, so far removed from the artists' ego even though it carried the Warhol name. But then, to see these connoisseurs of art, and Andy himself, so very much about ego and very little else. And Andy seemingly so bored for a pure aesthetics but so afraid to unmask the true aesthetics of his own act. Is he a genius of recycled ideas or myopic and misanthropic? God! These are small people! Why does Andy think they are giants? And then an epiphany. I realized Warhol really has no interest in painting. He has become the ringmaster in a circus. God! This is so sad. All this face paint and gesture and slight-of-hand and the occasional tragic loss of an aerial acrobat – it's all in the plan. Andy Warhol is *not* an artist. He surrounds himself with performers and he sits back with his tape recorder or his movie camera to capture every bump and grind of their torturous lives and calls it original art. This guy is a creep. Yes, as bad as Chapman. At least Chapman had the balls to end a life quickly. Warhol wants the slow death. So he can record and document. His people look upon him as some kind of talisman, but it all goes wrong for them. They struggle and fail and wither into obscurity while Andy happily records it all These people are repelling. They think they are *living* art!

I was soon out on the street. It was 11 p.m. and New Yorkers were blasting car horns, shouting out hotel windows, flagging taxis to cross Central Park to the Dakota to get a look at the scene of

John Lennon's death. It was a celebration. Revolting! And as day followed day, Raul and I made our way by Greyhound bus to the Mexican border. One of those days Raul placed to my ear the tinny speaker of his Sony transistor radio. It was Dennis Zamora. A re-run of an AP news release that had been taken up by every major network – Dennis on the steps of his new town house in Jackson Heights, Francine smiling by his side, a diamond ring sparkling on her finger, the *Rolling Stone's* lawyer whispering sound bites, and Dennis saying, "Yes, I am so sorry for the Lennons and their extended family and their friends and for John's fans everywhere. It was *not* my intention to get mixed up in his death, not at all. I had no idea Chapman would do this. But, yes, I did spend the weekend with Chapman as did certain others of my friends who have gone into hiding. I personally do not feel that evading responsibility is … (static) in *Rolling Stone* magazine … (static) exclusive … (static)." I flicked off the radio. My sadness deepened. And by the time the bus had arrived at San Diego, I had gone far into my meditations. I had decided the only honest way to portray the human spirit, its nature and soul, its ambition and destiny, is through my skeletal paintings, my explorations of the true insides of each of us that begins the same for us all. We are miracles of balance and complexity that we damage in our perverse quest for perfection, or that medical science performs on us. I would continue to work beneath the masks and the costume changes that we all embrace as required performance in this great circus of life.

I said, "Raul, before we cross over, get me drunk."

And he did. After swallowing the tequila worm, after emersion in the cantina of my revised life, and then in the dark of night, as I stumbled along the footpath crossing to Mexico with Raul and his companions of the drug trade, with the moon overlarge overhead, I was so plotzed I seemed to Raul to be speaking code. I spoke something about Claudia having a baby that Chapman killed. Something about Francine trading orgasm for notoriety. Something about Raul dumping me because I, Mason Fisher, was just too, too sad. And then, a year later in Bogota, when the Lennon series brought me the kind of fame and money I couldn't resist, I knew I had joined the circus. My sadness increased. Raul stayed with me just … well, just because. And now, twenty years later, as I sit in the courtyard in the rain, Raul is off with another man, or a woman. It really doesn't matter.

And the rain falls so hard upon the roof of our small house in Bogota it seems heaven has collapsed and all its golden columns of temples have broken into small bits and showered down upon the roofing tiles. Cats peer restlessly from beneath porticos. Birds fly with an urgency unseen in their gentle glide beneath the sun. And upon the paving stones of courtyard and streets, slick and gray with greasy rain, the steady drain of gutters from those roof tops carry like an insult the remains of a pulverized heaven down to the lowest, most humble, gravel-churning, lizard-dancing, offal-stinking retch of comingled refuse.

Under this sky I sit naked and weeping in the courtyard seated at the trestle table some buccaneer relative of Raul's had clung to in the frothy surf of Santa Marta many, many years ago.

The End

9 781937 677497